REVENGE

FORGE BOOKS BY HUGH HOLTON

Chicago Blues
Criminal Element
The Devil's Shadow
The Left Hand of God
Presumed Dead
Red Lightning
Revenge
The Thin Black Line
Time of the Assassin
Violent Crimes
Windy City

REVENGE

HUGH HOLTON

A TOM DOHERTY ASSOCIATES BOOK

NEW YORK

Holton

REVENGE

Copyright © 2008 by Elizabeth Cook

Book design by Ellen Cipriano

A Forge Book
Published by Tom Doherty Associates, LLC
175 Fifth Avenue
New York, NY 10010

www.tor-forge.com

Forge® is a registered trademark of Tom Doherty Associates, LLC.

Library of Congress Cataloging-in-Publication Data

Holton, Hugh.
    Revenge / Hugh Holton.—1st ed.
        p. cm.
    "A Tom Doherty Associates Book."
    ISBN-13: 978-0-7653-0139-0
    ISBN-10: 0-7653-0139-3
    1. Cole, Larry (Fictitious character)—Fiction. 2. Police—Illinois—
Chicago—Fiction. 3. Homicide investigation—Fiction. 4. Revenge—
Fiction. 5. Female offenders—Fiction. 6. Chicago (Ill.)—Fiction.
I. Title.

    PS3558.O4373 R38 2009
    813'.54—dc22

                                                2008038107

First Edition: January 2009

Printed in the United States of America

0 9 8 7 6 5 4 3 2 1

Prologue

Geneva, Switzerland
October 22, 1998
3:02 P.M.

The man crossed the bridge over the Rhône and entered the working-class Carouge neighborhood in Geneva. Not far from the Place Neuve, he entered one of the narrow crooked streets. He was careful to make sure that he was not being followed and also very watchful to ensure that none of his legion of enemies or the police were waiting for him up ahead. He was dressed in clean workingman's clothing and thick-soled boots. Everything from the inexpensive watch on his wrist to the wallet in his back pocket, stuffed with ten thousand American dollars, was brand new. His dark hair was worn long, and he sported a short unkempt beard, which was meant to obscure, if not disguise, his features. Although the day was overcast and the narrow streets he traveled were in shadow, he wore a cheap pair of dark glasses.

His name was Carlos José Perfido, and he was a professional criminal wanted for capital offenses in Europe, South America, and North Africa. He had once attempted to hide behind a dubious political ideology and call himself a freedom fighter. But his sole motivation for engaging in the kidnappings, murders, extortion, and bank robberies he had been responsible for on three continents was greed. During his eleven-year criminal career, Perfido had double-crossed the Mafia, Libyan dictator Mu'ammar Gadhafi, and the Russian KGB. There was a million-dollar price on his head, and many of Perfido's former colleagues were out to collect that bounty. He was rapidly becoming a man without a country. So he decided that it was time for Carlos José Perfido to vanish forever. But first he had to clear up some loose ends.

He came to a four-story apartment building that had been constructed before World War II. He stood in the doorway of a tavern across the street from the building entrance and studied every square inch of the surrounding area for possible danger. He realized there were any number of organizations looking for him that were so good, he would be unable to detect a surveillance until it was too late. Now he was forced to rely on his instincts, which had proved to be reliable in the past. Those instincts, coupled with his prior experience, told him it was safe to enter the building.

The first-floor corridor was dimly lit, quiet, and clean. The doors to six apartments led off the corridor, and Perfido proceeded to the second door on the left. Removing a key from his pocket, he let himself in.

The interior was small, consisting of a cramped sitting room, a narrow kitchen, and two closet-sized bedrooms. The furnishings were decidedly old-fashioned. But visitors to this place rarely noticed the décor, because of the clocks.

There were timepieces lining every square inch of wall space and on all the flat furniture surfaces. Each of the instruments was in perfect working order, and the combined symphony of their ticking made the small apartment pulse with sound. The occupants of this place found the noise comforting. To Carlos José Perfido, it was nerve-racking.

The old man was sitting at a table beneath a living room window, which was covered with a lace curtain. He was bending over a clock mechanism, studying its internal workings through a jeweler's eyepiece. He was unaware that Perfido was there until the international criminal was standing right beside him. The old man turned rheumy, bloodshot eyes up to stare with surprise at the newcomer. He had lived eighty-six years, and age had bent his back into a bow shape and left only a few wispy strands of white hair on his head. His hearing was virtually nonexistent, and his hands trembled. However, he was still a gifted watchmaker and creator of what many in the international criminal underworld referred to as "infernal machines of mayhem."

The old man's name was Isaac Weiss, and he had been born in Berlin, Germany, in 1912. When the Nazis came to power, Isaac's family, which had prospered in the jewelry trade for more than three centuries, recognized the potential danger Hitler posed. They sold all their holdings in Germany and escaped to Switzerland in 1935. The Weiss Clan spent the war years in comfort and prosperity, while Isaac attended the École d'Horlogerie, an eminent school of watchmaking in Geneva.

When the Nation of Israel was founded, Isaac left Switzerland to become a citizen of the new state. He fought in all the wars that had kept Israel in existence and during his military service learned to utilize his watchmaker training in the manufacture of bombs and other highly sophisticated weapons. Over the years, he had become a master at his craft and even learned a bit about making small precision firearms.

After leaving the army, Weiss became a freelance craftsman and developed a reputation for doing excellent work on a cash-and-carry-only basis. And despite the relative austerity of his Swiss residence, Isaac Weiss was a very rich man. A rich man who knew a great many secrets.

"Good afternoon, Isaac," Perfido said, looking down at the old man. "What are you working on?"

Weiss squinted not only to see his unexpected visitor a bit better, but also because he hadn't quite heard what he said. "Pardon? I didn't quite get that?"

Perfido realized that Weiss didn't recognize him, so he removed a folded slip of paper from his shirt pocket and placed it on the table next to the clock mechanism the old man had been working on. Weiss picked up the paper and, after he squinted to read it, recognition dawned.

"Carlos?" he said with fear and confusion. "What are you—?"

"Where is your niece?" Perfido asked, raising his voice to a sufficient volume so the nearly deaf man could hear him.

The watchmaker became visibly nervous, trembling uncontrollably.

"I don't know what you mean, Carlos?" the old man said in confusion; however, his face was betraying his terror. "What do you want with her?"

Now it would become necessary for him to hurt the old man. Perfido's only regret was that extracting the information forcibly would be time consuming, and he was in a hurry.

Grasping the back of Weiss's neck, Perfido pressed a thumbnail into the nerves in the mastoid gland behind the jawbone. The old man gasped in pain as his attacker said, "I need to know where your niece is, Isaac. We wouldn't want to leave any skeletons in our closet, now, would we?"

The watchmaker's gasps of pain became screams, which were muffled but not silenced by the cacophony of clock noises echoing through the small apartment. But Isaac Weiss's screams did not carry into the outer corridor or to any of the other apartments in the building, because advancing years had weakened the old man's voice.

The girl was thirteen years old and exotically beautiful in a dark, mysterious way. She had long black hair worn straight to hang to the small of her back and a slender figure that was just beginning to mature into womanhood. Her irises were of such a dark brown hue as to appear black and were haloed by long lashes that curled upward. Her nose was keen, and her lips full and sensuous. Most people who came in contact with her were forced to remark that she was quite stunning. But despite her beauty, there was no mistaking the mysterious, near haunted quality that seemed to hang about her like a shroud.

She lived in the Carouge section of Geneva with Isaac Weiss, whom she referred to as Uncle. Because of that, many thought the young woman was an Israeli. Actually, she was an American, and the watchmaker was not related to her at all. He was being well paid to look after her, but he was a very poor foster parent. They were supposed to be living in a villa attended by a staff of servants overlooking the Mediterranean, but Isaac Weiss preferred Geneva. The girl, who was unusually quiet and withdrawn, had never voiced an opinion, much less an objection, as to where they lived. She always had enough to eat, adequate clothing, and the opportunity to attend some of the most prestigious schools in Europe. The name she went by was Morgana Devoe, which was also a fabrication.

She was on her way home after classes at the École d'Horlogerie, where she had begun studying the watchmaker's art a year ago. As always, she was clad in dark clothing consisting of a black turtleneck sweater, charcoal gray jumper, black tights, a black sweater, and black beret. She carried a black leather attaché case, which showed signs of wear and tear. It had been a hand-me-down from her uncle and was one of her most prized possessions, because it contained her watchmaking tools and her textbooks. Morgana did not plan to be a watchmaker. In fact, at this stage of her young life, she had no idea what occupation she intended to pursue. Although she and the man she called Uncle lived in somewhat modest circumstances, she had always known she was independently wealthy. Her uncle had never directly disclosed this to her, but whenever she wanted anything that cost more than her monthly allowance, it was always provided for her. However, she had not grown up spoiled, but instead thoughtful and reserved beyond her years.

All her life, Morgana had been different. Even as a small child, she was not like other children, and she had no interest in playing with them or even attending children's events. She had never believed in Santa Claus, the Easter Bunny, or the Tooth Fairy. She didn't play with dolls or other toys. Before she could walk, she was fingering picture books. When she learned to read, she tackled projects many adults thought were far beyond her ability to comprehend. The child possessed a phenomenal memory and voracious curiosity. Perhaps the one thing that the nurse and housekeeper, who had been with her and her uncle during the child's early years, noticed was that Morgana didn't need anyone or anything. She did get hungry, become sleepy, and when she hurt herself, she cried. But she didn't *need* anyone. Before the housekeeper left, she remarked to Uncle Isaac, "That child hates people."

Morgana had overheard the housekeeper's comment, but it didn't bother her. She had grown up caring little for anyone with whom she came in contact. She found that people often got in the way of her pursuits and took up excessive space. She was too occupied with her studies to be bothered with them. At times, even her uncle's presence annoyed her.

She crossed the Place Neuve and entered her street. She had her evening planned in advance. Two hours of study, followed by a dinner, which she would cook, and then she planned to read a nonfiction book from the United States called *The Strange Case of Margo and Neil DeWitt*, which was written by a pair of American authors named Barbara Zorin and Jamal Garth. Morgana understood from a local librarian that the authors were preeminent in the field of mystery fiction. Uncle Isaac had recommended the book to her, but she was unable to understand why. He had never suggested reading material to her before, and when she questioned him about it, his only response was that *The Strange Case of Margo and Neil DeWitt* was a story that would someday be important to her. The ever-practical young woman doubted that, but she would read the book nonetheless.

She'd planned a dinner of Hungarian goulash and fresh baked bread with a tossed salad, which she would cook and serve with a red wine. After she cleaned up the small kitchen in their flat, she would begin the book. Morgana was a speed-reader and expected to finish the 312-page volume before midnight.

She entered the apartment and was halfway across the postage stamp–sized living room before she realized there was someone standing over her uncle. She turned and found herself less than ten feet away from Carlos José Perfido. Morgana recognized the man instantly—despite the beard, long hair, and dark glasses—because he was one of the strange people Uncle Isaac made precision devices for. She could also see that her uncle's neck had been broken. Morgana Devoe looked into Carlos Perfido's eyes and could detect quite accurately that he had visited the apartment and her uncle to kill her.

To Carlos Perfido, murder was a way of life. He had used it in business and to resolve complicated personal matters. Perfido would not need a weapon to kill her. In fact, he preferred to use his hands, because it wouldn't be messy, as would be the case with a knife or a gun. Moving a couple of steps closer to her would place him in the perfect position to snap that pretty neck. He was just about to make his move when he looked into his victim's eyes. What he saw there stopped the international killer dead in his tracks. Perhaps it was input from the instincts on which he relied so heavily. Instincts bordering on the psychic, transmitting to him that his intended target was dangerous.

His hesitation gave Morgana the only opportunity to escape that she was likely to get. She leaped for the door, flung it open, and dashed out into the corridor. Refusing to drop the attaché case, she sprinted down the narrow cobblestone street, which was completely deserted. Despite his hesitation back in the apartment, the man who had killed her uncle was right behind her now. She could hear the pounding of his feet on the pavement and could have sworn she could feel his hot breath on the back of her neck. If he caught her, it would all be over. This, Morgana would give the last ounce of her strength to prevent.

She retraced her earlier route back to the Place Neuve. There were people walking in the park, but no one whom she could call on for help. Even though she was in deadly peril, she refused to scream. This was a contest for survival between her and the man who had killed her uncle. If he caught her, she was dead. If she managed to escape, she vowed that someday she would kill him.

Carlos Perfido was less than five feet behind the girl as they sprinted onto the Place Neuve. Had it not been for the new thick-soled work shoes he wore, he would have caught her easily. As it was, the pursuit was directing too much attention to him. But he couldn't let her go that easily.

The killer was in excellent physical shape and could have chased the girl indefinitely. Then they began approaching the sea wall above the Rhône. There she would be trapped between him and the river. Now he had her.

Morgana knew she couldn't outrun him and that he would never abandon the chase until she was dead. So it would be necessary for her to go someplace where he either could not or would not follow her. Unlike her pursuer, she did not see the water as a trap, but instead as her salvation. She ran straight for the edge of the sea wall.

Perfido realized what she was doing, and there was no way he could stop her. He was forced to slow his pace and watch her run headlong off the edge of the sea wall and plunge into the river's choppy waters. He stopped at the river's edge and studied the spot where she had gone under. There was no sign of her. He stood there a moment longer, but a number of curious people were now approaching. With one last glance at the river, he turned and walked rapidly away, ignoring the spectators who had gathered.

Moments later, he was some distance from the river. The high-low wail of emergency vehicles heading in that direction echoed through the streets, so he sought refuge in a café on a commercial strip. He ordered coffee and a buttered scone from a waiter. Before he was served at a small table, Perfido placed a call from a public telephone box. This succeeded in getting a private car dispatched to pick him up from the café. Within two hours, he would be out of Switzerland and on his way to a new life and identity. He ate the scone and drank the coffee, which helped relax him. He rationalized that Isaac Weiss's niece had drowned in the Rhône. After all, she had been fully clothed and carrying the attaché case when she went into the water. The river was swollen due to recent heavy rains, and the currents were treacherous. Even if she did survive, it really wouldn't matter to him, because he was about to begin a new life in America, far from the criminal underworld of Europe.

The private car arrived, and after paying his bill, Carlos Perfido left the café. His plans from that point on proceeded without a hitch. The only problem was that he had left a loose end behind in Geneva, Switzerland. A skeleton that would someday come rattling out of the closet to kill him.

PART 1

CHICAGO, ILLINOIS

1

The Chicago Police Department Training Academy is located at 1300 West Jackson Boulevard, virtually in the shadow of the massive Sears Tower. For over a quarter of a century, this facility had educated and conditioned all entry-level police officers, as well as conducted periodic training classes for veteran cops and preservice sergeants, lieutenants, and captains. The two-story facility is equipped with state-of-the-art classrooms, a TV studio, library, computer lab, and a gymnasium. The one complaint that the officers using the academy continuously voice is that the building was not equipped with a swimming pool.

During the late twentieth century and the early years of the twenty-first century, there had been an aggressive building program aimed at replacing all outdated police facilities in the city. Police stations, including the old police headquarters building, which had been built before 1969, were demolished and replaced with modern structures. However, despite updated conference rooms and modern meeting facilities being in place, there were certain department traditions that remained in place. One of those traditions was having all CPD graduation ceremonies held at the police academy. Despite limited parking and the general congestion in the near-Loop area, the families, friends, and colleagues of new officers and those being promoted attended the events. On this warm June afternoon, a cadet graduation was scheduled.

Superintendent Orlando W. Wilson originally conceived the cadet program in the early 1960s during a top-to-bottom reorganization of the Chicago Police Department. The objective was to attract young people between the ages of seventeen and twenty-one to careers in law enforcement. Due to budget cuts in the mid-1970s, the program was abandoned. Now, due to the low numbers of entry-level police applicants, the police cadet program had been resurrected as the Windy City's attempt to compete with apprentice programs in the private sector and the U.S. military.

Following a six-week familiarization curriculum, 150 police cadets—eighty males and seventy females—were graduating prior to receiving assignments throughout the department. They would work as clerks and in other minor administrative positions while being paid an adequate wage. As a condition of their employment, the cadets were also required to carry a minimum of six credit hours toward a degree at an accredited college in the city. The cadets could pursue any academic course of study they desired, so long as they maintained a B average. The overall objective was to interest college-level people in law enforcement careers through direct contact with cops.

Besides the mixed gender of the graduating class, the cadets were a multiracial group with blacks, whites, Hispanics, and Asians forming a melting pot in microcosm of the city's diverse population. They were all required to wear a modified police uniform minus firearms. This uniform consisted of a dark blue saucer cap with the distinctive blue-and-white checkered border adorned with a gold cap shield inscribed with the words POLICE CADET; a robin's egg blue uniform shirt with navy blue epaulets and pocket flaps; dark blue wool trousers; and black leather shoes, garrison belts, and socks. As it was approaching the warmer months of the year in Chicago, the uniform's outer garment consisted of a short-sleeve shirt without tie.

The 150 new cadets looked quite impressive as they stood in ranks for inspection in the corridor outside the police academy gymnasium. The resurrection of the cadet program was being extensively covered by the news media, because it was touted by the current police superintendent and the CPD's director of news affairs as the beginning of a new era in American law enforcement.

Prior to the late-morning graduation, the assembled print-and-electronic-media types were aggressively looking for particular cadets to interview following the ceremony. These cadets would serve as spokespersons for the city's new crime-fighting initiative. They selected a white male who had been a star high school football running back but opted for an entry-level job with the police department, a Korean-American female with an IQ of 162, and a black male who joined the police department in order to follow in his father's footsteps. That young man was Larry Cole Jr., and his father was the current chief of detectives.

Larry "Butch" Cole Jr. had been appointed cadet group commander by the director of the Training Division. Such an appointment was not arbitrary, but based on a combination of the cadet's grades, on-duty decorum, and overall physical-training test scores. Success breeds jealousy, and there were those inside as well as outside the cadet program who had made groundless allegations that Butch Cole received the cadet group commander appointment because of "who" he was as opposed to "what" he had accomplished. The only possible advantage the cadet commander had over his fellow cadets was that his lifelong role model had been his father, one of the best law enforcement officers in the world.

The cadet commander was allowed to wear a pair of silver stars on the collars of his blue uniform shirt. He had called the cadet company to attention for the pregraduation inspection and had accompanied the director of the academy as she passed through the assembled ranks.

The cadet commander stood six feet two inches tall and weighed a muscular 195 pounds. He was well put together without appearing bulky, and moved with the graceful athlete's economy of motion. He was matinee-idol handsome, clean-shaven, and wore his hair cut short, which was a police academy requirement. One of the things both Butch Cole's friends and detractors agreed upon was that he looked so much like his father, it was uncanny.

On that past Father's Day, the *Chicago Times-Herald* newspaper ran a "Like Father, Like Son" contest. Fathers and sons who had a marked resemblance could enter the contest by submitting a photograph of the two of them together along with a short essay detailing the traits that also made them alike, in addition to the physical resemblance. Larry Cole Sr. and Larry Cole Jr. won the contest. Now those similarities were becoming even more pronounced as the son was following in his father's career footsteps.

The inspection concluded, the cadet company was marched into the academy gymnasium and directed to take seats on folding chairs in front of a dais, where the mayor, the superintendent, and a host of dignitaries waited.

The Chicago Police Department's command staff was assembled in a reserved section of the gymnasium next to the dais. They were arranged by rank from the highest position of division, chief to that of unit commander. There were three chiefs in charge of the patrol division, the organized crime division, and the detective division. Despite having a civilian dress assignment, Larry Cole was clad in the spring field uniform. It consisted of a white short-sleeved shirt, adorned with the CPD patch and City of Chicago flag; a gold badge inscribed with the rank CHIEF OF DETECTIVES; the silver stars of his rank on his shoulders; and a cap with the gold braid and scrambled eggs ornamentation of command rank. It was a mere coincidence that Cole's insignia of rank was the same as that of the cadet commander's. There had been a lot of highs in Larry Cole's life, but today, seeing his seventeen-year-old son become a member of the department put him on top of the world.

The visitors' section was located directly behind the cadet company. The cadet commander's mother was seated on the aisle in the second row of this section. The former Lisa Cole was a tall, beautiful, exquisitely built woman. She and her ex-husband had been divorced for ten years. She had initiated the legal proceeding to end her marriage after she developed an overwhelming fear for her son's safety. That fear began taking hold after serial killer Margo DeWitt kidnapped Butch and threatened to dismember him. After obtaining custody of their son, she had moved to Detroit. There she had remarried, but her son would never accept a substitute for his real father back in Chicago. After Butch graduated from Little Flower High School, Lisa had grudgingly allowed him to move back to Chicago to live with Larry Cole. Now she was forced to watch her son enter the profession that had brought about her divorce.

Although terrified by the sight of Butch in his police uniform, Lisa was making a valiant effort to keep up a presentable front. In addition to the stress she was under, she was also forced to deal with the fact that her former husband was still a damnably handsome, extremely sexy man. As she sat in the air-conditioned police gym waiting for the ceremony to begin, her eyes constantly strayed to his place in the front row of the command section. She found herself remembering what it had been like with him in bed. She forced herself to think of other things, but unwanted images kept intruding, and she felt a hot flash sear through her body from head to toe. To calm down, Lisa studied her surroundings.

Dressed in a sleeveless summer dress that made the most of her figure, Lisa sat next to her old friend Maria Silvestri and Maria's husband, Blackie, who was Larry Sr.'s best friend. Blackie had always reminded Lisa of a Mafia hit man, which he had come very close to becoming before he joined the force. Despite Blackie's tough outer appearance, when he saw Butch in a police uniform, his eyes filled with tears.

Seated beside Blackie were Lauren and Manny Sherlock, whom Lisa remembered from her years with Cole. As Lisa had arrived late and was forced to sit at the end of the row, she didn't get the opportunity to meet the women seated on the other side of the Sherlocks. One was wearing dark glasses and sported an enormous dark-brown French roll hairdo along with heavy pancake makeup and carmine lipstick. She was dressed in a loud flower-patterned print dress and a pair of spiked-heel shoes. Lisa speculated that this was Judy Daniels, whom Butch often talked about, but as always she couldn't be sure if it really was the woman known in Chicago as the Mistress of Disguise and High Priestess of Mayhem.

The other woman was of medium height, nicely built, and had blond hair and blue eyes. Lisa had heard that her ex-husband was involved in an on-again, off-again relationship with an investigative journalist and part-time jazz singer named Kate Ford. The former Mrs. Cole strongly believed that this blond woman was Kate Ford.

Lisa scolded herself for being jealous over the woman's presence. An ex-wife was not supposed to be concerned at all over whom her husband was sleeping with. Lisa was looking forward to this day being over so that she could go back to Detroit, where life was tame and a bit boring, but safe.

The formal graduation ceremony was anticlimactic. The mayor's speech was a rehash of clichés about the honor of public service. The superintendent of police rephrased his own press release about the police cadet program ushering in a new era in American law enforcement. One of Cole's old nemeses, the chairman of the city council police and fire committee, Sherman Ellison Edwards, lived up to his nickname of Alderman Foghorn Leghorn by giving a rambling, incomprehensible fifteen-minute speech about nothing. Finally, the speeches were over and the cadet group was lined up to march onto the dais, where they rendered a sharp salute to the superintendent and received their official police badges. The cadet badge was a modified version of a CPD police officer's star, and Butch Cole's bore number 102. A short time later, the ceremony ended.

There was a reception held in the cafeteria across the hall from the gymnasium. Punch, coffee, and cookies were served, while a trio of department photographers recorded the event. The cadet commander and the chief of detectives were asked to pose for photos with a number of graduates. Even Lisa Cole managed a smile for the camera when she stood between the two men in uniform who had played such an important part in her life.

The reception was coming to a conclusion when a female cadet came over to Butch and his extended cop family. She was a thin young woman with startling green eyes and short dark brown hair visible under her uniform cap, which appeared a shade large for her. "I wonder if I could take a picture with you and your father, Commander?"

Butch squinted momentarily at the cadet before saying, "Sure."

They stepped away from the group, and a photographer snapped the shot. At that moment, the heavily made-up woman in the flower-print dress—whom Lisa Cole had assumed was Judy Daniels—walked over and said, "Can I get a picture with you, too, Butch?"

The tall, handsome cadet grinned, which made him look more like his father than would seem humanly possible. "If you're trying to make me believe that you're Judy Daniels, you'll have to do a better job of it."

The woman returned his smile. "Do you remember the ice cream vendor named Mary Anne, who you thought was Judy Daniels when you were a little boy?"

Butch's grin faded a bit. "That was some kind of trick that Judy played on me, but she hasn't been able to fool me since then."

"As they say," said the green-eyed female cadet he'd just taken a picture with, "there's a second time for everything."

Chief Cole, Lisa, Blackie, Maria, Kate Ford, and Lauren and Manny Sherlock were stunned by the change in the female cadet's voice. But no one was more shocked than Butch Cole, because it was Judy Daniels who had spoken.

Pointing to the name tag that read DANIELS over her right breast, Judy Daniels added, "I tried to talk the director of training into letting me sit next to you during the ceremony, Butch, but she wouldn't have it. So I guess the photo that we took together and the witnesses"—she pointed to the group that was still staring at her in stunned shock— "will just have to do."

Butch looked at his father, and then the two of them began a laugh that infected everyone who had come to the Chicago Police Academy to attend Larry Cole Jr.'s graduation. The Mistress of Disguise and High Priestess of Mayhem had struck again.

"Why don't we go over to Mama Mancini's on Taylor Street for some beer and pizza?" Blackie said. "Just soda for you, kid," he said to Butch.

"We can't tonight, Blackie," Cole said. "Butch and I have got to rush home and change. Barbara Zorin's play *Murder at the Opera* is opening tonight at the Goodman Theater, and we promised to attend."

Blackie shook his head in dismay. "What is this police department coming to? We have a cop graduation and then everyone rushes off to see a play."

Again the group broke out in collective laughter.

2

T he Albert Ivar Goodman Theater is in the Goodman Performing Arts Center, which is the cornerstone of the North Loop Theater District in Chicago. Located at Dearborn and Randolph Streets, the Albert, as it is called to distinguish it from its smaller companion theater, the Owen, seats 850 people on the main floor and mezzanine levels. The playhouse was constructed with not only the comfort of theatergoers in mind, but also for enhanced acoustics and a setting intended to heighten the feeling of intimacy between the audience and the actors. Visitors to the Albert and the Owen

Theaters often remarked that it was almost as if they were part of the stage production.

The Goodman Theater had been a cultural mainstay of the Windy City for nearly a century, and a long list of prestigious theatrical productions had been staged there. From the works of Shakespeare and Tennessee Williams to the performances of Sir Laurence Olivier and Brian Dennehy, the Goodman had a well-deserved reputation for excellence. On this June night, the Barbara Zorin/Jamal Garth play *Murder at the Opera,* starring acclaimed stage actor Richard Banacek, was opening at the Albert Ivar Goodman Theater.

Opening night is a time of intense stress for everyone connected with a stage production. The rehearsals and costume fittings were over, and now it was time to tread the boards before a live audience. A space had been reserved in the center section of the first row on the main floor for theater critics from the *New York Times, Chicago Tribune, Chicago Times-Herald,* and *Time* and *Newsweek* magazines. As the 7 P.M. curtain time approached, the scene backstage was one of controlled chaos. Four separate sets were required for the two-and-one-half-hour production. *Murder at the Opera* was actually a performance within a performance. The plot revolved around the murder of the principal male lead in the opera *Magic Man,* which Chicago mystery writer Barbara D'Amato had written. *Murder at the Opera* would be told in flashback and deal with events surrounding the mysterious death of Sean Price, a magician, during the opening scene of *Magic Man.* Richard Banacek would play the Sean Price character.

Banacek was a talented stage actor who had made a name for himself in numerous supporting roles on Broadway and in leading man roles in local productions from coast to coast. Possessing a beautiful baritone voice and no little degree of acting talent, Banacek was perfectly suited for the male lead in *Murder at the Opera.* Yet the five-foot-nine-inch, 175-pound middle-aged actor had never been able to break into the big time. In fact, it was rumored that he had avoided movie and TV work with such regularity, he was no longer being asked to fill roles that would have provided him financial security. Despite such eccentricity, Banacek was still very much in demand. In the role of ill-fated magician Sean Price, Banacek would be alone at center stage for the opening scene and, despite his character's death during Act One, play a major part in each of the succeeding acts. During the opening, he would be required to sing, dance, and perform a number of magic tricks ranging from pulling scarves and flowers from a top hat to making a live, fully grown tiger miraculously appear onstage. Every precaution was being taken with the reportedly domesticated five-hundred-pound, cat, but its presence kept the cast and crew in a heightened state of anxiety.

As the time for the opening curtain approached, Barbara Schurla Zorin, a petite silver-haired woman with a pleasant smile and easygoing manner, paced slowly through the backstage scene of preproduction controlled chaos. Although she maintained a relaxed outward appearance Barbara possessed a high state of internal tension. She hadn't produced a play in twenty-five years, and that had been a college production. Barbara and her co-producer Jamal Garth were two of the most successful mystery authors in the country, and it was this prominence that caused *Murder at the Opera*'s financial backers to approach them with the stage project. The play was conceived as a moneymaking venture by a group of LaSalle Street bankers, who noticed that since the beginning of the twenty-first century, everything connected with mysteries was extremely popular. It was at a Midwest Chapter of Mystery Writers of America dinner meeting that the story that would become *Murder at the Opera* was conceived by authors Barbara D'Amato, who wrote the original *Magic Man* stage play, Mark Richard Zubro, Jamal Garth, and Barbara Zorin. That was eighteen months ago, and since then, *Murder at the Opera* had become Zorin's whole life—eighteen hours a day, seven days a week. Now it all came down to the first performance with the opening curtain going up in less than half an hour.

The tiger cage was already positioned backstage, and as Barbara Zorin approached, the huge animal was stretched out on the cage floor, paying little attention to the hustle and bustle of stagehands rushing around it. The young woman in a red, white, and blue leotard, who served the dual roles of the magician's assistant in the play and also the actual tiger handler, stood next to the cage, staring in at the jungle animal. She was unaware of the producer's presence until Barbara spoke to her.

"Don't you ever get nervous being in such close proximity to a dangerous animal?"

The magician's assistant merely glanced at Barbara before looking back at the tiger. "That's what makes it so beautiful, Mrs. Zorin. The tiger can rip the life from a human being with a single graceful swipe of its paw and at the same time remain one of the most majestic creatures in nature."

The young woman had a smattering of inconsequential lines during the performance. At one point, fictional Detective Cullen Knight of Scotland Yard, who was investigating the magician's onstage murder, would consider the assistant a suspect. She would quickly be cleared and fade into the background as more prominent suspects were discovered. However, her value as a thespian was secondary, because she had such a great way with the tiger.

In the trick that the fictional magician Sean Price performed onstage, the magician's assistant would get into the cage, and the magician would cover it with a red cloth. After uttering a magical incantation, the magician would remove the cloth to reveal that the tiger had replaced the assistant. An impressive feat, which was expected to draw gasps as well as applause from the audience. Despite this, the tiger's presence still made Barbara Zorin nervous.

The animal's gaze shifted from the magician's assistant to the producer. Now Barbara knew what a rare beefsteak felt like. "Well, be careful," she said to the young woman.

As the producer walked away, the magician's assistant looked up from the tiger cage at her receding back. The actress's gaze was that of a predator examining a piece of raw meat.

Barbara moved on to inspect the set, which was constructed to resemble the lobby of a playhouse in post–World War II London, where a great deal of the action of *Murder at the Opera* would take place. She was adjusting the drapery over a recessed alcove when Jamal Garth came rushing over to her.

The author had close-cropped snow-white hair and a full mustache. Beads of perspiration on his ebony forehead indicated the internal stress he was experiencing. In something of a panic, he said, "We've got a problem, Barb."

She felt a chill run through her. "What's wrong?"

"I can't get Richard to come out of his dressing room."

She glanced at her watch. "It's six minutes to the opening curtain, and the tiger act opens the play."

"I know that," Garth said hurriedly. "But he's locked himself inside, and he's not talking to anyone."

"This is a disaster," she said, rushing toward the dressing rooms with Garth in her wake.

Richard Banacek was a creature of emotion rather than intellect. He approached the roles he played on the stage from a spiritual rather than a mental or physical perspective. How he *felt* about the part was paramount and had succeeded in making him one of the most sought-after actors in America. That sense of the spiritual bordered on the verge of psychic phenomenon, and a number of people in the audiences he had appeared before remarked that they could actually feel a charismatic aura emanating from him during a performance.

The actor was seated in front of his dressing room table staring at his reflection in the mirror. He was dressed in the white tie and black tails of his Sean Price, the Magician role. His hair was dyed jet black, and his thin, pale face was clean-shaven. His dark eyes possessed a bright, near luminous quality and seemed capable of peering into the soul.

Richard Banacek was a startlingly handsome, intelligent man with a brilliant career. But the reflection cast in the dressing room mirror of the Albert Ivar Goodman Theater was a fraud. Plastic surgery had altered the flesh around his eyes, the shape of his nose, and the cut of his jawline. However, there were still some similarities between what he had been before and what he was now. Hiding behind the facade of the talented thespian was Carlos José Perfido, the international criminal who had vanished in Geneva, Switzerland, eight years ago.

There was a knock at his dressing room door. He did not answer it, nor did he take his eyes from his reflection. The instincts that had kept him alive during his criminal career and led to him establishing himself as a successful actor were telling him that he was in grave danger.

The knocking on his door was repeated, followed by Barbara Zorin calling out, "Richard, you've got to come out. There are only a couple of minutes before the curtain goes up."

He ignored her.

The actor attempted to rationalize the uneasy feeling he was experiencing as no more than opening-night jitters. His skin was clammy, his stomach queasy, and he couldn't shake the feeling that some dangerous entity was looming over him. Since he had assumed the Richard Banacek identity, his instincts for detecting unforeseen danger had lain dormant. Now, within a space of a mere thirty minutes, they were acting up as if he were in mortal peril.

The knocking became more insistent. "Richard, could you at least let me in so that we can discuss this?" the Zorin woman pleaded. "If you can't go on tonight, the entire production will be ruined."

Banacek continued to stare at his reflection. Perhaps he was simply being silly. This was a play being staged in the heart of the theatrical district in one of the most densely populated cities in the world. All advance notices had him performing brilliantly in the lead role of the murdered magician in *Murder at the Opera*. What could happen to him on a stage in front of 850 people?

"You could break a leg, Richard," he said to his image in the mirror. Then, before Barbara Zorin could knock on the door again, Banacek rose dramatically from his dressing room chair, donned his top hat, cocking it at a rakish angle, and said, "The show must go on."

The opening-night curtain for *Murder at the Opera* went up on time.

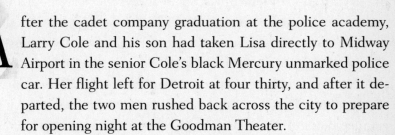

3

June 16, 2006
6:50 P.M.

After the cadet company graduation at the police academy, Larry Cole and his son had taken Lisa directly to Midway Airport in the senior Cole's black Mercury unmarked police car. Her flight left for Detroit at four thirty, and after it departed, the two men rushed back across the city to prepare for opening night at the Goodman Theater.

The chief of detectives showered and changed into a black tuxedo. His son donned a tuxedo as well, only Butch was wearing his father's waist-length white dinner jacket with the black buttons. The jacket was called a Michael Jordan Number Twenty-three and had been purchased for the chief of detectives by Judy Daniels and Barbara Zorin a year ago. To-night Butch would be wearing it, and when he slipped on the Number Twenty-three and stood in front of his bedroom mirror, he found that the jacket fit him almost as well as it did his father.

"We're running a little late, Butch," Cole called from the living room. His condominium was less than a mile from the Goodman Theater complex, but it was too late for them to walk, and parking in the downtown area was always difficult.

Butch came out of his bedroom carrying a backpack.

"What are you going to do with that?" his father asked.

"After the play, I'm going to a cadet graduation party on the north side. I was going to change at the theater. Barbara's letting me use one of the dressing rooms backstage."

"You're not going to stuff my dinner jacket into that backpack, are you?"

"No, sir," Butch said. "I was going to ask you to bring it home for me."

That conveyed quite accurately to Cole that his son would be riding his fire engine red Honda motorcycle to the theater. Although Butch was an excellent driver, Cole always worried about his safety on the two-wheel conveyance. The chief of detectives was well aware that there were a great many dangers out on Chicago's streets.

On top of that, Butch had received his first assignment as a police cadet, which was to the Second District in the Area One Police Center complex at Fifty-first and Wentworth. Cole had been the detective commander at that facility for six years, and it was one of the busiest police operations in the city. His son would be assigned to administrative tasks inside the facility, but the Second District station could be a very dangerous place indeed. Cole remembered that a criminal named Steven Zalkin had detonated a number of explosive devices in the building a few years back.

The watch commander Butch would be reporting to was an old friend of Larry Cole's. In fact, the two veteran cops had shared a number of adventures over the years. Under the captain's supervision, Butch would learn a great deal about police work in the Windy City.

"We'd better get going," Cole said, heading for the door.

"Oh, Dad," Butch said as they left the condo and boarded an elevator for the ride to the sublevel garage. "Could you put my backpack in your trunk?"

"It would be my pleasure, son," Cole said, taking the backpack. Then, as this was as good a time as any, he added, "You made me very proud of you today."

Butch smiled back at his father and responded, "And I've been proud of you all of my life."

Dressed in his father's dinner jacket and a red visored helmet, Butch rode his Honda XJ7 motorcycle across Randolph Street toward the Goodman Theater complex. By the time he turned off Randolph onto Dearborn Street, a few stragglers were entering the Albert Theater in preparation for the curtain going up on *Murder at the Opera*. He drove his motorcycle into the alley behind the theater and up onto a loading dock. There was an ancient security guard perched on a metal folding chair outside the stage door. The guard's uniform dwarfed his emaciated figure.

"Excuse me, sir," Butch said to the guard, who barely took his nose out of the book he was reading to acknowledge the young man's presence. "Mrs. Zorin, the producer of the play—"

"Yeah, kid," the security guard said impatiently without looking up. "She told me you were going to park your bike here on the dock. She gave me this autographed book as compensation for my trouble. I would have preferred a couple of bucks, but this novel ain't too bad. That is, if you like murder mysteries."

Butch glanced at the dust jacket. The title was *Reluctant Witness* by Barbara Zorin, and he had read it.

"Can I go through here?" Butch said, pointing at the stage door.

"Sure. That Zorin woman said it's okay for you to go in that way. Course, I can't be responsible for your motorcycle. My job is to watch the stage door, not be no parking lot attendant."

"I understand, sir. The bike's locked, and I'll be taking my helmet with me. Have a good evening." With that, he entered the theater.

Stashing his helmet behind a stack of lumber backstage, Butch headed for the lobby. He could hear the orchestra warming up and knew the play would be starting soon. He was walking past a row of props, which were positioned on one of the sets, when he heard a low animal growl coming from behind him. Startled, he spun around and looked right into the feline face of the huge tiger in its cage. His heart was pounding in his chest when he heard a woman's soft laugh. From someplace close by, but hidden from view, she said, "What's the matter, honey? Cat got your tongue?"

Butch backed slowly away until he reached the lobby entrance. The theater doors were just about to close on the main floor and he hurried over to give his ticket to an usher. Butch took the stub and was about to head for his seat when another latecomer walked up to the usher. Butch glanced back and looked into the face of the most beautiful young woman he had ever seen.

Her jet-black hair was worn shoulder length and framed a delicate face with exotic dark eyes, long lashes, and well-defined eyebrows, a keen nose and full sensuous lips. Wearing a black "after five" dress with a single strand of white pearls at her throat, she was slender but not frail, possessing prominent breasts and athletic legs. The young police cadet was so absorbed with this exotic woman, he didn't realize she had taken her ticket stub back from the usher and that he was blocking her from proceeding into the theater. At that moment, she looked directly at him.

Their eyes met for no more than a few seconds, yet in that brief period, something electric passed between them. Had Blackie Silvestri been present, he would have informed the young man, who was as close to him as a son, that he had just been hit by what was referred to in old country Italian folklore as "the lightning bolt."

Finally, the young woman moved her lips to say a shy, almost whispered, "Excuse me."

This galvanized Butch, and like a man awakened from a deep sleep by a bucket of ice water, he jumped out of her way, saying, "I'm sorry. I . . . uh. . . ." Then words failed him.

Carrying her ticket in one hand and a black clutch bag in the other, she walked past him into the theater. She had gone about ten paces when she turned around to look back at him. When she saw that he was still staring at her, she blushed and turned abruptly, which caused her to lose control of the leather binocular case she carried on a strap slung over her shoulder. The case almost fell to the floor, but she managed to catch it. When she continued on her way, Butch was not far behind her.

Larry Cole had arrived at the theater a full five minutes before his son and was now in seat 7L of the Albert Ivar Goodman Theater. The last seat in the row was 7M, which Butch held the ticket for. As they had left the apartment at the same time, Cole expected his son to arrive at any second. The orchestra was playing a medley of show tunes, and the opening curtain was scheduled to go up in less than two minutes. The chief of detectives settled in with a copy of *Playbill* magazine, which had been handed out at the usher's station. The current *Playbill* edition listed the particulars of the *Murder at the Opera* performance, including the biographies of all the play's contributors, producers, writers, actors, and the director.

Cole was looking forward to Richard Banacek's performance. The cop had seen the actor in a number of local stage productions, and Cole had remarked on more than one occasion that Banacek possessed the brilliance and dramatic range of such noted actors as Jack Nicholson and Kevin Spacey. Yet despite possessing tremendous talent, Banacek had never gone much beyond off-Broadway stage productions.

When Richard Banacek was cast in one of the principal roles in *Murder at the Opera,* Cole had been introduced to him by Jamal Garth following a rehearsal. At the time, the pale, thin, dark-haired actor had been polite but oddly withdrawn in the policeman's presence. To Cole, who had been a cop for most of his adult life, it was obvious that Richard Banacek was hiding something. However, without a legitimate reason to look into his background, Cole would just have to sit on his suspicions.

The theater was filling to capacity rapidly, and the house lights blinked a couple of times, signaling that the play was about to start. Cole turned around to see if he could locate Butch when he heard two men arguing.

The verbal combatants were standing at the back, but their argument drew the attention of everyone in that section of the theater. Cole recognized both men.

The tall black muscular man with the shaven head, hard features, and a stocky build was Franklin Butler, a former NFL fight end—and a prominent attorney. Butler's primary legal specialty was a mystery. He had represented clients in both criminal and civil cases, but was rumored to have organized crime connections that spanned from Chicago street gangs to the operations of La Cosa Nostra and the Russian Mafiya. From information contained in confidential CPD

Organized Crime Division intelligence reports, Butler was rumored to have moved into money laundering for any segment of the criminal element that could pay his fee. Cole found Butler's presence unsettling at the opening night performance of *Murder at the Opera*. Particularly because the alleged mob lawyer was arguing with C. J. Cantrell, one of the play's financial backers.

Charles Jason Cantrell was a third-generation La Salle Street banker who was reportedly worth over a quarter of a billion dollars. His father and grandfather before him had made fortunes buying and selling anything of value in Chicago over the past seventy-five years. C. J.'s father, Carlton Michael Cantrell, used the initials C.M. and had once come close to being indicted for bank fraud in the late 1960s. C. M. Cantrell managed to get off by bribing the right judicial officials, themselves later indicted in a massive Cook County Court scandal some years afterward.

C. J. had a reputation for honesty, but he was plagued by the curse of continuous financial failure. Despite his millions, everything that he touched turned out disastrously, whether it was a stock deal or a bank merger. The financial pages of newspapers from coast to coast reported that C. J. Cantrell had recently lost over $100 million in bad investments and failed mergers. Whether that was true or not was a matter of some speculation. Now C. J. was one of the financial backers of *Murder at the Opera,* and it was anticipated that the play was going to be a tremendous success both artistically and financially.

For all that Franklin Butler was tall, black, and powerfully built, C. J. Cantrell was short, white, and rotund. He stood five feet four inches tall and weighed 230 pounds. He had an unruly mop of curly dark brown hair, a jowly face, and kewpie doll eyes, and he resembled an inflated balloon with a painted face on it. To see the short egg-shaped

Cantrell arguing with Franklin Butler was somewhat ludicrous; however, their words were far from amusing.

"I warned you, Cantrell!" Butler shouted, towering over the smaller man.

Refusing to be cowed, Cantrell stood his ground and yelled back, "Don't threaten me, Butler! I'm going to vote the way I see fit and not be intimidated by you or anyone else."

The usually unflappable Franklin Butler was in a rage, as evidenced by the veins standing out like a road map on his dark forehead. For a moment, Cole, still seated in row seven, thought that Butler was going to physically attack Cantrell. Then the lawyer happened to notice the scrutiny directed at him by a number of the theatergoers in that section. This resulted in Butler's undergoing an amazing transformation. Within the blink of an eye, the tension drained from his body, the veins on his forehead vanished, and he even managed a smile.

Franklin Butler said, "No sweat, C. J. Do whatever you think is right, and good luck with the play." With that, he turned around and walked toward the rear of the theater.

Cantrell remained in place, continuing to fume following the confrontation. Finally, face flushed and breathing hard, he stomped off to find his seat. No sooner had the preproduction argument ended, than Butch Cole came down the aisle.

"Where have you been?" Cole said as his son slid into seat 7M and the house lights dimmed.

But the younger man was twisted around in his seat, staring at someone on the opposite side of the aisle a couple of rows back.

Cole attempted to follow his son's line of sight, but due to the lights being extinguished, he was initially unable to see who Butch was so absorbed with. Then the stage lights came up and Cole saw the beautiful young woman in seat 9N. To the veteran cop she looked familiar, but he was unable to place her. He had to admit one thing: His son had tremendously good taste. The lady in black with the strand of white pearls around her slender neck was a dead ringer for a young Elizabeth Taylor.

The curtain began to rise and the orchestra began the opening number. Turning back to face front, Cole said to his son, "I think she's going to be here for the entire performance, Butch. So you'll get a chance to see her at the intermission."

Reluctantly, Butch turned around and said, "I sure hope so, Dad."

4

T he curtain rose on a set depicting the exterior of the Savoy playhouse in London. A tall, stately, white-haired man dressed in a dark blue double-breasted suit and black derby hat strode onto the stage and said, "It is the summer of 1947 and the world is still recovering from the ravages of World War Two. In London, the cinema and playhouses, such as the Savoy behind me, are packed to capacity every night of the week. This evening's performance features stage magician Sean Price in the musical comedy *Magic Man*. The overall production was panned by a theater critic for the London *Daily Mail*, who stated, and I quote." The narrator removed a folded newspaper from his suit jacket pocket. "'*Magic Man* is a second-rate perfor-mance more suited for a carnival sideshow than a London stage.'"

The line brought mild laughter from the audience in the Good-man Theater.

Returning the newspaper to his pocket, the narrator continued, "Yes, perhaps *Magic Man* is a less notable theatrical work than *Mac-beth, Othello,* or *The Mousetrap,* but tonight the stage performance will take a turn from the whimsy of magic to the dastardly crime of murder. Then I, Chief Inspector Cullen Knight of Scotland Yard, will be called upon to literally bring down the curtain. But first—as the magicians say—Abracadabra, the show must go on."

The stage lights dimmed briefly, and when they came back up, the Savoy playhouse set and Inspector Cullen Knight were gone, re-placed by a man in a black cape and top hat standing at center stage with his back to the audience. A single spotlight was trained on him, and the backdrop was in total darkness. Slowly, the actor turned around to reveal Richard Banacek in a white tie and black tails. He leaned forward on a black ebony cane and, after the opening applause for the popular actor subsided, the orchestra began to play and Ba-nacek sang the opening song, "Abracadabra."

The young woman in the black dress opened her binocular case when the opening curtain went up and the actor portraying the role of Chief Inspector Cullen Knight appeared on stage. From the case, she removed a pair of bulky Zeiss binoculars that would have been more suitable for long-range outdoor use. She raised the glasses and looked through the eyepieces. With the range of the instrument at its lowest setting, the image of the actor portraying Cullen Knight filled the left lens. She was unable to see anything at all through the right lens. That did not alarm her.

The woman, with whom Butch Cole had become smitten at first sight, was Morgana Devoe. Since Carlos Perfido had killed her uncle and chased her into the Rhône in Geneva eight years ago, she had been searching for him. When she discovered that he had become American actor Richard Banacek, Morgana had devised a dramatic means to assassinate him.

Still sighting in on Inspector Knight, Morgana reached up with the index finger of her right hand and located a switch built into the side of the binoculars' housing. Pushing the switch upward activated the right lens. Her view of the stage through this lens was remarkably different. The crosshairs of a gun sight had been placed over the lens, as well as a computerized distance calibrator installed. Moving the activation switch backward or forward enabled her to adjust the sight. The view through the right lens was not so expansive as was the case with the left lens. That was because the binocular housing had been modified to contain a nine-millimeter pistol barrel, a firing mechanism, and a four-round bullet clip. The device had been perfected by Isaac Weiss for the Mossad and was accurate up to 150 feet. The calibrated scale revealed that Inspector Knight, standing at stage right, was sixty-two feet away from Morgana's 9N seat. When Richard Banacek appeared at center stage in the second scene, the scale registered him at a distance of forty-seven feet. Keeping the murderer-turned-actor in her sight, she waited.

Butch was turned at an angle, so that he could see the stage and at the same time, with a minimal amount of effort, keep an eye on the woman in seat 9N. He heard little of Inspector Knight's opening monologue and merely glanced at the stage when the magician began to sing and dance through the "Abracadabra" number. Within less than a minute, he was looking back over his shoulder. He saw the young woman raise the binoculars and adjust the lenses. Momentarily, her use of the magnification device puzzled him, because their seats were so close to the stage. Then his father whispered, "You're going to hurt your neck if you keep turning around like that."

"Yes, sir," Butch said, sitting straight in his seat and focusing his total attention on the play. Actually, he felt embarrassed for behaving like a lovesick puppy in front of his father. After all, Larry Cole Jr. was the Chicago Police Department's cadet group commander.

Richard Banacek, in his role of magician Sean Price, danced from one end of the stage to the other as he sang "Abracadabra." During the song-and-dance number, he pulled a rabbit from his top hat and a seemingly unending string of brightly colored scarves from up his sleeve. Making the rabbit and the scarves vanish, he danced over to an ornate lacquer cabinet, which appeared on cue out of the blackness of the darkened stage. Opening the cabinet, he used his cane to probe its vacant interior. Then he closed the door and spun the cabinet around through three complete revolutions. He made a bright red cloth appear out of thin air and draped this cloth over the cabinet before stepping back and singing the word "Abracadabra." When he yanked the red cloth away and it vanished, the lacquer cabinet had been replaced by the shapely magician's assistant dressed in a red, white, and blue leotard.

Magician and assistant danced stage left as he sang, "In the world of magic, nothing is ever as it seems. At least not for long."

An empty animal cage with iron bars appeared at stage right. The magician swung his assistant in a wide arc to deposit her gently inside the cage. He closed and padlocked the cage before again pulling the red cloth. Draping the cloth over the cage, he again sang, "Abracadabra."

When he snatched the cloth away, the assistant was gone and the tiger stared out at the audience through the bars. A collective gasp escaped from the 850 theatergoers in the Albert Ivar Goodman Theater. This was followed by thunderous applause.

True showman that he was, the actor playing the magician danced to center stage. He waited patiently for the applause to subside before he sang, "In the world of magic, nothing is ever as it seems. Abracadabra."

Then he began a rapid pirouette, during which his costume, which had been chemically treated, changed colors from black to red to blue and, finally, back to black again.

The audience was completely enthralled by the performance, and from his seat in the last row of the theater, Franklin Butler watched the drama within a drama within a drama unfold.

Morgana Devoe's distance calibrator read forty-eight feet. The spinning actor at center stage was directly in the crosshairs of her sight. During the opening song, he had moved around so much, she was unable to get a fix on him. Now he was stationary even though the pirouette and his multicolor changing costume made him no more than a blur in her lens. This was her chance. Her plan was to empty the four rounds of nine-millimeter ammunition into his body. At this range, assisted by the delicate instrumentation of the computerized mechanism, she couldn't miss. The trigger was located beneath the targeting lens. She had practiced with this weapon and was capable of hitting a bull's-eye with a tight shot group at the maximum 150-foot range. All she had to do was pull the trigger and she would avenge the death of her uncle eight years ago. She couldn't recall a day during those years that she had not dreamed of this moment. Now that it was finally here, her resolve began deserting her.

Morgana ground her back teeth together with such force that her jaw muscles ached. The magician would not continue the pirouette indefinitely, and when he stopped there was no telling when she would get another opportunity to exact her measure of vengeance. The pirouette slowed and this galvanized Morgana into action. She pulled the trigger twice. The binoculars bucked and, despite the baffles built into the firing chamber to muffle the noise, the crack of the discharging pistol shots sounded unusually loud to her.

She waited long enough to see him stop spinning, stare quizzically at the audience, and begin collapsing to the stage. Before he hit the floor, she was out of her seat and walking rapidly toward the exit. She kept the deadly binoculars clutched tightly in her hand.

The secret of doing a dancing pirouette without getting dizzy is to pick a stationary spot to focus the attention on during the spin. This helps the dancer maintain his equilibrium. Richard Banacek had completely overcome the pangs of anxiety he had experienced back in his dressing room at the instant the spotlight framed him at center stage.

To the actor, performing before a live audience was the most sensually stimulating activity he could engage in short of sexual intercourse. During his now-defunct criminal career, dangerous acts, such as bank robberies, assassinations, and shootouts with the police, had provided similar stimulation, but at a much greater risk. And despite the personal peril being minimized by his change of profession, he still found some degree of erotic danger present when he stepped in front of a live audience.

Banacek's opening number, featuring the song "Abracadabra," had gone off exactly the way it had been rehearsed with the exception that his comely assistant in the striped leotard moved as if her feet were encased in cement. But each of the gags, right up to the tiger trick, came off very much to the actor's satisfaction and the enjoyment of the audience. As he went into his pirouette, he focused on the tiger cage. The beast was locked inside, studying the magician with the yellow eyes of a man-eating predator. Banacek was certain that if the iron bars had not been present, the tiger would quickly make a meal of him.

The pirouette was one of the actor's dancing masterpieces. It consisted of ten 360-degree high-speed turns that took a total of five seconds. He had one more verse of "Abracadabra" to sing, and then they would move on to the next scene in the play.

He came out of his seventh spin, feeling inertia beginning to slow him down. On the eighth revolution, he saw a flash followed by a hard blow at the center of his chest. He was halfway through the ninth revolution when he felt a sharp pain in his upper right arm. But the pain in his chest became all encompassing. Richard Banacek managed to face the audience before he fell to the floor of the stage and died.

When the magician suddenly collapsed, the audience was momentarily confused. The *Playbill,* as well as advance publicity concerning the performance, had advertised the magician's murder during the first act, but the manner in which Banacek had fallen to the stage without preamble was amateurish to the point of being crude, from a theatrical standpoint. Despite the collective unease of the 850 theatergoers present, there was a smattering of nervous applause. Then, after some moments passed during which the actor failed to move, a murmur of dissatisfaction swept through the theater. Finally, the curtain came down.

Standing in the wings of the Albert Ivar Goodman Theater, Barbara Zorin saw Richard Banacek's unexpected fall. As the author of the *Murder at the Opera* stage play, she knew the actor's collapse was not in the script. In fact, his stage death would not occur in view of the audience, so something was very wrong.

She stared ominously at the unmoving actor, hoping that he would somehow rise and manage to work his fall into the play. Such improvisation was the mark of the gifted performer. But Banacek remained motionless.

The director and stagehands shook themselves out of the shock that had taken hold, and the curtain came down. Barbara was one of the first to reach the fallen actor. One of the stagehands turned Banacek over to reveal an ever-expanding bloodstain on the front of his shirt. Barbara had written about death and done enough research for her mystery novels to realize that Richard Banacek was not only dead, but he had been shot as well. She also knew the procedure for protecting the crime scene.

The stagehand was reaching to loosen the actor's collar when Barbara ordered, "Don't touch him."

The stagehand, a thin young man with blond hair who had taken the backstage job as an entrée to an acting career, stared quizzically at her.

"Get up and go out in the audience," she stated in an authoritative tone. "Chief of Detectives Larry Cole and his son are in seats 7L and 7M. Ask them to come back here as quickly as possible. Be discreet when you talk to them, and try not to let anyone else know what has happened. Do you understand?"

He nodded, got to his feet, and rushed off to do what she had instructed.

The murmur of the disgruntled audience carried through the closed curtain. She turned to find a stunned Jamal Garth standing a short distance away.

"He's been shot," the author said with a confused frown. "How could—?"

"Larry Cole is out in the audience, Jamal," Barbara said. "I sent a stagehand to get him. But the theater manager must make an announcement to calm the audience before we have a riot on our hands."

Hearing angry voices coming from the theater, the author rushed off to locate the stage manager.

Barbara then had the stage cleared until Larry Cole could arrive. Left alone with the dead body and the caged tiger staring out at her through the bars, she muttered, "Talk about life imitating art."

From seat 7L of the Goodman Theater, Larry Cole had witnessed Richard Banacek's sudden collapse and realized instantly that this was not part of the scheduled performance. He also heard a pair of soft popping noises, which he couldn't accurately identify, coming from somewhere behind him on the right at the same time the actor fell. He had turned to look in the direction from which the strange sounds had come in time to see the young woman, whom Butch had been eyeing, hurrying toward the exit. Without knowing exactly what was going on or why, Cole saw no reason to pursue her at the moment. Before he could mention the woman's departure to his son, Butch was already out of his seat, following her.

The curtain came down and the audience began grumbling. Cole was about to go backstage and inquire if he could be of any assistance when the stagehand approached. Leaning down across the seat Butch had just vacated, he relayed Barbara Zorin's message to Cole.

The chief of detectives had been a cop for a long time and was able to put together what had occurred. And it alarmed him.

Standing up, Cole said to the stagehand, "Tell Mrs. Zorin that I'll summon police assistance and an ambulance right away."

"You're not coming backstage with me right now?" the stagehand asked with confusion.

Pulling his department-issue Motorola combination radio/telephone from his tuxedo jacket pocket, Cole replied, "I've got to check on something first." With that, he rushed toward the exit that his son and the woman in black had just taken.

Reaching the lobby, he saw Butch and the young woman standing on the other side of the empty lobby. Relieved, Cole placed a call to the CPD's Office of Emergency Communications before walking over to join them.

As he approached, he knew that there was something wrong simply by looking at his son's face. The young woman, who was even more radiant under the illumination of the theater complex's ornate lobby, stood in front of Butch. She had her head down and exuded a

pronounced tension. Cole could see that his son was equally troubled. He also noticed that Butch had the woman's binocular case in
one hand and his recently issued police cadet badge in the other.

Glancing from the young woman to his son, Cole asked, "What's
going on?"

Displaying no little degree of confusion, he explained, "I followed
this young lady out of the theater to find out her name. When I stopped
her, she asked if I was a police officer. I told her that I was and she demanded to see my badge." He glanced at her in case she had something to add, but she remained mute and stood motionless, staring at
the floor.

Butch added, "When I showed her the badge, she gave me this."
He held up the case. "She told me that there's a gun concealed inside
the binoculars, which she just used to kill Richard Banacek."

To say the least, Larry Cole was dumbfounded.

The murder of Richard Banacek had been committed in front of 850 eyewitnesses. There was no possible way the responding police officers could interview all of them as to what they had seen or heard. At least not tonight. What the six uniformed officers and four plainclothes detectives who reported to the theater were instructed to do by Chief Larry Cole was to verify the identities of all those present. Then their names, addresses, and telephone numbers were to be recorded so that the investigating detectives could talk to them later, if necessary. Cole went up on the stage and personally made the announcement to the audience. The procedure was carried out with only two problems developing.

An elderly socialite with snow-white hair took offense over the tedium of the police operation and raised very vocal objections. "I didn't come here to be interrogated like a common criminal. I demand to be allowed to leave this theater at once!" she screamed at the young female officer stationed at one of the exits.

Before the officer could respond, Larry Cole stepped in front of the disgruntled woman. "This is a homicide investigation, madam," he said quietly, "and we need your cooperation."

"Well, you're not going to get it," she railed. "Now get out of my way."

Cole didn't move. "I'm sorry, but you leave me no choice. You are under arrest for obstructing justice."

"You're joking," she said defiantly.

"No, I'm not," he said, solemnly motioning to a pair of officers standing nearby.

Within seconds, the socialite was handcuffed and on her way to the central detention facility. Larry Cole was definitely not joking.

The only other problem experienced during this phase of the investigation was encountered when a middle-aged man sporting a distinguished Vandyke beard was unable to produce any means of verifying his identity. The detective recording his information summoned the chief of detectives.

"Did you leave your wallet at home, sir?" Cole asked.

"Uh, yes," the man said, shoving his hands into his pockets to conceal the fact that they were trembling. "I can go home and get my driver's license for you. I'll bring it to the police station anytime you'd like."

Cole shook his head. "An officer will have to accompany you. Where do you live?"

All the color drained from the man's face. "Is all of this really necessary?"

With a hard, riveting stare, Cole said, "I'm afraid that it is."

It was later discovered that the distinguished gentleman sporting the Vandyke beard was a bigamist wanted in four states.

The remaining 848 theatergoers and twenty-seven members of the production company who were in the theater at the time of the murder cooperated fully with the investigation.

The time-consuming process was still going on when Cole returned to the stage to check on the Crime Lab's progress in collecting evidence. All the overhead lights were on, and the curtain remained closed, concealing the crime scene from the audience. The tiger had to be removed from the theater, because once the predatory cat detected the scent of the dead man's blood, it became highly agitated. Cole was amazed by the relative ease with which the magician's assistant in the skimpy leotard herded the five hundred-pound beast from the stage and placed it in a transport cage.

The body had been removed and the Crime Lab technicians were crating up the evidence they had collected and putting away their equipment. Captain Mike Zefeldt, who was in charge of the Crime Lab crew, spied Cole and came over to report.

"Everything is consistent with what you told us about the shots being fired from the audience, Boss," said Zefeldt, a Hercule Poirot look-alike with a fifty-pound advantage in weight; however, his mustache was identical to that of the fictional Agatha Christie detective. "We can account for three rounds: two in the deceased and one which struck the back wall of the set."

The young woman who had confessed to the murder of Richard Banacek had identified herself as Morgana Devoe. She had surrendered to Butch, which Cole knew would probably give him future nightmares. The weapon she used was the most sophisticated piece

of concealed ordnance that Cole had ever seen. He was still unable
to shake the uncanny feeling that the young female killer seemed familiar to him. Larry Cole was quite certain that before this investigation was concluded he would know a great deal about the stunningly
beautiful Morgana Devoe.

There was also something about what she said earlier that was
bothering him.

Following her surrender, Cole, accompanied by Butch, escorted
Morgana to the theater manager's office, which was located just off
the main lobby. There Cole had advised her of her Constitutional
rights as Butch looked on. When he recited the Miranda warnings,
she listened patiently, looking up at him with those big brown eyes
that exuded innocence. Cole felt as if he were arresting a child. When
he finished, she openly confessed to committing the murder.

Cole opened the leather case but did not touch the deadly binoculars. He had instead turned them over to the Crime Lab technicians
for examination. During her confession, Morgana stated that she had
fired two rounds at Banacek.

Now Captain Zefeldt was telling Cole that three rounds had been
discovered: two in the dead man's body and one in the rear wall of the
stage set.

"Did you check out her binoculars?" Cole asked Zefeldt.

"Just a minute, Chief," the captain said before calling out to a
technician on the other side of the stage. "Hey, Jerry, did you check
out those binoculars the boss gave us?"

The Crime Lab technician was a middle-aged black man with a
receding hairline. "Sure did, Cap," Jerry called back, reaching into a
portable metal evidence locker and removing a sealed plastic bag.
Carrying this bag, he walked over to join Cole and Zefeldt.

Jerry held up the evidence bag so that they could see its contents.
The housing of the right barrel was open, revealing the sighting and

firing mechanisms. "I've never seen anything like this before in my life. The inner workings are as delicate as a fine clock mechanism. A genuine master craftsman put this thing together."

"Did the girl tell you where she got it, Boss?" Zefeldt asked Cole.

The chief of detectives shrugged. "She said she made it herself."

The Crime Lab technicians were too stunned by this revelation to comment. Finally, Jerry continued his verbal report. "The gun has a spring-loading clip with a four-round capacity and is calibrated to be accurate over a distance of one hundred feet."

"How many rounds were fired?" Cole asked.

Jerry responded. "Two."

This surprised Captain Zefeldt and Chief of Detectives Larry Cole.

"Are you sure, Jerry?" Zefeldt asked.

"Yeah, Cap. I checked it out myself. There were two rounds discharged, and the expended shell casings were ejected into the binocular housing. A very self-contained lethal weapon."

Cole looked at Zefeldt. "We've got to find out the origin of that third bullet, Mike. Run a ballistics test on the weapon when you get back to headquarters. I want to know if the round you retrieved from the back wall of the set was fired from Morgana Devoe's gun. Have your people do a match on the bullets that the medical examiner removes from Banacek's body. I want to know where that third bullet came from."

Morgana Devoe was transported to detective division headquarters at 3510 South Michigan Avenue. Although she surrendered without incident and had so far cooperated with the investigation, she was in handcuffs when a burly pair of male uniformed officers escorted her to a police wagon parked in front of the Goodman Theater. The news media arrived, and the image of the elegantly dressed young woman appeared on nightly newscasts. The beautiful arrestee was dubbed the "Murderess of the Opera."

At headquarters, she was escorted into a drab interrogation room with white cinder block walls, and tables and chairs bolted to the dark blue carpeted floor. The handcuffs were removed and she took a seat on one of the straight-back, uncomfortable metal chairs. She cast a lonely gaze at her surroundings and noticed the pair of closed-circuit cameras mounted on the ceiling. She knew that someone was watching her and that she would remain under official surveillance for the rest of her life. The thought made her shiver. She wondered if killing the murderer of her uncle had been worth throwing her life away.

In the drab atmosphere of the police interrogation room, Morgana drifted into the past.

She recalled coming home from school on that October day eight years ago and finding Carlos Perfido standing over Isaac Weiss. Her escape from the apartment and run to the river was a blur, but the one thing paramount in her mind was escape. She made the decision to jump into the Rhône. She didn't think her uncle's killer would follow her, because the odds of her staying alive in the turbulent water were very slim. She knew that if she fell into Perfido's hands, the odds of her staying alive were zero.

The instant she hit the water, two things struck her at once: she had indeed managed to elude the killer, and she was now in equally deadly peril. The water was ice cold, and she was dragged beneath the surface by the treacherous current. She fought with all her might against the black water surrounding her, but she was held fast in an undertow that swept her along at a dangerously fast pace. She broke the surface once and managed to take in some air, but she also swallowed a great deal of water. Then she was dragged under again. The cold depths of the Rhône enveloped her, and she was about to surrender herself to the arms of death when she struck the sea wall. She managed to grab hold of the cement surface. She drifted in and out of consciousness, and then she was pulled from the water.

She awoke three days later in a hospital. She had nearly drowned and was suffering from exposure. A Geneva police detective arrived a short time later to question her about the murder of Isaac Weiss. She had little to say to the bald little man, who looked more like a banker than like a cop. Her uncle's death would be between her and Carlos Perfido.

A week later she was released from the hospital. The clothing she had nearly drowned in was all that she had to wear. Despite being wrinkled during her ordeal, the jumper, blouse, and stockings were still serviceable. Her beret and shoes were gone. She was surprised to discover that she had managed to hold on to her attaché case, which was with the rest of her personal belongings.

The police detective drove her back to the Carouge section of Geneva and even checked the apartment for her, which was something she did not request. The detective made some remarks about the necessity for a social services investigation to be conducted because she was a minor without an adult guardian. Morgana had no intention of becoming a Swiss ward. As soon as the detective left, she began making plans to secure her independence.

Being alone in the apartment where her uncle had died made her uneasy. She was also forced to face the possibility that Perfido would come back for her. Within a week of her release from the hospital, she had moved from the Geneva apartment into a hotel room in Zurich. She had enough money to live on temporarily, but she would need a steady source of income. She obtained the name of her uncle's solicitor in Geneva and made an appointment to see him. What she learned from the lawyer not only shocked her, but also left her financially secure for the rest of her life.

Morgana Devoe had been on her own since then and had spent a great deal of time and money searching for the man she had murdered earlier tonight.

The ceiling cameras in the interrogation room where Morgana Devoe was being held were connected to a pair of monitors in the chief of detectives' office. Butch Cole, still clad in his father's white dinner jacket, was staring intensely at the young woman. Even though she confessed that she had killed Richard Banacek, Butch could not bring himself to believe she was a murderer.

There was a knock on the office door followed by Manny Sherlock coming in. The sergeant was a tall man in his mid-thirties who wore a pair of horn-rim glasses that gave him a slightly owlish look. He sported an unruly mop of curly black hair that defeated any attempt at control by a comb and brush. Manny had been one of the youngest detectives in the history of the Chicago Police Department. In a sense, because he had been under the command of Larry Cole for most of his police career, the sergeant thought of Butch as a little brother.

Manny smiled when he saw the chief's son. "It didn't take you long to get on the board, Butch. You only graduated from the academy this afternoon and you've already made your first homicide arrest."

Manny had expected the remark to draw at least a smile, but when Butch continued to stare solemnly at the monitors, the sergeant detected that there was something wrong. "You want to talk about it?"

It took Butch a moment to respond. Finally, he shrugged and said, "I can't believe that she's a killer, Manny."

Manny also looked at the monitor. "She's a very attractive young lady."

Butch caught his meaning. "It's not just her looks. I've got a feeling about her."

"Don't let Blackie hear you say that. He hates hunches. When your father called me, he said that she not only surrendered to you at the theater, but she also confessed to shooting the actor."

Butch sighed. "That's right."

"There's one more thing that your father told me," Manny said. "You followed her out of the theater after the murder and stopped her in the lobby."

Butch merely nodded without taking his eyes off the monitors.

Manny continued. "She still had that trick weapon and she could have easily killed you, too."

The young man's shoulders sagged. "Yes, she could have, Manny, but she didn't."

Manny placed a protective hand on the cadet's shoulder. "I've got to take a statement from her. Do you want to sit in?"

"Could I?" Butch said, his spirits brightening for the first time since Morgana Devoe had surrendered to him.

"Let's go," Manny said.

Attorney Franklin Butler's chauffeur-driven black Lincoln limousine picked him up in front of the Goodman Theater. Settling into the leather backseat, he instructed his driver to take him home. Opening the liquor cabinet, Butler removed a bottle of Ambassad 25 Scotch, dumped ice cubes from the mini-refrigerator into a crystal goblet, and poured a double shot of liquor. Before taking a sip of his drink, he toasted himself. The earlier problem he'd had with C. J. Cantrell was minor in the general scheme of things.

The black limo traveled east to Michigan Avenue before turning north onto the Magnificent Mile. Butler lived and worked in DeWitt Plaza. His legal practice had made him a millionaire many times over. However, he wanted more. A great deal more.

Franklin Butler had succeeded in everything he had ever attempted in his life. He was born in Aiken, South Carolina, the fourth of six children born to a veterinarian father who specialized in the treatment of farm animals, and a mother who prided herself on being the best cook in the farm country where they lived. His three older brothers, older sister, and younger sister still resided in South Carolina and had entered occupations related to their parents' lifelong agrarian pursuits. Two of his brothers were veterinarians; the other was a farmer. His sisters owned successful catering businesses. At an early age, Franklin Butler realized that his destiny lay far away from the rural pursuits of Aiken, South Carolina.

In school, Butler excelled at all levels both academically and physically. He was a straight-A student and a star performer in football, basketball, baseball, and track. He was indeed talented both mentally and physically, but the primary reason behind his accomplishments was that he drove himself unmercifully not only to succeed, but also to be perfect at everything.

He could have attended any college he desired on a full scholarship, but the prospect of a regular college curriculum and even participation at Level I sports did not present a sufficient challenge for him. He applied for and was accepted to the United States Military Academy at West Point. There he found the exact challenge he was looking for. At least for the time being.

The strict discipline and demands of the Point placed Butler in his natural element. He learned early on that there were few cadets who could compete at his level. In fact, before he entered his third year, there was no cadet in his class who could even come close to him. And everything he accomplished in his studies, in close-order drill, in the physical training, and on the football field was due primarily to his overwhelming desire to succeed at all costs.

It surprised no one on the West Point staff when Butler graduated first in his class; however, a number of the officers who had encountered him questioned how effective the super-achieving second lieutenant would be in the command of mere mortal human beings.

Butler was in the West Point graduating class of 1971. Playing one season in the NFL, he was an all-pro fight end for the Bears. At his request, however, he was sent to Ranger Training with the Eighty-second Airborne at Fort Benning, Georgia, the following season. After jump school, First Lieutenant Butler was assigned as the company commander of a Ranger unit in Vietnam. He arrived in country in time to take over a group of soldiers who had never been in combat.

Company C of the Eighty-second Airborne Division, First Battalion, First Brigade was assigned to the joint forces military compound outside of Tuy Hoa City, South Vietnam. As soon as the soldiers of Company C set foot on the metal prefabricated airfield, Lieutenant Butler began rigorously training them for combat duty. Eight days later, the company was sent out on a long-range patrol. The mission objective was for Company C to make contact with the enemy and then call in their location for artillery and air strikes from base camp. On the second day of the LRP, Company C encountered the Viet Cong.

A vicious firefight erupted while the forward observer attempted, in vain, to make radio contact with the rear echelon to obtain artillery and aerial support. Butler's Rangers were outnumbered five to one by a veteran fighting force. By rights, Company C should have been completely destroyed, and the Viet Cong came very close to doing just that, as the Rangers suffered over 75 percent casualties. But Butler forced his troops not only to fight, but also to inflict over 250 casualties on the opposing force. When reinforcements did arrive, the jungle was the scene of unprecedented carnage even for the senseless slaughter that the Vietnam War became known for. When it was all over, Lieutenant Franklin Butler was a hero.

Butler did two more tours of duty in Vietnam before the American forces withdrew. During the thirty-nine months he spent in country, he became a bona fide legend. But whether that legend was considered good or bad depended on who was being asked.

To his superiors, he was a highly dedicated officer and a miracle worker in combat. To his peers and contemporaries, he was a self-centered, fanatical, gung ho glory boy whose foolhardy combat exploits were going to someday get him and a lot of good soldiers killed unnecessarily. To the troops Butler commanded, he was the closest thing to a deity they had ever encountered on this earth.

By 1975, Butler had risen to the rank of major and was one of the most highly decorated soldiers to come out of the South East Asian conflict. It was rumored through the army grapevine that Franklin Butler would eventually become Army Chief of Staff or the Chairman of the Joint Chiefs. Given Butler's fanatical, single-minded approach and dedication to the soldier's profession, his projected rise was not a bad bet. Only the highly decorated major had other plans. When his military commitment was up, he surprised everyone by resigning from the army.

Butler approached his health and physical fitness with the same zeal that he had pursued his brief career with the Bears and the Rangers. He ran seven miles a day and engaged in a grueling weight-training program five days a week. Although he did consume an occasional cocktail, he did not smoke nor did he allow smoking in his presence. He did not eat red meat or pork.

He engaged in sexual intercourse with different women between five and six nights a week, depending on the demands of his busy schedule. His appetite was insatiable, and he often engaged in strenuous sex for four to five hours at a stretch. He hired thousand-dollar-a-night sex partners from a mob-owned call operation, and he used condoms to protect himself from disease. To keep from forming any attachments with the girls—and because few whores would tolerate him as a repeat customer—he required the call operation to supply him with a new girl for each session.

The hookers often compared notes on their prominent client.

They universally concluded he was well-endowed, a powerful sexual athlete, and that he tipped well. They were quick to warn the new girls, however, that Franklin carried a black leather paddle in his briefcase, and if they took the date, they would get to know it well. Instinctively sadistic, he overindulged in hard, sometimes prolonged bare-bottom spanking.

Otherwise he treated them with the kindness and compassion that a man would usually reserve for an inflatable sex toy.

Had Franklin overheard their professional critique, he would have been pleased, even flattered. After he had married and sired three darling daughters—whom he babied, spoiled, and never spanked—he continued his nightly trysts with these ladies of the evening.

His shrewish wife—who had long ago moved into a separate bedroom—knew intuitively that he saw other women. Obsessively suspicious of his late-night hours, she'd begun threatening to take their daughters and leave—a threat that invariably plunged him into dark despair.

Now Franklin feared that she'd put a private eye on him and was making good on her threat.

The black limousine pulled up to the long-term parking garage on the south side of DeWitt Plaza. Using a computerized access card, the muscular chauffeur, a white ex-marine, opened the gate and drove inside. He deposited his charge at a private elevator on the twelfth and highest level of the garage. Butler exited the backseat and used another computerized access card to summon the elevator car, which provided service to the penthouse only. When the elevator arrived, he rode up to the forty-eighth floor alone.

He stepped off into the spacious corridor on the lower level of the three-story penthouse. A bank of commercial elevators was on the opposite side of the corridor, which provided access during business hours from the twenty-fifth floor, where a security officer was stationed twenty-four hours a day. The forty-eighth floor of DeWitt Plaza was where the offices of FRANKLIN BUTLER—ATTORNEY AT LAW were located. He employed a staff of eight lawyers, six paralegals, and four secretaries in the eighteen rooms on this level. The previous occupants of the twenty-million-dollar multistoried penthouse had also used the forty-eighth floor to conduct business.

Butler crossed the wide corridor to a spiral staircase that led up to his private quarters on the forty-ninth and fiftieth floors. Those levels were as spacious and lavishly furnished as the suite of offices below. The lawyer lived there alone, and this arrangement was very much to Butler's liking.

Major Franklin Butler did not abandon his military career without having a definite plan of action in mind. During his years in Vietnam, he had come to the realization that he was being grossly underpaid for risking his life in the service of his country. His voracious reading of American history revealed that the poor and disenfranchised had fought and died for two hundred years in wars to protect the country, while the rich stayed safely at home and even made fortunes from selling arms. Butler assessed his position in society. He was a commissioned officer with a brilliant future. He had a chestful of metals, and if he played his cards right and didn't step on the wrong toes, he could retire as a general with a generous pension by military standards after twenty-five or thirty years of service. Then he could move back to South Carolina and raise chickens and pigs for the rest of his life. Or he could go for the jackpot.

With the money he had saved during his seven years of military service and the G.I. Bill, Butler applied for and was accepted to Harvard Law School. With the same dogged single-mindedness that had characterized his military career, Butler received his LL.D. degree with honors. Then he went to work building his own fortune.

The living room on the forty-ninth floor of DeWitt Plaza provided a panoramic view of the Magnificent Mile of North Michigan Avenue and the western shore of Lake Michigan. The sixty-square-foot space was in darkness, and Butler's deep voice pierced the gloom when he said, "Lights." Lamps and indirect ceiling lights blinked on. The furnishings had cost him over two million dollars, but Butler didn't consider this place his permanent residence. He had much bigger things planned, and so far, all was going well.

There were computers and telephones throughout the penthouse, which could instantaneously put him in touch with anyone on this planet. Activating a secure line, he pushed a button on the speed dial. When the connection was made, he said, "The girl performed exactly as I anticipated. Perfido is dead, and she was taken into custody at the theater. That is unfortunate, but not a disaster. Tomorrow I will move on to the next phase of the plan."

With that, he broke the connection.

A short time later he was in his private gym on the top floor of De-Witt Plaza. He was doing squats with a barbell loaded with three hundred pounds of iron. In the wall mirror, he admired his fifty-two-inch chest and twenty-inch arms. He was pleased he still had a full head of black hair, which he wore in a short three-inch ponytail.

He loved his palatial penthouse.

He loved his apartment building. This building on North Michigan Avenue had once belonged to multibillionaire serial killers Margo and Neil DeWitt. Now it belonged to Attorney Franklin Butler. He also had plans to get his hands on the rest of the DeWitt estate, which was worth over fifty billion dollars.

6

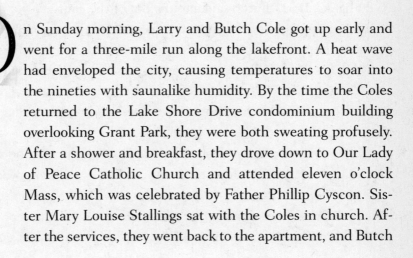

O n Sunday morning, Larry and Butch Cole got up early and went for a three-mile run along the lakefront. A heat wave had enveloped the city, causing temperatures to soar into the nineties with saunalike humidity. By the time the Coles returned to the Lake Shore Drive condominium building overlooking Grant Park, they were both sweating profusely. After a shower and breakfast, they drove down to Our Lady of Peace Catholic Church and attended eleven o'clock Mass, which was celebrated by Father Phillip Cyscon. Sister Mary Louise Stallings sat with the Coles in church. After the services, they went back to the apartment, and Butch changed into his cadet uniform. Then his father drove him to the Second District Police Station at 5101 South Wentworth. This was to be Butch's first day on the job following his graduation from the police academy.

When they pulled up in front of the police station, Cole was about to park the car preparatory to accompanying his son inside when Butch said, "Do you mind if I do this alone, Dad?"

"I was just going in to say hello to the watch commander," Cole said.

"Could you maybe drop in on him some other time after I've been here for a while?"

Cole understood what was going on. Butch wanted to do this by himself, at least as far as his first day on the job went. The father understood his son's desire for independence at this moment, and despite the pride he felt, he was also experiencing a certain degree of sadness. Butch was becoming a man.

"Okay, I'm going to headquarters to check on the investigation into Richard Banacek's death." He noticed his son's heightened interest. "I'll keep you posted on any new developments."

"Thanks, Dad," Butch said, getting out of the car.

Cole stopped him. "I want you to be careful in there. It can be a very dangerous place."

With a smile, the cadet responded, "As Uncle Blackie says, 'I'm always careful.'"

Cole waited until his son entered the building before he drove away.

When Cole arrived at detective division headquarters, he signed in at the front desk before checking with the skeleton weekend staff to see what was going on around the city. He then proceeded to his office, where he found a thick file containing all the reports on the Richard Banacek homicide. All the newspapers that had covered the story had also been left on his desk. The chief sat down and began to read.

Every media outlet in the country carried the story of the beautiful young woman accused of murdering actor Richard Banacek while he was performing onstage before a live audience. Actually, as of the morning of June 18, Morgana Devoe had not been charged with murder, but was being held on an illegal-weapons charge pending further investigation of the murder. The reason for that was the third bullet.

The firing mechanism concealed in Morgana's binoculars fired nine-millimeter standard pistol ammunition. Two rounds from the four-round magazine had been fired. One nine-millimeter bullet was recovered from the actor's right arm. The wound caused by this bullet was not fatal. The other bullet from the exotic weapon was found lodged in the back wall of the set. The bullet recovered from the dead actor's chest was a .45-caliber dumdum round, which had been altered to explode on contact and do maximum damage to the target. It had struck Banacek in the sternum, smashed into the chest cavity, and completely destroyed the heart and lungs. The force of the bullet would have knocked the actor some distance across the stage if the projectile's velocity had not been diminished by a silencer. So now the police were looking for a second gunman, also firing from the audience. The problem was that they had no way of knowing what direction the shot had come from due to Banacek's performing a pirouette at the time he was shot.

Blackie had come up with the initial theory that Morgana Devoe had an accomplice in the audience, one who fired at the same time she did. However, Cole didn't buy that. After firing at Banacek, she had immediately left the theater, and had Butch not been following her, she would have made good her escape. No one else left at that time, which would have been consistent with an accomplice being involved. Also, Morgana's bullets were standard-issue nine-millimeter, and the fatal .45 round had been lethally altered. In addition to that, Morgana had confessed to the crime in such an open manner that Cole was certain she wasn't hiding anything, such as the presence of an accomplice at the scene.

Despite the confession, Morgana had not provided them with a motive for the crime. When Cole had asked her why she shot the actor, her only response was that she had what she called, "compelling personal reasons."

Cole knew that by tomorrow morning, they would have a fairly extensive dossier on the young murderess. So far, they had learned she possessed an American passport under the name Morgana Devoe and had arrived at New York's JFK Airport from Zurich, Switzerland, on June 5. She had transferred fifty thousand dollars from a Geneva bank account to an account in her name at the Northern Trust Bank in Chicago. She had flown to Chicago on June 9 and had been living in a five-hundred-dollar-a-night suite at the Swissotel on Wacker Drive. Cole was having Blackie, Manny, and Judy look into her background going all the way back to the day she was born. Cole was also having Richard Banacek checked out.

The chief of detectives didn't believe that crime victims should be investigated in the same manner as crime perpetrators, but Richard Banacek's personal history presented the police with a complete mystery. All the actor's references prior to 1998 were bogus, and the autopsy discovered that the dead actor's fingerprints had been burned off with acid. Cole planned to find out what the connection was between Richard Banacek and Morgana Devoe, and at the same time discover who had actually killed the actor onstage.

He finished the reports and newspaper accounts of the murder during the performance of *Murder at the Opera*. He felt sorry for Barbara and Jamal, whose play had been cancelled after the death of their leading man. It was reported in the *Chicago Times-Herald* Arts and

Entertainment section that it was doubtful whether the play could ever be revived. Banacek's murder during the first act would be viewed as a jinx, and actors were exceptionally superstitious. Thinking of the play made Cole recall the tiger trick, which had been quite impressive.

Something suddenly struck Cole concerning the list of theater personnel that had been interviewed after the shooting. Going back to the list in the file, he found that there was one name missing: the magician's assistant and tiger handler. Her name was Pamela Hoffman, and she was a member of the stage actor's union. But that was all they had been able to find out about her. Cole remembered that she had been permitted to leave the theater when the tiger became agitated after catching the scent of the dead man's blood. The tiger was being temporarily housed at the Lincoln Park Zoo, and apparently Pamela Hoffman had dropped it off and had not returned to the theater. Cole placed a note in the file to have the investigating detectives check her out.

Now, even though Butch had wanted to enter the Second District for his first day on the job alone, Cole could see nothing wrong with calling the watch commander and discreetly inquiring as to how his son was doing. Cole dialed the number and heard the phone begin ringing on the other end.

Captain Gary Harmon, who was scheduled to be the third-watch commander in the Second District on this summer afternoon, had a very similar morning to Larry Cole's and his son's. The captain, a handsome black man with thick wavy hair, had exercised on a stationary bicycle and lifted weights in the wood-paneled recreation room of his modest south side home. Then he ate breakfast, showered, and dressed in a lightweight dark blue suit and open-necked white cotton shirt. He attended the eleven o'clock Mass at St. Columbanus Catholic Church, where he had been a lector for over thirty years and read both Scripture readings. After returning home, he consumed a tuna salad sandwich on whole-wheat toast and a glass of iced tea. As he was changing into his police uniform, he remembered that Larry Cole's son would be reporting for work today. Harmon was looking forward to mentoring the young cadet. Over the years, the captain and Larry Cole had crossed paths amicably many times. Cole's son would be treated like one of Harmon's own children.

Carrying a black leather portfolio, he left the house and walked out to his black Lexus sedan parked at the curb. He was about to get behind the wheel when a sleek silver gray Corvette pulled up and double-parked next to the Lexus. He frowned when he saw that the Vette was equipped with tinted windows, which were a violation of the Illinois Vehicle Code. Then the passenger-side automatic window was lowered to reveal a stunningly built young woman clad in a skimpy halter top and tight shorts seated behind the wheel. Her face was partially obscured by a pair of enormous sunglasses.

"Excuse me, Captain," she said, flashing a dazzling smile. "I recently moved in down the street, and I was wondering if you could help me."

Gary Harmon was a divorcé in his early fifties, but he kept himself in good shape and felt that he was as virile as any man half his age. At least once a night. And a neighbor with the obvious physical attributes of the Corvette driver might just be able to improve his average.

He walked over and bent down to look inside the car. The Vette had a pronounced new leather smell mixed with the woman's musky perfume. "How may I be of assistance?" he said, flashing a smile.

"It's my trip computer," she said, pointing at the dark screen set in the dashboard. "I've only had this car a short time, and I need to program it to get directions to Indianapolis."

This was easy. Such computers were becoming standard equipment in most top-of-the-line new cars. There was one in his Lexus, and the captain knew how to use it, so programming her car would be simple enough.

"Do you mind if I get in?" he asked.

"I'd be ever so grateful."

She unlocked the door, and he climbed into the bucket seat. He was silently amused to find that she hadn't even turned her computer on. Harmon was glad that he had allowed himself plenty of time to get to the station, because he was going to have to take her slowly through the trip computer's operation.

He pressed the ON button, and as the screen began brightening, he turned to glance at her. What he saw initially confused him before alarm set in. She was pointing a .45-caliber Smith & Wesson semiautomatic pistol at him. The gun was equipped with a wicked four-inch, sausage-shaped silencer, and the sexy young woman gave him every indication that she was quite good with the firearm.

"Now, you just relax, honey, and do what I say," she said, adopting a deep southern drawl, "and little Magda won't put a messy, very fatal hole in you. I want you to reach up slowly and use your right hand to buckle your seat belt."

With no other options available to him, Harmon complied.

"Now slip those beefy forearms beneath the lap strap," she ordered.

With his jaw muscles rippling in anger, he said, "Do you want to tell me what this is all about?"

"What would you say if I told you that I planned to make you my love slave?" she said mockingly.

"I don't think you want to hear what I would like to say to that right now," he said angrily.

The part of her face that was visible behind the sunglasses turned hard. "Then do us both a favor, Captain Harmon, and keep your mouth shut. As long as you do exactly what I tell you, there's an excellent chance that you'll survive this encounter."

With that, she raised the tinted window on the passenger side of the Corvette and drove off with her captive.

Police Cadet Butch Cole was forty-five minutes early for his scheduled reporting time for duty on his first day on the job. This was at his father's recommendation, and it gave him a chance to take a look around the station. The Area One Police Center, in which the Second Police District was located, had been formally named the Robert M. Harness Police Center in honor of one of the first African-American police commanders and most legendary law enforcement officers in Chicago Police history. Commander Harness had joined the force in 1933 and retired in 1970. There was a plaque dedicated to him in the station lobby, and Butch spent a few minutes reading the bio of the cop who had been known as "the Crusher."

There were also photographs in the lobby of officers who had been killed in the line of duty while assigned to the Second Police District. Butch also examined these, discovering that the oldest photo was of Patrolman Robert Granger, who was killed on April 9, 1932, at 5730 South Prairie Avenue and the most recent was of Police Officer Michael A. Ceriale, who was killed on August 15, 1998, at 31 West Root Street.

Butch was still examining the lobby photos when someone called to him, "Hey, kid, give me a hand, will you?"

He turned around to see a heavyset black man struggling to get through the front doors. The reasons for his difficulty were the two shopping bags bearing the Jewel Food Store logo and large metal roasting pan he was carrying. Butch rushed over to help.

"Thanks," the man said, handing over one of the shopping bags, which Butch found to be fairly heavy. "It's my turn to bring lunch."

He led the cadet across the lobby to a door set in the wall next to the L-shaped police station front desk. He knocked hard twice, and an attractive young female police aide, who was wearing a uniform similar to the cadet's, opened the door. "Well, it's about time, Sarge," she said with a smile.

The man who Butch had assisted was wearing a loud yellow, red, and green Hawaiian shirt over dark blue trousers and black oxford shoes, which tipped him off that he was a cop. Now Butch had discovered that he was also a sergeant.

Beyond the door leading off the lobby was an office equipped with an enormous copying machine, a refrigerator, a microwave oven, and two long narrow tables that had been covered with red-and-white checkered paper tablecloths. After placing the metal tray and shopping bags on one of the tables, the sergeant turned to Butch and extended a thick-fingered hand. "Sergeant Quentin Davies, Cole, but as your father will tell you, most people call me Q. I'm the desk sergeant on the third watch."

The police aide was standing by, watching them. "I guess that you two have met before."

"Not really," Sergeant Davies said, "but I'd know that head and the set of those shoulders anywhere. In that uniform, our new cadet couldn't be anyone else but Chief Larry Cole's son."

The aide extended her hand and said, "I'm Tara Spellman. Although Captain Harmon and Sergeant Davies run the third watch, I do all the paperwork and other miscellaneous administrative tasks, which they are much too busy to perform."

The sergeant interrupted. "Tasks like giving our new cadet a tour of the station after you put the food away." He turned to Butch and added, "It's kind of difficult to get a decent meal on Sunday, kid, so we take turns bringing in a spread. I hope you like soul food."

"Yes, sir," Butch responded. He was beginning to feel at home already.

"Give Tara a hand while I go change into my uniform. We always eat at six thirty after the last roll call. I hope you brought your appetite."

The cadet grinned. "I'm always hungry, Sarge."

There were four administrative support personnel assigned to the Second District desk under the supervision of Sergeant Quentin Davies. Today that staff consisted of Administrative Aide Tara Spellman, Police Cadet Larry Cole Jr., and limited duty Police Officers Perry Montoya and Anna Falk. Montoya was a thirty-year-old Hispanic with jet-black hair worn in a crew cut. He was forced to walk with a cane because he was recuperating from a near-fatal automobile accident that had occurred during a high-speed police chase of a stolen vehicle. Anna Falk, a slightly built young blond woman in her mid-twenties, was seven months pregnant. Falk had the distinction of being one of the most highly decorated officers currently assigned to the Second District. Despite her delicate condition, putting Falk behind the district desk was tantamount to hitching a thoroughbred horse to pull a plow.

As the 2 P.M. third-watch shift starting time approached, all of Sergeant Davies's desk personnel were in place. There was only one person missing, and that was the boss of the watch, Captain Gary Harmon.

Sergeant Davies donned a uniform shirt, which was clean, ironed, and starched but had seen better days. The patches were a bit faded, and the buttons in the ample midsection area appeared ready to pop off. But Sergeant Q. Davies had a well-deserved reputation for being one of the hardest-working desk sergeants in the busiest police station in the city.

Butch Cole was put to work the moment he set foot behind the desk. The computers, telephones, and fax machines were all in continuous operation, and the administrative staff was in constant motion, trying to keep up with the flow of data. Sergeant Davies oversaw everything from one of the double desks at the center of the enclosed area. Officer Montoya sat opposite the sergeant in what was called the "hot seat," where he was responsible for handling all the arrest reports, warrant listings, and court scheduling sheets for the prisoners that passed through the facility each day. Officer Falk was perched on a high swivel chair and served in the combination capacities as station receptionist, information officer, and report taker. Because they were the youngest and most agile members of the desk crew, Aide Spellman and Cadet Cole were responsible for answering the phones and monitoring computer and fax transmissions.

At a quarter past two, Sergeant Davies looked up at the twenty-four-hour clock on the west wall of the desk area and said, "Has anyone heard from the captain?"

Each of the veterans replied in the negative. The heavyset sergeant was obviously concerned about the missing watch commander.

"Do you want me to give him a call?" Anna Falk said.

The sergeant considered that briefly. "We'll wait awhile. Maybe he had car trouble."

"In a brand-new Lexus?" Montoya questioned.

"Tara, now's as good a time as any to give our new cadet a tour of the facility," the sergeant said. "Just don't be too long."

"Yes, sir," the aide said. "C'mon, Cole. We'll start in the lockup."

Butch followed her toward the detention area. As they walked down the corridor, he said to her, "Everyone seems really worried about the watch commander being late."

Tara Spellman was grim. "That's because he has never been late before in the six years that he's been assigned here."

The lieutenant came in through the south entrance from the parking lot. He was dressed in a sharply creased uniform and walked with a shoulders-back, gut-sucked-in military gait. He stood over six feet five inches tall and was rapier thin. When he came up to the station desk, Montoya noticed him and said to Sergeant Davies, "We've got company."

The sergeant turned around on his swivel chair to face the new arrival. "What can I do for you, Lieutenant?"

The lieutenant had slate-gray eyes, which made the coldness of his gaze assume arctic proportions. "Isn't it customary to stand when you are in the presence of a superior officer, Sergeant?"

Quentin Davies stared quizzically at the lieutenant. Actually, it was not a common practice within the Chicago Police Department for subordinates to stand in the presence of higher-ranking officers. However, Sergeant Davies had been around long enough to know when to humor officious types like this lieutenant. Getting to his feet, Davies said, "Begging the lieutenant's pardon, but we are quite busy right now."

It wasn't really an apology, but the lieutenant didn't press it. "Where's the watch commander's office?"

"Right there, sir," Davies said, pointing to a door across the south corridor from the station desk. "But the captain's not in right now."

The lieutenant's chilly gaze did not alter. "And he won't be. I'll be the third-watch commander tonight."

With that, he turned and entered the office, leaving a stunned desk crew behind him.

Tara Spellman used a heavy brass key attached to a circular metal ring, which she had removed from Sergeant Davies's desk, to unlock the heavy metal door at the entrance to the detention facility. With a flourish, she motioned for Butch to go in ahead of her. After he crossed the threshold, she followed him inside and relocked the door behind them.

The lighting inside the central processing area was adequate, but turned to a low setting. There was a pronounced disinfectant smell in the air, which barely masked the waste and decay odors that had seeped into the old walls of this place over the years. There were six officers assigned to the lockup: three men and three women. All of them were busy processing prisoners when Police Aide Spellman and Cadet Cole entered. The lockup keepers—or "turnkeys," as they were called—could only acknowledge Cole's presence with a nod or grunt when Tara introduced him. While the turnkeys continued to work either fingerprinting, photographing, or searching arrestees, Tara explained the procedures.

"Everything done back here is computerized," she said. "The photographs and fingerprints are placed immediately into the system, and a search of all want and warrant files is conducted."

"How long does it take to receive a response from the Automated Fingerprint Identification or Criminal History Record Information Systems?" he asked.

"From eight to sixteen hours if the computers don't go off-line."

He was unable to mask his surprise. "Why so long?"

"Do you know how many people are arrested in Chicago every day? The systems process the inquiries quickly, but they have to do one at a time with the rest being queued. That's why the procedure takes so long."

"I see," he said. And to an extent, he did.

They proceeded to the cellblocks, first the male side and then the female side. Each of the cells was equipped with two metal benches, which the prisoners could either sit or lie on, a metal toilet, and a metal sink equipped with a drinking faucet. If a prisoner required toilet paper, a turnkey would have to provide it on request. A pay telephone was available in each cellblock so that the prisoners could make their incarceration phone call.

"There is one female cellblock and two male cellblocks," Tara explained. "We have a capacity of fifty women and one hundred men, but we seldom ever reach those numbers. Sergeant Davies keeps us hopping to make sure that anyone eligible for bond is promptly released or sent to court at the earliest possible opportunity."

When they entered the women's cellblock, Tara yelled out, "We've got a man on the floor. Make sure that you're decent, ladies." Then she said to Cole, "Walk a couple of paces behind me, and if I tell you to stop, freeze in your tracks. The department was sued a few years ago by a woman who claimed that male officers were spying on her while she was locked up here."

"Did they?"

"The IAD conducted an investigation after a *Chicago Times-Herald* exposé, but the complaint couldn't be sustained. As far as the lawsuit went, the last that I heard . . ."

She had walked by two cells, one containing a young woman with long dark brown hair wearing a black dress and the other one vacant, when Tara realized that the cadet was no longer with her. She stopped and turned around to find him standing at the cell door, where the young woman was being held. Tara heard Cole say, "Hello, Morgana."

The prisoner crossed the cell to stand on her side of the bars facing him. "Hello, Officer Cole," she responded.

Police Aide Spellman said under her breath, "Now this is what Sergeant Q. Davies would call a revolting development."

"I'm not getting any answer at the captain's place," Anna Falk said in frustration. "I left a message on his answering service."

"Can't we call Operations Command and find out what's going on?" Perry Montoya said.

"Yes, we can," Sergeant Davies said, looking up from the stack of reports he had been working on nonstop since the tour of duty began, "but we would be violating the chain of command."

In frustration, Falk said, "Sarge, how can we just let this guy walk in here and take over like this?"

"Because he's a lieutenant of police, Anna," Davies snapped. "And I've been around long enough to know what one looks like. The captain could be ill or have some type of emergency forcing him to take off and the lieutenant was assigned to take his place."

"But wouldn't the captain have called us?" Montoya said.

"Why should he?" Davies countered.

"Because that's what Gary Harmon would do," Falk said.

Sergeant Davies was unable to argue with that. Finally, tired of the questions and his own misgivings about this watch-commander situation, he said, "There is one person the captain would have called, because he would have had no choice." Davies reached for the telephone on his desk and began punching in a number.

"And who would that be?" Montoya asked.

Falk answered, "The district commander."

The desk crew had been so absorbed with the watch-commander problem, they were unaware of the two men in dark business suits who had walked up to the desk. One was black and the other white. "Excuse me, Sergeant," the broad-shouldered white guy with the lantern jaw said.

Sergeant Davies turned around and looked at them just as the district commander's phone started ringing. Slowly, he replaced the receiver on its cradle. The two men were cut from the same mold despite their racial difference. They were big, tough-looking, and wearing suits that had not come off any department store rack. Q. Davies would have made them for feds, but they both flashed Chicago Police detective badges. "What can I do for you?" Davies asked.

"We're from the chief of detectives' office," the black guy said.

"We need to sign out Morgana Devoe and take her back to headquarters for further interrogation."

"You'll have to get the watch commander's approval," the sergeant said.

The white man's lips curled in what could have been a smile as he said, "I know."

Tara Spellman's stepbrother had been arrested for domestic battery about a year ago. During an argument with his wife, Danny Spellman had thrown a TV tray at her and cut her bottom lip. Although the injury had been relatively minor, the wife had flown into a rage and called the police. Danny was arrested. Tara was on duty that day, and when she found out that her stepbrother was in custody, she had gone back to the lockup to see him. This had succeeded in getting her a strongly worded rebuke from Sergeant Davies.

"I don't care if it was your father back there, Tara," he scolded. "You are a Chicago Police Department employee. As such, you will leave your likes and dislikes, friends—and that includes relatives—and enemies, preferences and prejudices at home. Anyone incarcerated in our lockup is a prisoner, and you will behave toward them in that manner. Once they are released from custody it's a different story. Do you understand me, Police Aide Spellman?"

It was the sternest tongue-lashing she'd received in the five years she had been working for the CPD, and she had taken it to heart. Now the young cadet was violating the precept of nonfraternization between prisoners and police personnel.

"How are you feeling?" the cadet asked the prisoner.

Morgana Devoe shivered and rubbed her hands over her exposed arms to warm herself. "This place is very uncomfortable and I am cold."

"Perhaps we can get you something to put on," he said, looking to Tara for help.

"I need to talk to you right now, Cadet Cole," the aide said.

It was apparent from the shocked look on his face that he was surprised by her harsh tone. Tara escorted Butch Cole out of the female cellblock.

"Sergeant Davies would give you and me both hell if he found out that you were talking to that woman," Tara said.

The cadet was confused. "What's wrong with me talking to her?"

"All of our contacts with prisoners must be strictly in the line of duty," she explained. "It's against regulations to fraternize."

"I wasn't fraternizing," he said defensively. "I'm the one that arrested her for murder at the Goodman Theater the other night."

Now it was the police aide's turn to be shocked, but before she could make any comment, one of the female turnkeys called to her. "Hey, Spellman, since you've got so much time on your hands to give guided tours, do us a favor and take this arrestee up front to Sergeant Davies."

Tara and Butch Cole turned around to find that a heavyset female turnkey, clad in the dark blue police utility uniform of all lockup personnel, had removed Morgana Devoe from her cell. Now the accused murderer had her wrists cuffed in front of her and was waiting for them at the female cellblock entrance.

The tall lieutenant examined the cramped watch commander's office with disdain. He walked around and took a seat behind the ancient metal desk. Removing his cap, he glanced up at the wall clock and compared the time to that on his Chase-Durer Special Forces chronograph. The wall clock was two minutes and forty-five seconds slow.

The nametag over the lieutenant's right breast pocket stated that his name was Kelly and that his unit of assignment was the Fifteenth Police District on the west side of the city. The five-pointed lieutenant's badge over his left breast bore the brass numbers 667. There was, in fact, a Lieutenant Kelly assigned to the Fifteenth District with that badge number. However, that Lieutenant Kelly would report for duty at four o'clock that afternoon. There was a slight resemblance between the real Lieutenant Kelly and the man who had walked into the Second District station, but the likeness was superficial at best. The imposter would not stand up under prolonged scrutiny, because he had no more than a rudimentary knowledge of Chicago Police procedure. But the fake lieutenant not only possessed nerves of steel; he was also a very dangerous man if crossed. It was anticipated that he would not have to remain in character for more than half an hour. In fact, that time span was generous. All the elements of the plan should be carried out successfully within a period of far less than thirty minutes.

Lieutenant Kelly had been seated in the Second District watch commander's office for twenty-two seconds shy of seven minutes when there was a knock on the door.

"Come," he called out.

Sergeant Davies entered carrying a stack of papers. "I didn't want to disturb you, Lieutenant, but I've got a couple of detectives here. They want to take one of our female prisoners out for interrogation at headquarters."

The lieutenant studied the sergeant through his lifeless gray eyes. When Davies began displaying visible signs of unease, the lieutenant said, "Do you want me to sign the authorization for the prisoner's transport?"

"Uh, yes, sir," the sergeant stammered. "It's standard procedure."

The imposter extended his hand to take the papers. Davies handed them over. For a moment, the lieutenant shuffled through the arrest slip, complaints, and other miscellaneous reports in Morgana Devoe's arrest file. Then he turned to the back of the original copy of the incarceration formset and scrawled an illegible signature in the appropriate authorization box. Handing the papers back to Davies, he said, "Oh, Sergeant, if I'm ever detailed to this place again, I expect to find you attired in a presentable uniform."

Sergeant Q. Davies hesitated before leaving the watch commander's office. Over his shoulder, he said, "Sure thing, Lieutenant. Whatever you say."

The imposter realized he was overplaying his hand, but he was enjoying himself. Why shouldn't he have some fun on this job by making the fat sergeant squirm? Lieutenant Kelly, badge number 667 of the Fifteenth District, would vanish soon enough.

Just as he had that thought, the telephone on the watch commander's desk began ringing.

Larry Cole sat in his office at police headquarters and listened to the telephone ring. He had dialed the direct line number to the Second District watch commander's office and had expected Gary Harmon to answer. After the sixth ring, Cole was about to hang up when the receiver was picked up. However, Cole was met with complete silence.

"Hello," Cole said, aware that there was someone on the other end of the line.

There was no response.

"Hello," Cole repeated.

Still silence. Then the connection was broken.

Cole stared at the instrument for a moment before redialing the number. This time it rang continuously without being answered. Puzzled, Cole hung up and dialed the Second District desk.

85

After two rings, the phone was answered. "Second District, Officer Falk."

"Officer Falk, this is Chief Cole. How are you today?"

"Hello, Chief. How's it going?"

"Who is your watch commander this afternoon?"

Falk paused for a second. "You're not going to believe this, boss, but I don't know."

Police Aide Spellman and Cadet Cole escorted the handcuffed Morgana Devoe to the front desk. The muscular black and white detectives were waiting for them. Butch felt a strange unease when he saw the two men in plainclothes. Blackie, Manny, and Judy, from his father's personal staff, had been handling all facets of the Richard Banacek homicide. The young cadet was also aware that there were over three thousand detectives assigned under his father's command and that any of them could be called on to assist in the investigation. But somehow the men who were picking up Morgana didn't seem right.

Then Butch recalled the advice Blackie Silvestri had given him the night before his first day in the police academy: "Although they might not come out and say it, kid, a lot of the cops you come in contact with on the job are going to know that your father is the chief of detectives. Some will admire you; some will hate you, which really won't matter in the long run, because you will be judged on who you are and what you do as opposed to who your father is. So my advice to you is do your job to the best of your ability, keep your eyes open and your mouth shut."

"Yes, sir," Butch had said to Blackie.

So, as the detectives took charge of Morgana Devoe, Butch Cole kept his misgivings to himself.

Sergeant Davies handed a document to the white detective.

"That's the transportation copy of the arrest report formset, which must be returned with the prisoner."

"No problem, Sarge," the lantern-jawed man said. "We're going to take real good care of this young lady for Chief Larry Cole."

Sergeant Davies and Tara Spellman looked at Cadet Cole, but the young man remained mute.

"Let's go, sweetheart," the black detective said to Morgana.

As the trio headed for the building's west exit, the prisoner turned and cast a forlorn glance at the cadet. There was no mistaking the sadness in her eyes.

"Sarge," Officer Falk called to Davies from her seat behind the desk, "I've got Chief Larry Cole on line three for the watch commander."

"Call the lieutenant on the intercom and tell him the chief is calling, Anna," Davies said in exasperation.

"He's not answering, Sarge," she defended.

At that moment, Lieutenant Kelly, with his uniform cap placed squarely on his head, stepped out of the watch commander's office. "I'm going out to my car," he said to Davies.

"The chief of detectives is on the phone for you, Lieutenant," Davies said.

"Tell him that I'll call him back," he said, continuing to walk toward the south exit.

A stunned desk crew remained behind. After a moment of protracted silence, Anna Falk said, "What shall I tell Chief Cole?"

Davies shrugged. "Ask him if he'd like to stop by later for a soul food dinner?"

7

The Corvette in which Captain Gary Harmon was being held captive was parked in a self-park, multistoried garage on Wabash Avenue north of Wacker Drive in the downtown area of the city. The female kidnapper, who called herself Magda, had selected a deserted level, and during the thirty-four minutes they had been sitting there, no vehicles or pedestrians were observed in the garage. The driver sat in a relaxed position, leaning back against the headrest with the silenced .45 pistol held loosely on her lap. She had the sports car's stereo system turned to a hard rock station, which was tuned loud enough to vibrate the tinted windows.

The police captain, his forearms restricted by the seat belt lap strap, was attempting to remember every detail that he could about this woman, her gun, and the car she was driving. At this stage of his kidnapping, Gary Harmon was fairly sure that he was going to survive. His rationale: If she wanted to kill him, she had ample opportunity to do so, since she had picked him up. She had not asked anything or demanded anything. Her sole objective was apparently to maintain control of him. But the nagging questions were, Why had she kidnapped him, and how long did she plan to hold him?

The dash-mounted cell phone rang. She turned the radio off before answering it. She said a simple yes into the mouthpiece. The caller's message took less than five seconds to transmit. Without another word, she hung up the phone and raised the .45. The captain experienced a bad moment because he was certain she was going to shoot him in the head. She did jam the gun against his temple, but to his tremendous relief, she did not pull the trigger. Using her free hand, she quickly and expertly frisked him, removing his nine-millimeter Glock pistol and extra bullet clips from his belt. She ejected the chambered round and bullet clip from his gun and, using her thumb, flicked all the bullets from the clips onto the floor of the sports car. Then she tossed his empty gun and magazines into his lap.

"Good-bye, Captain," she said, unlocking the door. "It's been nice knowing you."

She still had the .45 pointed at him, and he was so absorbed with the unwavering barrel that he didn't move right away.

"I said good-bye, Captain Harmon," she repeated angrily.

Extricating himself from the seat belt and clutching his gun and clips to his chest, he stumbled out of the Corvette. He had barely set foot on the concrete surface of the parking garage, when she was behind him.

"Face the wall," she barked.

Face to the wall, Harmon knew what to expect. In fact, he was grateful that the blow to the back of his head was a gun-butt and not a bullet.

Cadet Butch Cole's first day on the job was proving to be anything but routine. In less than two hours following the start of his tour of duty, he had seen the woman, who had confessed a murder to him, escape from custody. And from what the young cadet had learned from his father and Sergeant Davies, Morgana Devoe's escape was one of the most brilliantly executed such operations in the history of American law enforcement.

Despite the maelstrom of investigative procedure swirling around the Second Police District on that Sunday afternoon, the normal administrative duties still had to be completed. Cadet Cole, Aide Spellman, and Police Officers Anna Falk and Perry Montoya worked the station desk to complete the routine tasks required to process and book prisoners along with taking crime reports from citizens walking into the station off the street. The completion of the work was complicated by a pack of media types arriving at the station after it was discovered that the notorious Murderess of the Opera had escaped.

Sergeant Q. Davies was upstairs in the Area One Detective Division offices, as the police sought to piece together exactly what had occurred. Chief Larry Cole arrived at the station and had taken unofficial charge of the investigation. A short time later, Lieutenant Blackie Silvestri showed up, having been yanked from a quiet Sunday dinner with his wife, Maria. Then Assistant Deputy Superintendent Geno Bailey arrived.

Butch was entering information into the CHRIS computer when Bailey stormed into the station. Tara Spellman was tutoring the cadet in the computer's operation, and on seeing the ADS, he heard her say, "Now we're in real trouble."

Bailey was wearing the command officer's summer uniform with the silver eagles of his rank on the shoulders of his white shirt. He walked past the station desk at a pace just short of a run. He was the highest-ranking field officer on duty that afternoon. The thin, intense, middle-aged man had gray hair cut short, a thick Neanderthal forehead, and eyebrows that stretched in a continuous line from temple to temple. Under other circumstances, his apelike appearance would have been amusing, but when Tara told Butch that ADS Bailey had a long-standing animosity toward Sergeant Q. Davies, all the young cadet's humor vanished.

"Things will work out, Tara," he said, completing the final CHRIS entry.

"It's good to know that we have an optimist in the house," she said with a pronounced lack of enthusiasm. "You don't know Geno Bailey."

"You're right on that score," Butch said, "but you don't know my dad and Blackie Silvestri either."

Lieutenant Blackie Silvestri had been a cop all his adult life. In fact, when he thought back to his early years as a punk on the mean streets of the city's west side, he realized that he had always thought like a cop, although in his formative years only from the standpoint of someone who operated on the wrong side of the law. So it was that he knew that most crimes were random acts prompted either by emotion or greed. However, there were also crimes that were methodically planned and carefully executed. Morgana Devoe's escape from custody was such a crime.

Blackie was a solidly built man. The lieutenant's favorite expression was a no-nonsense scowl, which the unknowing thought was an indication that he possessed a mean spirit. Nothing could be further from the truth. What Blackie's scowl was most indicative of was an intense analytical mind. Now his expression was at its most furious as he examined the evidence that had so far been discovered about the escape of the infamous Murderess of the Opera.

Blackie, Chief Cole, and Sergeant Q. Davies were in the Violent Crimes CO's office on the second floor of the Area One Police Center. When the ADS on duty arrived, they would conduct what was called a "round table" in an attempt to discover as much as they could about the escape. Blackie knew that whatever had gone down was indeed bizarre. Then, when Geno Bailey walked in, things got decidedly worse.

Blackie moaned audibly at the sight of the ADS, which brought a sharp glance from Cole. Even though the chief of detectives outranked Bailey, it was still the street deputy's show. Cole was going to be particularly careful in his dealings with this particular ADS, because his son was involved in the investigation.

Bailey heard the noise Silvestri made and, staring directly at the lieutenant, said, "Is there something that you want to say to me, Lieutenant Silvestri?"

Blackie returned the deputy's stare. "No, Deputy. It's always a pleasure to see you, sir." The sarcasm was evident.

Geno Bailey realized that he was being patronized and that there was nothing he could do about it right now. However, the prisoner escape from the Second District lockup was his investigation, and he would call it as he saw fit. And he planned to enjoy every minute of it.

The administrative investigation that ADS Geno Bailey conducted was aimed at discovering possible culpability in the escape from custody of Morgana Devoe. The detective division would conduct the criminal investigation, and a wanted message, containing descriptions of her and all her possible accomplices, had been broadcast to every police agency in the country. But it was still necessary for the internal inquiry to be conducted.

The first witness called was Captain Gary Harmon, who had flagged down an Eighteenth District police car after the kidnapper released him in the North Side parking garage. A description of the kidnapper and her sports car was also broadcast along with descriptions of the phony detectives and police lieutenant. Now Captain Harmon was required to answer questions before the "round table" being chaired by Assistant Deputy Superintendent Geno Bailey.

Although still obviously ruffled following his kidnapping, Captain Harmon gave a coherent, concise account of what had occurred earlier on that summer day. When he finished, ADS Bailey questioned him.

"You were in full uniform at the time that this woman approached you, isn't that right, Captain?"

"Yes, I was."

"During the course of your—" Bailey paused for effect. "—ordeal at the hands of an attractive woman in hot pants who was driving a Corvette, did you make any attempt to escape?"

"An attempt did not present itself for me to safely do so, sir."

Bailey made a note on the yellow legal pad on the table in front of him. Without looking up, he asked, "She also disarmed you?"

"Yes, sir," Harmon said tightly. "But she gave me back the gun after she unloaded it and emptied my extra bullet clips."

"I see," Bailey said, now looking up and gracing Harmon with what could only be characterized as a mocking smirk. "I have no further questions." As Cole and Blackie had no questions, the captain was dismissed.

Sergeant Quentin Davies was next.

"Sergeant Davies," ADS Bailey asked, "do you recall the badge number of the lieutenant who told you that he was taking Captain Harmon's place as the third-watch commander today?"

"Yes, sir. The number was 667."

"Did you verify the legitimacy of this star number with Operations Command?"

"No, sir."

Bailey displayed surprise. "May I ask why?"

"The lieutenant was in full uniform and appeared legitimate, Deputy."

"Now we know that appearances can be deceiving, don't we, Sergeant?"

Maintaining his control, Q. Davies responded, "Whatever you say."

"Now let's move on to these phony detectives, who walked into this facility and waltzed out with a felon," Bailey said.

The interviews, to include those of the desk and lockup personnel, took over three hours. When they were concluded, Cole, Blackie, and Bailey compared notes. The facts were fairly consistent in each account of what had occurred that afternoon. The only discrepancy was that Cole and Blackie found that the police personnel involved were blameless and ADS Bailey's finding was completely the opposite.

"Captain Harmon and Sergeant Davies must bear the supervisory culpability for the escape," Bailey pronounced. "I am going to recommend that they both be suspended for fifteen days."

Blackie looked ready to explode, but Cole stepped in before Bailey could add the lieutenant's name to the suspension list. "This was a sophisticated criminal conspiracy, Geno. The bogus lieutenant, the phony detectives, and the woman in the Corvette were all working in concert to free Morgana Devoe. There was not one single, solitary shred of evidence presented here to indicate that the phony cops were anything but legitimate. They carried the operation out on a tight schedule with military precision. I'd also be willing to bet that we haven't heard the last of them, whoever's behind this, or Ms. Morgana Devoe."

Assistant Deputy Superintendent Geno Bailey was frightened of and intimidated by Larry Cole. In fact, despite the disparity in their ranks, the ADS wasn't really comfortable finding himself in such close proximity to the macho, scowling Blackie Silvestri. The reason behind this fear was that Bailey was a deeply insecure individual, who should never have become a Chicago police officer. Had it not been for powerful political connections, Bailey would have ended up sorting mail in the post office or driving a garbage truck. Life is not fair, and Bailey had not only managed to become a police officer, but he had also been promoted into a position in which he could hurt good, hardworking cops like Gary Harmon and Q. Davies. The ADS would enjoy not only the harm he would do, but also showing up the great Larry Cole. Bailey intended to do that by including the highly damaging information in his report that Cadet Larry Cole Jr. had been fraternizing with Morgana Devoe only moments before her escape.

"Well, Chief," Bailey said, shoving the yellow pad into his attaché case and putting his uniformed cap on, "we all must have our priorities in life." Getting to his feet, Bailey added, "I'll send you a copy of my report." With that, he walked out.

"What a jerk," Blackie said when he and Cole were alone.

"Don't sweat him, Blackie," Cole said. "He's a dim-witted pencil pusher who wouldn't know a complicated criminal investigation if it fell out of the sky and hit him in the head. We can expect the worst in his report, but the only way to counter what he writes is for us to find out what happened to Morgana Devoe today and why. Let's go."

When they reached the main floor, the delicious aroma of hot food reminded Cole and Blackie that it had been quite some time since they'd last eaten.

"Something sure smells good," Blackie said.

"Butch mentioned something about the desk crew taking turns bringing a meal for Sunday dinner," Cole said.

"Do you think they have enough for us?"

Cole laughed. "We can ask them."

The tables in the office behind the desk now held trays and dishes containing fried chicken, barbecued ribs, black-eyed peas, collard greens, potato salad, and corn bread. A case of canned iced tea was chilling in a metal tank filled with ice. The desk and lockup personnel had already eaten and were back at their posts. Gary Harmon and Q. Davies were just finishing up their dinner when Cole and Blackie came in.

"Can a couple of broken-down, hungry detectives join you?" Cole asked.

"Come on in, guys," Harmon said. "We've got plenty left, and what we can't finish we give to the homeless people who live in the station lobby."

The four cops spent the next few minutes absorbed with the soul food dinner. Finally, Q. Davies said, "Bailey's going to do a hatchet job on us for letting that Devoe woman escape."

Cole swallowed a hunk of corn bread and chased it with iced tea before saying, "The assistant deputy superintendent was preoccupied with looking at the 'what' of the escape, as opposed to the why. That will be the key to this whole thing. I promise you that we'll get to the bottom of why she escaped before this is all over."

Morgana never realized before in her young life how much fresh air and sunshine are taken for granted. Even though she had been deprived of such minor pleasures for only a short time, she felt her spirits soar when she stepped into the police station parking lot and felt the warm kiss of the hot summer sun. Momentarily, she forgot that she was in custody. She stopped, closed her eyes, and tilted her face up to absorb the sun's rays. The two men walking on either side of her stopped when she did and waited for her moment of freedom to pass.

Then they led her to a white four-door Chevrolet that was parked in the lot a short distance from the station exit.

The black detective assisted her into the backseat and checked her handcuffs before he got into the front passenger seat. The white detective got behind the steering wheel and drove the white Chevy from the parking lot onto the Dan Ryan Expressway. The car windows were rolled up and the air-conditioner turned to a low setting. To Morgana, after the chilliness of her jail cell, the police car was quite comfortable. She didn't know where the detectives were taking her or why, but she was so tired that it really didn't matter. She leaned back against the soft fabric covering the seat cushions and began to doze. The image of the handsome young cadet she had left behind at the police station came to her in a dream, and she mumbled in her sleep, "I'm sorry, Butch."

The past three days had been the strangest of Morgana's life, and not necessarily because of the death of Richard Banacek, whom she knew to be Carlos Perfido. Yes, she had hesitated before firing at him, but she had mustered up the nerve to finally pull the trigger. Then, as she had learned from all those gangster and spy stories she had read, Morgana immediately fled the Goodman Theater.

She was halfway across the lobby when Butch Cole called to her. With the exotic weapon concealed in the binoculars still clutched in her hand, she turned to face the young man. However, there was not an instant in which she considered using the weapon to gain her freedom. Her only regret was that she had not met him before she shot Banacek. When he came up to her in the lobby, she could detect a definite aura of authority in his manner. It was in his posture and the way he carried himself. She was certain that he was either a professional soldier or a police officer. But that wasn't why she surrendered to him. She'd been trying to come up with the reason since her arrest, but the answer eluded her. At least a logical answer.

From infancy Morgana Devoe had experienced little emotion and had never felt really close to any human being. Her earliest memories had been of an orphanage in Geneva, where there had been little or no contact between the infant wards and the staff. When Isaac Weiss took her from the orphanage, she was three years old and had developed a fierce streak of independence. She could feed, clothe, and bath herself. She also had little to say to Weiss or the small staff of servants that attended them in a modest town house outside of Paris until Morgana was eight. The child possessed a phenomenal memory and a genius-level IQ. She could read English, French, and German by the time she began attending school. She developed a dislike for the cook, maid, and combination butler/chauffeur who attended her and Isaac. This was not due to the servants being menials, but because she thought they were stupid. She at first tolerated and then grew fond of Weiss. She even began calling him Uncle, because he was not only very intelligent, but he could also seemingly do anything he set his mind to. It was not a term of endearment, but instead one of respect, because he possessed a superior intellect to hers. She developed a certain affection for him, but she could never honestly say she loved him. When Perfido killed Weiss, she did feel a sense of loss, as well as one of responsibility, which had driven her to avenge his death. Her motivation was not affection.

After her uncle's death, Morgana had learned from his Geneva solicitor that she would receive a substantial inheritance. That sum had been ten million American dollars.

Once she obtained the money—following a brief battle in the Swiss courts, which she won—she moved into a small villa on Lake Lucerne. The place had been obtained for her and staffed with domestics by the same firm her uncle had employed. There she learned to live well and without the need for the continued presence of anyone else.

Over the years, she devoted a great deal of her time to an exhaustive, expensive search for Perfido. She also hired tutors from Paris to come to Lucerne and complete her education in philosophy and engineering up through master's degree levels. During that period, she had been quite comfortable with her lifestyle. The only part of her life she was not comfortable with was that she had never been able to find out "who" she was.

Morgana attempted to trace her heritage and discover the identity of her parents. She returned to the orphanage from which Isaac Weiss had rescued her at the age of three. There she was able to discover only that she had not been adopted, but that Weiss had presented proper guardianship papers for her. The corporate law firm of Lilly, Draper, and Williams in New York had prepared those documents. She had her Geneva solicitor make inquiries with the New York firm, but the official response was that their relationship with their clients was confidential. The only item of information Morgana's Swiss representative was able to discover was that Lilly, Draper, and Williams worked exclusively for the multinational DeWitt Corporation.

Morgana made the connection the instant that she heard the name DeWitt. Before he died, Uncle Isaac wanted her to read a book by a pair of American authors titled, *The Strange Case of Margo and Neil DeWitt.* Carlos Perfido's intrusion into her life had prevented her from accomplishing the task.

By the time she made the connection between the New York law firm, the DeWitt Corporation, and *The Strange Case of Margo and Neil DeWitt,* Morgana had been on her own for three years. She had carefully transported all her uncle's clocks, tools, and books from the apartment in the Carouge section of Geneva to her villa in Lucerne. The library was the largest room in the villa, and the sound made by the numerous timepieces housed there infused the place with a relaxing mechanical symphony. When she was in the library, she always thought of Isaac Weiss, who was the only real family she ever had.

She even had the worktable he had been seated at when he was killed moved into the library. Although the dead man was frequently in her thoughts, she could not say that she actually missed him.

She found the copy of *The Strange Case of Margo and Neil De-Witt* among the books on philosophy, engineering, and watchmaking on one of her bookshelves. After dinner on a winter evening in February 2001, she sat down to read the book. She found the experience oddly unsettling.

The tale was of a unique relationship between a pair of serial killers who were married to each other. Operating in Chicago, the woman had victimized male children, and the man young women, whom he had also raped. The DeWitts were two of the wealthiest people in the world, possessing an estimated fortune of thirty billion dollars. In the end, Neil DeWitt was killed by a police officer when he attempted to murder a witness to one of his murders, and Margo De-Witt had been shot to death after she kidnapped a high-ranking Chicago Police official's son with the intention of dismembering the little boy. In the book, there were photos of the DeWitts, the authors— Barbara Zorin and Jamal Garth—and the police official and his family, consisting of his wife and his son. When Morgana came to that section, she found she was drawn to the policeman's family photo, feeling a particularly strong attraction to the little boy, who was about six or seven years old at the time. Morgana Devoe was experiencing an alien emotion. She had no way of knowing that five years in the future, she would meet Larry Cole Jr. in the flesh.

She was about to return to the text when something compelled her to turn back to the photo of Margo and Neil DeWitt. In the hardcover edition of the book that Morgana was reading, the picture of the DeWitts was a black-and-white reproduction. The couple was dressed in formal attire and exuded the relaxed arrogance of the extremely wealthy. As had been the case with the policeman's family, Morgana found herself drawn to this picture as well. However, her reaction to the DeWitts was much different from what it had been with the Coles. Suddenly, despite the warmth provided by the central heating plant installed in her villa overlooking Lake Lucerne, Morgana experienced a violent chill, which struck her with such force that she dropped the book. When she reached to pick it up, some unseen force stopped her. When she finally did retrieve it from the floor, she returned the volume to the bookcase.

On that winter night, Morgana Devoe was forced to face the possibility that the remaining contents of *The Strange Case of Margo and Neil DeWitt* held the answers to her past. There was also the possibility that the book Isaac Weiss had recommended to her was a complete waste of her time. Before pursuing that line of inquiry about her past any further, she realized she would need a great deal more information than what was contained in the story of a pair of dead serial killers. From that point on, Morgana made Carlos Perfido her top priority. However, the photographs contained in *The Strange Case of Margo and Neil DeWitt* constantly haunted her.

Now, in the backseat of the white Chevy, Morgana found herself haunted by Larry Cole Jr. and in her fitful sleep, she again called out the name "Butch."

The two police detective imposters who had implemented Morgana Devoe's escape from custody did not consider themselves career criminals. They would prefer being referred to, at best, as soldiers of fortune or, at worst, nefarious entrepreneurs. They had spent over a half century in the United States Army and had now placed their skills on the open market for the highest bidder.

The white man, who had done most of the talking back at the Second District station, had been born Alphonso Gaskew in Boston, Massachusetts, in 1958. He enlisted in the United States Army at the age of fifteen after lying about his age. He served one tour of duty in

Vietnam before the ignominious withdrawal. At the time, Specialist Fourth Class Gaskew was in Captain Franklin Butler's Ranger Company. And even though Al Gaskew would retire from the U.S. Army as a sergeant major after twenty-seven years on active duty, he considered Captain Butler the best officer he had ever served with.

The black man was Sherman Goolsby, and he was originally a native of Oakland, California. His tour of duty in Vietnam had predated Gaskew's by two years. Goolsby had been assigned as a second lieutenant and forward observer to Captain Butler's Ranger Company. Not until Lieutenant Goolsby arrived in Vietnam did he become aware that his life expectancy in combat was less than sixty seconds. But after joining Franklin Butler's outfit, the lieutenant decided that if he was going to die, then he would gladly do so with honor under this particular commanding officer.

Goolsby not only survived the war, but also spent twenty-six years on active duty, retiring as a brigadier general. His last duty assignment was with Army Intelligence, his area of expertise being Western Europe.

Morgana Devoe had fallen asleep before they left the police station parking lot. Goolsby, who occupied the front passenger seat, was turned at an angle, enabling him to keep an eye on her. Even though they had freed her from police custody, when she found out who they really were, she might not necessarily view them as allies. Her slumber was troubled, and she called out periodically. The only words they were able to understand were the names Butch and Isaac.

The fake white Chevrolet police car the ex-soldiers were in would appear legitimate under most circumstances. It was a clean, no-frills, late-model four-door sedan equipped with a multichannel Motorola police radio, which was concealed in the glove compartment. The radio was on and turned to the frequency that CPD detective division field units operated on. Although they were supposed to be taking

Morgana Devoe to Chief Larry Cole's office, the white car turned off Lake Shore Drive at Chicago Avenue miles north of police headquarters just as the police radio began broadcasting a wanted message regarding the escape from the Second Police District. Before the police dispatcher mentioned Morgana's name or the description of the men who had aided in her escape, Goolsby turned the radio off. The handcuffed woman in the backseat did not wake up.

Less than five minutes later, the white car entered the DeWitt Plaza parking garage. Using a key card to gain access, former Sergeant Major Gaskew drove the car slowly up the ascending ramps, which contained only a handful of parked autos on this lazy Sunday afternoon. They entered a reserved parking area on the twelfth level, which required another access card to allow them through a secured overhead door.

Beyond this door was an area that could easily accommodate up to fifty cars. There were only seven vehicles in evidence, with one of those being Franklin Butler's Lincoln limousine. Standing next to a black Range Rover was the tall rapier-thin man with cold gray eyes, "Lieutenant Kelly," badge number 667. He had shed the police hat and now wore a desert battle dress uniform shirt over the white police shirt. As the phony police car approached, he had assumed a ramrod-straight parade rest stance.

The bogus lieutenant was Major General Daniel Thomas Wayne, retired. He had also served in the Rangers in Vietnam, but he had been a battalion commander, and Captain Franklin Butler had served under him during three tours of duty in the South East Asia war zone. When Gaskew and Goolsby saw Wayne, they sat up a bit straighter.

After parking the car, the former soldiers got out and conferred briefly with the former major general.

"Any problems?" Wayne asked.

"Negative," Goolsby responded.

"Okay, get her out of the car."

"Yes, sir," Gaskew said.

Morgana Devoe was bleary-eyed from sleep as they helped her out. She was unaware of where they were as they escorted her to a private elevator in the parking garage. At that moment, the young woman didn't know she had simply been moved from one jail to another.

8

June 19, 2006
9:02 A.M.

T he windows of Morgana Devoe's suite in the Swissotel on
Wacker Drive provided impressive views of Lake Michigan,
the Chicago River, and the Magnificent Mile of North Michigan Avenue from the Times-Herald Tower to DeWitt Plaza
and the John Hancock Building. The five-hundred-dollar-
a-night accommodation the young woman had been living
in for the past two weeks was nicely furnished with objects
possessing a pronounced European flavor. Entry from the
twenty-third-floor corridor was into an alcove, where a walk-
in closet was concealed behind a sliding door covered by
a floor-to-ceiling mirror. A carpeted corridor bisected the

entryway. Taking this corridor to the right led into a small living room; to the left, a bedroom equipped with a queen-sized bed. There were two bathrooms and a wet bar in the suite. The bathroom servicing the lone bedroom was equipped with a bidet and a two-headed shower with gold fixtures.

It was a luxury suite in downtown Chicago that Morgana Devoe had called home before she shot Richard Banacek on the stage of the Goodman Theater. On this overcast summer morning, as a steady rain fell on the city, Sergeant Judy Daniels was in the twenty-third-floor suite, attempting to find out all she could about the young woman who had been so mysteriously snatched from police custody the previous day.

Since her successful attempt to fool Butch Cole had been carried out at the police cadet graduation, the Mistress of Disguise and High Priestess of Mayhem had been experimenting with her hair. Her primary efforts had been aimed at not only radically changing the styles, but also the colors. Altering her features with prosthetics and the tint of her skin with makeup went without saying. She also modified her attire to suit the personality of the particular disguise she had donned.

On Saturday afternoon, when she arrived at the Swissotel, she had been a frizzy-haired redhead with freckles and a prominent nose that dominated her thin face. When she presented a search warrant for Morgana Devoe's suite to the effeminate, self-important assistant manager with the phony French accent, Judy noticed that he stared openly at her rather large false proboscis. On Sunday morning, her hair was worn in a blond pageboy, she wore blue contact lenses and had applied a peaches-and-cream coating of makeup to her face. Her efforts were rewarded when the manager said, "There was another officer here yesterday. Could you people at least give me some idea when you will be through with this hotel?"

As Morgana Devoe's suite was paid up through the end of the week, Judy was not going to rush her investigation. When she arrived at the Swissotel on Monday, she sported black hair swept back from a high forehead into a tight bun tied at the nape of her neck, thinly arched eyebrows, and black lipstick. The Mistress of Disguise and High Priestess of Mayhem was disappointed when she discovered at the concierge station that the assistant manager she had been dealing with was off on Mondays.

After obtaining a passkey card from the assistant manager on duty—a tired-looking brunette whose tacky choice of wardrobe fired Judy's imagination—the police sergeant returned to Morgana Devoe's twenty-third-floor suite. The black-on-yellow crime scene tape Judy had left on the door yesterday was still in place, and she considered releasing the suite after she finished today's examination. Actually, she had already gone through everything in the two previous days, but still she was drawn back. Something was bothering Judy Daniels about Morgana Devoe.

The two-room suite had not been cleaned in three days, but it was still quite tidy because that was the way its occupant had left it. Even the slept-in bed was neatly mussed. Carrying her laptop computer case and purse draped over her shoulder, Judy began a slow walk through the suite. Everything was exactly the way she had left it yesterday. The living room was pristine, and it was obviously the place where the young would-be murderess spent the least amount of time. The sofa, matching easy chairs, cocktail table, and small dining area for two over by the windows had not been touched. The bar was in this room, and even though Judy had inspected it before, she checked it again.

Like any other young woman her age, Morgana had consumed snacks and soft drinks from the overpriced refreshment compartment in the refrigerator. She was particularly fond of Coca-Cola, salted peanuts, and chocolate bars. Judy mused that when Morgana got older, she'd have to watch not only her weight, but also her complexion.

The detective sergeant checked the bathroom that led off the living room. The paper seal was still on the toilet, and it didn't appear that Morgana had used this facility at all. Judy moved on to the bedroom.

It was as obvious now as it had been on Judy's previous visits to the Swissotel that Morgana spent the majority of her time in this room. At least while she had been in the suite. There was a half-full glass of water on the night table beside the slept-in bed. An assortment of toiletries and cosmetics were arranged on the counter in the second and largest bathroom in the suite. Then there was the desk.

The ornate Victorian-era writing table was in the far corner of the room next to the wooden cabinet containing the television set. A stack of manuals on watchmaking and a black leather notebook containing a white lined notepad were stacked neatly on the surface. In the center desk drawer, there was a leather case containing small precision tools, a box of standard Remington nine-millimeter semiautomatic ammo, and a few miscellaneous items of a type any tourist might pick up. It was these items that Judy found to be the most fascinating about Morgana Devoe.

There was a Chicago Cubs' button, a brochure from the Field Museum of Natural History, a small illustrated booklet on the history of the National Science and Space Museum, and a hastily drawn portrait of Morgana. The drawing was of a type that had been done by a street corner artist, such as those that frequented Navy Pier or the Old Town area. There was also a Ticketmaster envelope, which had contained a single ticket for a performance of *Murder at the Opera* at the Albert Ivar Goodman Theater at 7:00 P.M. on June 15, 2006. Other than the expensive but singularly drab clothing and shoes in the closet, these personal items told Judy about the young woman who had lived in this place.

Pulling out the chair, Judy sat down at the desk, placing her laptop computer case and purse on the floor. As she continued to study the items in the drawer, she attempted to form a personality profile of the young woman. Morgana Devoe was obviously intelligent, curious, and capable of precision mechanical and watch repair. She was serious-minded beyond her years, which her wardrobe and selection of no-frills, utilitarian underwear indicated. But she did possess a certain degree of vanity, which was indicated by the pencil sketch.

Judy asked herself, Was having your portrait done by a street corner artist really indicative of vanity? But it was to this drawing on cheap drafting paper that the Mistress of Disguise and High Priestess of Mayhem always returned to. The artist had worked quickly to fashion a superficial image of Morgana that was sad to the point of melancholia. However, Judy noticed another quality present. It took her longer to decide exactly what that elusive characteristic was. She finally decided on arrogance, but in so small a quantity as to be virtually nonexistent. And when Judy looked at the sketch of the escapee with arrogance in mind, another image from the past attempted to force its way from the depths of her subconscious.

Judy had been attempting to grasp that elusive memory for three days, and now she almost had it. Unzipping her computer case, she placed her laptop on the desk surface. Turning the computer on, she inserted a digital video data disk in an access port. The small cylinder contained an extensive archive of all the major felony cases that had occurred in Chicago in the past twenty years. She began searching for a decade-old case, which she had been directly involved in. It took her less than thirty seconds to find what she was looking for. She called up the photos of the principals involved. It was all that she could do to stop herself from screaming at the top of her lungs in the exclusive Wacker Drive hotel room. Then she reached for the telephone.

"Manny, it's me. Where's the boss?"

A steady rain was still falling on the city when Sergeant Manny Sherlock parked the chief of detectives' black Mercury on Dearborn Street north of Randolph. He flipped the passenger-side visor down, revealing a CHICAGO POLICE DEPARTMENT—OFFICIAL BUSINESS placard adorned with the CPD emblem. Then he turned off the engine and followed Chief Cole and Lieutenant Silvestri into the Goodman Theater. Barbara Zorin and Jamal Garth were waiting for them in the lobby.

"Thanks for coming, guys," Cole said, shaking hands with the authors.

"Sorry about your play," Blackie said. Although the tough lieutenant wasn't much for stage plays, he had a definite appreciation for opera. "Having one of your main characters murdered in the first act is a disaster."

The authors exchanged conspiratorial glances before Jamal said, "It looks like things are going to work out for us, Blackie. We've had calls from a Broadway producer and a movie production company in Hollywood. It may sound a bit morbid, because Richard won't be buried until Wednesday, but the producers want us to incorporate his onstage death and the young woman's arrest into the performance."

"Talk about art imitating life," Manny said.

Jamal Garth looked at the young sergeant and said, "You don't know how many times Barbara and I have said that over the last couple of days."

The reason the cops were visiting the theater was to take one final look at the Albert Ivar Goodman stage before releasing the crime scene back to normal use. Also, because Barbara and Jamal had worked closely with him in the past on criminal cases, Cole wanted to fill them in on what had been uncovered concerning Banacek's death.

As they walked down one of the carpeted aisles of the Albert, Cole said, "We've discovered some interesting facts about your star performer. Besides Banacek having no verifiable biography, his fingerprints were burned off with acid, and we discovered some unusual items in his Wrigleyville apartment."

They had reached the stage, which was still cordoned off with barrier tape. Before ascending the steps, Cole stopped and turned to face them. "Banacek lived in a converted condo building on Pine Grove, north of Addison. The original structure was built in the 1930s and remodeled a number of times over the years. After Banacek moved in, he had the place gutted, new walls put in, and the floors stripped, sanded, and buffed. Apparently sometime during this process, the actor built a secret compartment into the bedroom floor beneath an old, heavy chest of drawers. Inside that compartment we found an Uzi submachine gun, five hundred rounds of ammunition, twenty-five thousand dollars in cash, a couple of fake passports, one from Argentina and the other from Paraguay, some jewelry, and an interesting scrapbook detailing the exploits of a criminal named Carlos José Perfido."

"Isn't that the guy who vanished in Europe some years back?" Blackie asked.

"The same," Cole responded. "Chief Inspector Gordon Edwards of Scotland Yard is an old friend of mine, and he e-mailed me everything Interpol and the Yard had on Perfido. The information came in this morning and covered Perfido's criminal career from his first bank robbery in Paris in July 1979 until the kidnapping of a Madrid doctor's daughter in January 1998. The girl was rescued and the ransom money recovered. Over a period of six to eight months, each of the kidnappers was caught, with the exception of Perfido. A hefty bounty was put on the criminal's head and administered through the Vatican Bank. A number of inquiries were made about providing the information that would result in the ransom being paid, but Perfido remained at large. One of the inquiries was from an Israeli national named Isaac Weiss. Supposedly, this Weiss had Mossad connections, and his information was taken seriously. Weiss was an octogenarian watchmaker living in Geneva, Switzerland, with his young niece. He offered to make arrangements to turn Perfido over to the Swiss police, but before anything could be set up, the watchmaker was murdered. There was enough evidence uncovered at the time to indicate that Perfido killed Weiss. That evidence also points to Isaac Weiss's niece being our very own Morgana Devoe."

"Larry, are you saying that Richard Banacek was this Carlos Perfido?" Barbara Zorin said.

"Until we come up with evidence to the contrary, we're going to conduct our investigation based on that supposition, because right now it fits. On the day that Isaac Weiss was murdered back in October of 1998, a bearded man—who was about the same age, height, and weight as Perfido—pursued Morgana Devoe through the streets of Geneva. According to witnesses, he would have caught her, but she jumped in the Rhône and almost drowned in the river."

"Now that is what I would call a determined young lady," Garth said.

"I agree," Cole responded. "After she was fished out of the river, she refused to cooperate with the detective investigating her uncle's murder, nor would she provide any information about the man who had chased her."

Barbara ventured the question, "Do we know why Perfido killed this Isaac Weiss?"

"I think that I can answer that for them, boss," Blackie said.

"Be my guest," Cole said.

The lieutenant produced a manila envelope from his pocket and removed six photos from it. Handing the pictures to the authors, he explained, "Isaac Weiss worked as a weapons expert for the Israelis from 1946 until 1990. Even after his retirement, he had been known to construct exotic weapons to specification for clients who could pay his fee. From the quality of his workmanship, I would say that Weiss charged a pretty penny. Now what you've got there are photos of a fountain pen, a wristwatch, and a pair of binoculars."

Barbara and Jamal, with Manny looking over their shoulders from his six-foot-four-inch height, examined each of the pictures as Blackie spoke. The items were displayed intact and also in a dismantled form.

"The fountain pen is a signature Mont Blanc Edgar Allan Poe model, which has been modified to fire a nine-millimeter cartridge. The Rolex wristwatch has a miniature electrical battery contained within it that powers a very thin laser beam. The laser isn't much of a weapon, but it will cut through solid metal, such as what might be found in a lock mechanism or the chain connecting a pair of handcuffs."

"If you aim that beam at someone's eye," Barbara said, "you'll do a lot of damage."

"The binoculars were used by Morgana Devoe to shoot Richard Banacek," Blackie continued. "The actor had the fountain pen and the watch on him at the time of his death, so he was ready for trouble."

Barbara handed the pictures back to Blackie. She said, "Each of those is definitely a work of art."

Cole interjected, "Now we know that Weiss was looking to turn Perfido in to the European police, and it could have become fairly easy to do if the wanted man came to the watchmaker's apartment in Geneva to pick up the custom-made fountain pen and watch. Somehow Perfido surprised Weiss and killed him. Morgana walked in on the murder, Perfido pursued her, and she got away by jumping in the river. Now the weapons that Weiss made are impressive, but they're actually little more than toys."

"One of those toys killed Richard Banacek," Garth said.

"No, it didn't," Cole countered, shocking the authors of the now-infamous stage play *Murder at the Opera*. "Banacek was killed with a .45-caliber dumdum bullet fired from a silenced weapon. The medical examiner estimates that the fatal round was fired from a distance of from six to twelve feet."

"That means it came from the stage," Barbara said.

"Exactly." With that, Cole turned and ascended the steps with the others following him. Everything was the same as it had been on the night of the murder. The location where the actor had fallen was outlined with white tape, and the props for the "Abracadabra" number were still in place.

Cole pointed at the lacquer cabinet at stage left. "That's what, maybe twenty-five to thirty feet away?"

"About that, boss," Blackie said.

As one, they all turned to look at the tiger cage, which was less than ten feet from the body outline on the floor. "Does anyone know how the tiger trick works?" Cole asked.

"I do," Barbara Zorin said, walking over to the cage, which still bore the strong scent of the jungle cat. She moved around behind the cage and vanished from view. They heard her say, "When Banacek was shot, the tiger was visible. Now I'm going to make the assistant appear." The mystery writer popped up from the bottom of the cage.

"How did she do that?" Manny said in awe.

"It's magic, kid," Blackie responded, deadpan.

When they reached the cage, Barbara was climbing out.

"So Pamela Hoffman, the magician's assistant, was inside there?" Cole said.

"There are two separate compartments," Barbara explained. "While the tiger is in view, the assistant is hidden, and vice versa."

Cole shone a pocket flash into the area where the magician's assistant had been concealed. What he was looking for became instantly visible.

"There's a small hole in the front housing of the cage and a spent .45 cartridge at the bottom of the compartment," Cole said. "Manny, get the Crime Lab back down here. We now know where our second shooter fired from."

Manny removed the combination radio and cell phone from his pocket and was about to make the request when the instrument rang. It was Judy calling from the Swissotel, attempting to locate Chief Cole.

9

M
organa Devoe awoke to find herself lying in an enormous canopied oval-shaped bed. She had been covered with black silk sheets while she slept and clad in a white silk nightgown. She sat up in bed and took in her surroundings. The bedroom was spacious, taking up twice as much square footage as her Swissotel suite. The one characteristic about this place that stood out most prominently for her was that the room was virtually empty. The only furnishings were the canopied bed and a nightstand on which a pitcher of water and a single glass rested.

After she swung her feet to the floor, Morgana's toes

sank into a thick carpet. The lights were turned low, but there was enough illumination for her to see by. Her mouth and throat were dry, and she poured a glass of water. As she sipped the cold liquid, she discovered a Band-Aid in the crook of her right arm. While she slept, someone had drawn her blood. At that moment she realized she didn't belong here. She was supposed to be in jail.

Confused, but not alarmed, Morgana searched her memory for some clue as to how she had gotten to this place. She remembered the cold, damp cell she had been incarcerated in after her arrest. She recalled Butch Cole, looking very handsome in his police uniform, coming to her cell door. Then there had been the two men who had taken her from that place. She attempted to picture them in her mind, but she had encountered so many police officials in the past few days that they had all begun resembling each other. The exception to this was Butch and his father, whom everyone referred to by the title Chief. To Morgana, the Coles were very different from the other officials.

The two men had taken her from the police station and placed her in the backseat of an American-made car. Then? . . .

Everything from that point on was vague. There was a dim recollection of another man in a parking garage, but she couldn't remember much about him at all. The question that raged through her mind at that moment was, Why had they taken a sample of blood?

The lights in the room brightened, and a door, which had been concealed from view by the dim lighting, opened on the other side of the room. A shaft of bright light forced Morgana to look away until her eyes could adjust. When she looked back, she saw the silhouette of a woman framed in the doorway. For a long moment, the figure remained stationary. The door was closed, and the area became dark once more. Initially, Morgana thought she was alone. Then she detected movement at the foot of the bed. When she turned to look in that direction, the woman was standing there.

Morgana Devoe did not frighten easily. Her life experiences had imbued her with an inner strength that enabled her to face difficulty with a steely calm. Even after her arrest for the murder of Richard Banacek, she had not surrendered to despair. She had not even attempted to contact a lawyer, even though she could easily have afforded one. And apparently that situation had worked itself out, at least temporarily, in her favor because she was no longer incarcerated. However, seeing the woman standing at the foot of the bed filled Morgana with an apprehension nearly as intense as the fear she had felt on that long-ago fall afternoon when she stumbled across Carlos Perfido standing over a dead Isaac Weiss.

There was nothing about this woman that was easily identifiable as being menacing. She was tall, but not exceptionally so. She was tastefully slender without appearing emaciated. Her features were somewhat large for her face, but they were not unattractive. Her hands and feet were a bit large in proportion to the rest of her body, and she possessed a coiled spring tautness with a pronounced predatory feline quality present. When she spoke, her voice was low and husky. "You've been asleep for quite some time, Morgana. You must be hungry. By the way, you don't mind if I call you Morgana, do you?"

She shrugged and responded, "I don't mind."

For a moment the woman fixed her with an intense gaze that appeared to border on insanity. But just as quickly, the intensity of the gaze vanished. "As I said, you are undoubtedly hungry. I will have something prepared for you. There is a lavatory over there." She pointed at an area shrouded in the same darkness as the one through which she had entered. "In it you will find everything you require to shower. There is also a change of clothing. When you are finished, I will be waiting outside for you."

The woman turned to leave. Morgana called to her, "Excuse me."

She stopped, but did not turn around. "Yes?"

"Where am I?"

"You'll be told in good time, Morgana." Then she was gone.

Attorney Franklin Butler was the acting chairman of the board of directors of the DeWitt Corporation. There were currently six members of the board, and there was one vacancy. C. J. Cantrell, one of the producers of the *Murder at the Opera* stage play, was one of those members. Over the weekend, C. J. had seen his financial fortunes plunge to the verge of ruination before calls from Broadway and Hollywood held the promise of future riches following the murder of Richard Banacek. For the time being, Cantrell was in the black, which was one of the reasons why he was in such a good mood on that rainy morning. The other reason was that at the DeWitt Corporation board meeting, the rotund little man was going to get a chance to stick it to the arrogant Franklin Butler.

Charles Jason Cantrell did not consider himself a blatant racist, although technically he was. He didn't use racial slurs in polite company and he didn't knowingly associate with bigots. However, his politics were to the right of ultraconservative, and he was a firm believer in the superiority of white American-born males over all other gender and racial classifications of humanity. This attitude made it particularly difficult for Cantrell to subordinate himself to Franklin Butler. C. J. was about to remedy that situation.

The board meeting had been scheduled three months ago to vote on a permanent chairman of the board of directors of the multinational corporation. Butler had held the position for over two years. Other than Butler and Cantrell, the other board members consisted of a sitting circuit court judge, the president of the Cook County Medical Association, the curator of the Chicago Historical Society, and the former editor-in-chief of the *Chicago Times-Herald* newspaper. The seventh board member was the former president of Chicago State University, who died in late May. The former college president and Franklin Butler had been the only African-American members with seats on the board.

At the 10 A.M. meeting time, the six surviving board·members filed into the conference room that could accommodate thirty on the forty-eighth floor of DeWitt Plaza. They were now split down the middle, with Butler possessing three votes for election as permanent board chairman and C. J. Cantrell controlling three votes against. Because of that divergence, filling the vacant seventh seat would be a major undertaking—and could take months, if not years. C. J. Cantrell had won this round.

The meeting was over in less than ten minutes, and the results entirely predictable. As Cantrell walked out with the others, he shot the acting chairman a mocking glare. Butler wouldn't even look in his direction.

For some moments, the black attorney, who was dressed in a natty blue pin-striped suit, remained seated at the conference table, lost in thought. At that moment, he was planning to kill C. J. Cantrell, even though such an act would not be necessary for Butler to permanently assume the coveted chairman of the board post.

There was a knock on the closed conference room door. "Come," Butler called out.

The door opened, and the young woman who had attended Morgana Devoe only a short time before came in. Her name was Susanne York, although she had a number of aliases. She was Butler's personal assistant. The duties that went along with her title were a mystery, but to the DeWitt Corporation acting chairman of the board, she was indispensable.

"Morgana is having breakfast in the dining room," Susanne York said.

Butler roused himself from his contemplative mood and said quietly, "Escort her to my office when she's through eating."

"Have the test results come back yet?" she asked.

Butler nodded.

When he did not elaborate, she pressed, "Were they positive?"

He turned to look at her before saying a matter-of-fact, near whispered, "Of course they were positive."

She digested the information slowly before smiling, gracing him with a slight bow, and walking out of the conference room.

It took Morgana a few moments to discover the bathroom door, which was set flush in the wall of the room she had slept in. The entrance, like the door through which the strange woman had entered, was virtually undetectable from the wall's surface on sight. There was a lever at waist level, which operated on a spring-operated principle. She pressed the lever, and the door slid sideways, revealing a spacious black-marble-lined washroom on the other side. From a mechanical standpoint, Morgana found the door's operating mechanism intriguing, and she closed the door and tried it once more just for fun before proceeding inside.

She found brand-new athletic shoes, sweat socks, blue jeans, and a denim blouse hanging on a coat tree. Toiletries, a comb, brush, and toothbrush were arranged on the counter beside a sink deep enough to bathe in. The shower and combination tub had six nozzles and was equipped with a whirlpool bath. There was also a sauna. By comparison, this facility made Morgana's Swissotel suite resemble a shack.

After showering and dressing in the clothing that had been set out for her, she left the bathroom and crossed the bedroom to the door that the strange woman had entered through. The opening mechanism was the same, and the door slid open in the same manner as the bathroom door.

On the other side of the door was a dining room lined with floor-to-ceiling windows that provided a view of the north shore of Lake Michigan. The rain and clouds of this rainy day made visibility poor, but it was obvious to Morgana that she was high above the streets of Chicago.

The table in the dining room could seat twelve, but was set for only one. It was covered with a white linen cloth and expensive silver candelabra. At the lone place setting were matching china dishes containing half a grapefruit, a glass of orange juice, water, and a coffee service for one. She sat down and, because she was hungry, began to eat. She was nearly finished with the grapefruit when another sliding door opened and the strange woman entered. A thin middle-aged man dressed in the burgundy waist-length jacket and black trousers of a waiter accompanied her. He was carrying a tray, which he placed on the table. He uncovered the lid, revealing a plate containing scrambled eggs, fried bacon, potatoes, and buttered toast.

"I think that you will find this adequate," the woman said. "I'll be back to check on you in a few minutes." Then she and the waiter were gone.

Morgana was not used to eating large American breakfasts like the one she'd just been served. In Europe and since her arrival in the States, she had been going the simple Continental breakfast route. Now her appetite forced her to consume the entire high-fat, high-calorie meal.

No sooner than she took the last bite of toast and chased it with a swallow of orange juice did the woman return. At the sight of her, Morgana realized she was beginning to develop a marked dislike for this person.

"Did you have enough to eat?" the woman asked.

Morgana nodded.

"Good. Now, if you'll come with me . . ."

Morgana didn't move. "I want to know why I'm here," she demanded.

The woman again revealed the wild insanity in her gaze. It lasted for only a few seconds, but still Morgana caught it, "All of your questions will be answered by the person that I am taking you to see."

After a brief hesitation, Morgana rose from her chair and followed the woman from the dining alcove. They entered a wide marble-lined corridor. A frosted-glass skylight provided ample illumination for the area where sculptures on pedestals and paintings were arranged along the walls. Morgana's education in Lucerne enabled her to recognize some of the artwork as priceless.

"Permit me to introduce myself, Morgana," the woman said as they walked along. "My name is Susanne York."

"Is this your place?" Morgana asked.

The woman's laugh had a harsh, unpleasant tone. "No. It belongs to the corporation and is leased by my employer, whom you are going to meet."

They came to a winding staircase that led down. The next level was laid out in the same basic configuration as the one above, right down to the texture of the marble and the quality of the artwork. There were a pair of highly varnished double doors set at fifty-foot intervals on each side of this lower corridor and a single pair of such doors at the far end. It was to those doors that Susanne York led Morgana Devoe.

York knocked twice on the center door panel before opening the door. She allowed Morgana to enter in front of her; however, York did not follow her. Morgana was unaware of her absence until the door shut behind her. She found herself standing inside the largest private library she had ever seen. She thought she was alone until a deep male voice said, "Come in, Morgana."

He was sitting on a leather couch, which was arranged between two hand-carved wooden end tables. Morgana could not see him clearly, because of the antique reading lamp that partially obscured him. From her vantage point by the door, she could tell that he was black, powerfully built, and expensively dressed. Morgana made no move to go farther into the room.

A moment or two passed before he got to his feet. He had a book in one hand, which he closed, marking his place with a bookmark before placing it down on one of the tables. He allowed his hands to hang loosely down at his sides, but he stood ramrod straight. Something about his posture reminded her of Butch Cole.

"My name is Franklin Butler, Morgana, and I am your lawyer."

"I don't remember hiring you," she said quietly.

The slightest hint of a smile crossed his face. "But you do need me."

Their eyes locked as she said, "Do I?"

His smile didn't alter. "Why don't we get to know each other a bit better, and then you can decide if you want me to represent you or not?"

She didn't respond.

"Won't you have a seat?" Butler offered, motioning to the couch he'd been sitting on when she came in.

There was a large leather armchair adjacent to the couch. She walked over to it and sat down on the edge with her knees pressed tightly together. He returned to the couch.

"I trust that you slept well?" he said.

"I was apparently drugged, and while I was unconscious, someone extracted a sample of my blood." Her tone was conversational, but there was a cold edge present.

"I assure you, Morgana, that whatever was done was in your best interests. Including that very necessary blood test. I am quite certain that when all of the details of what has occurred and why are revealed, you will find everything quite acceptable."

Her gaze remained on him a moment longer, and then she looked around the room. "Is this some type of advancement in American penology?"

A frown dented Butler's forehead. "I don't understand what you mean?"

"The last thing that I recall was being in Chicago Police custody, charged with the murder of actor Richard Banacek. Now I am here. So I'd like to know if this is some new form of jail, and if not, what am I doing here?"

Butler remained silent for a time, and then with a shrug said, "I arranged your removal from police custody, Morgana, which I assure you will have no lingering negative consequences. As for this place—" He swung his arm up to take in their surroundings. "—it belongs to you."

"I live in Switzerland," she snapped.

"But you are an American citizen," he countered. "And this room, the room you slept in last night, the penthouse complex itself, and, for that matter, this entire fifty-story building is your personal property."

She remained silent, continuing to stare at him.

After some time passed and she made no comment, he said, "Morgana, have you ever heard the names Margo and Neil DeWitt?"

"That's the craziest thing that I ever heard, boss," Blackie said. "The DeWitts didn't have any kids."

"How do we know that, Blackie?" Cole responded. "There was a great deal that we were unable to discover about the DeWitts. The DeWitt Corporation has continued to operate and flourish for all of these years, and no heir has ever been found—or at least none that has been named."

Manny Sherlock was driving the unmarked black police car north on Michigan Avenue. They were on the way to DeWitt Plaza to pay an

unexpected call on Attorney Franklin Butler, who was the current oc-
cupant of the three-story penthouse formerly occupied by the DeWitts.
Cole also knew that Butler was the acting chairman of the board of the
DeWitt Corporation. Judy Daniels was going to meet them there.

"But how did Judy come up with a connection between Margo
DeWitt and Morgana Devoe?" Blackie asked.

Cole was sitting in the front passenger seat. The chief of detectives
stared through the rain-streaked windshield at the traffic on the Magnificent Mile. Without turning around to look at the skeptical lieutenant in the backseat, Cole said, "I've been trying to put my finger on
who Morgana Devoe reminded me of since the moment I laid eyes on
her. It took our own Mistress of Disguise's unusual perception to make
it clear. Now Morgana is not a dead ringer for the DeWitt woman, but
there's enough of a resemblance for us to make some inquiries."

Blackie chewed on his bottom lip, as a substitute for the cigar he
craved. "Aren't we going out on a limb on this one, Larry?" Blackie used
the chief's first name in private conversations only when the lieutenant
was deeply troubled. Although Manny was present, the young sergeant
was considered a member of the family. "I mean, there have got to be
hundreds, if not thousands, of women walking around looking like our
dear departed Margo DeWitt."

"You've got a point, Blackie," Cole said. "And this could be a
waste of time, but whoever put together Morgana Devoe's escape employed extensive resources applied with military precision. So we're
going to find out if there is any connection between our escapee and
the most notorious female serial killer in the history of American law
enforcement."

Morgana was listening to every word that Franklin Butler said, but it
was as if her consciousness had fled her body and she was viewing

everything from a great distance. What the lawyer was saying to her was at once enlightening and at the same time devastatingly shocking. A saying Isaac Weiss frequently repeated when he was alive came back to her: "Be careful what you wish for because you might just get it." Now she knew who her parents were and where she came from, but at that moment she sincerely wished she had stayed in Europe.

"From everything that I have been able to discover, Morgana," Butler was saying, "you were conceived shortly after Margo and Neil were married in the winter of 1985. Your mother went to the family chalet in the Alps and remained there until you were born. Then she made arrangements for you to be cared for in Switzerland."

"Why?" The question startled Morgana. Although she had spoken, it sounded as if the voice was that of a complete stranger.

Butler used his most comforting professional voice in telling the young woman about her parents. One of the reasons that he was such a successful attorney was due to the skill he had cultivated in playing to a judge or a jury, which he considered the same as an audience. Now he was playing to Morgana Devoe. Employing an understanding tone, he responded to her question by saying, "Your mother was an unusual person. She had a unique way of viewing life and . . ." After pausing for effect he added, ". . . death. Perhaps she thought that having to care for an infant daughter was beyond her ability to handle."

"Are you saying that my mother was afraid that she would kill me when I was an infant?" She was valiantly attempting to hide it, but she was in obvious pain.

"We can't ignore that possibility," he admitted.

"What about my father?"

"From everything that I've been able to discover about your parents, it seems that Neil DeWitt was somewhat henpecked and would go along with whatever your mother said. There are also indications that Margo was responsible for his death."

Morgana clasped her hands in front of her. Her grip was so tight that the knuckles were white. "I thought that Neil DeWitt was shot to death by a police officer."

"He was," Butler said, "but an autopsy revealed that he'd been administered a massive dose of a tranquilizer called Dalmane. Apparently, your mother gave it to him without his knowledge."

"I see," Morgana said, even though she didn't and never would. "Did you know them?"

"I never had the pleasure, but it was because of your mother that the corporation hired me. You see, before your father's death, the operation was run by a somewhat ultra–right wing conservative gentleman named Seymour Winbush. Mr. Winbush kept minorities and women relegated to minor positions within the corporation. When your mother took over, she initiated an affirmative action program, which resulted in me being recruited from a law firm in Atlanta, where I was a junior partner. I joined the DeWitt Corporation shortly before your mother's death, but I never met her."

There were so many questions that Morgana wanted to ask and things she needed to know, but she couldn't bring herself to make inquiries right now. But there *was* a question that demanded an answer right now. "What do you want from me, Mr. Butler?"

Staring directly into her eyes, the attorney responded, "I want you to receive what rightfully belongs to you, Morgana."

Manny pulled up in front of DeWitt Plaza. Before Cole got out of the car, he said, "Blackie, I want you and Manny to check out this magician's assistant, Pamela Hoffman. She gave an address on Wrightwood near Halsted at the Goodman Theater, but I'd be willing to bet that not only her name but her address is phony, too, or she's long gone by now. Just in case she did stick around, get some backup from the Twenty-third District before you pay her a visit."

"You got it, boss," Blackie said. "If we don't come up with the magician's assistant, we'll check with Actors' Equity. Hoffman had to show a current actor's union card in order to participate in the play."

"Before she was the magician's assistant, she was referred to the production as an animal trainer by the people they leased the tiger from," Cole said.

"We'll check everything out and see you back at headquarters," Blackie said, slipping into the front seat that Cole vacated.

As the police car pulled away, Cole entered the DeWitt Plaza lobby. Once inside, he waited. There were any number of young women in evidence, but the chief of detectives had to wait for Sergeant Judy Daniels to approach him. That was simply because he could not recognize her in whatever disguise she had selected to wear today. Cole had become so used to this that he actually didn't give it a second thought. He had been standing there for less than a minute when an efficient-looking young woman with black hair worn in a spinsterish bun approached. She was wearing horn-rimmed glasses and a business suit, and when she walked up to him, she said a severely polite, "Good morning, sir."

"Good morning," he responded. "Judy?"

"At your service, Chief," she said. "How do you want to handle this: the direct way or in the clandestine manner?"

"Just for my own information, what is the clandestine manner?"

She cast a quick glance around to make sure that she couldn't be overheard. "The utilization of stealth, subterfuge, and dirty tricks."

Cole shook his head. "I'll keep that in mind, but right now we're going to employ the direct way. Let's go."

They had to take two elevators to reach the penthouse. The final car deposited them in a carpeted foyer on the forty-eighth floor. A middle-aged woman was seated at a desk across from the elevators. She was typing at a computer terminal as the cops approached. On the wall behind her desk the words, THE DEWITT CORPORATION— FRANKLIN BUTLER, ACTING CHAIRMAN AND ATTORNEY AT LAW were displayed in large gold letters.

The receptionist stopped typing and turned to greet them with a less-than-cordial, "May I help you?"

Cole displayed his gold badge and said, "I'm Chief Larry Cole, and this is Sergeant Judy Daniels. We're with the Chicago Police Department and would like to talk to Franklin Butler in regards to a homicide investigation."

The receptionist's severe manner did not thaw a single degree. "Do you have an appointment?"

"No, we don't," Cole said, taking a step forward to tower over the officious woman. "But I'm sure Mr. Butler will see us if you inform him that we're here."

Appearing visibly uncomfortable, the receptionist picked up a telephone from her desk and punched in an in-house number. "There is a Chief Cole and a Sergeant Daniels from the police department here to see the chairman and they don't have an appointment. Yes, I'll hold."

The receptionist waited with obvious impatience for approximately twenty seconds. Then, "Thank you. I'll inform them." Hanging up, she said, "Someone will be along to escort you to the chairman's office." With that, she went back to her computer.

Cole and Judy walked over to an area equipped with a white leather sofa, a pair of matching easy chairs, and an ornate wrought-iron cocktail table with a glass top. Cole remained standing as Judy sank down in one of the chairs. Rubbing the soft leather surface, the Mistress of Disguise and High Priestess of Mayhem said, "Now this is nice. Very nice."

Cole looked around. "Butler has made some changes in this place, but it's pretty much the same as it was when the DeWitts lived here."

The clicking of a woman's heels on the hard surface of an uncarpeted floor carried to them from an adjoining corridor. The cops turned to look up just as a tall striking woman strode into view. When she approached them and stepped onto the carpet, the clicking of her heels ceased and she seemed to glide toward them like a silent wraith.

Before she reached the reception area, Judy stage-whispered to Cole, "She's wearing a disguise."

"Good morning, Chief Cole and Sergeant Daniels," the woman said. "My name is Susanne York, and I am Attorney Butler's assistant. Please come with me."

They followed her from the reception area down the wide marble-lined corridor. As they walked along, Cole gave their escort a cursory examination. Under ordinary circumstances, he would have taken her appearance for granted, but Judy had alerted him that the woman was disguised. Despite him not being much of an expert on such things, Cole noticed that the texture of the woman's face was a bit too smooth, possessing a decidedly artificial appearance. She was wearing color-treated contact lenses and a wig. However, her appearance was merely academic right now.

She ushered them into a large office with a view to the south that overlooked Michigan Avenue far below. The west wall was covered with photographs, citations, and diplomas from Franklin Butler's military and legal career. The east wall was vacant, giving the office a stark, utilitarian atmosphere. The attorney that they had come to see sat facing them in front of the windows behind a no-frills metal desk equipped with a black vinyl covered chair.

"Chief Cole and Sergeant Daniels, do come in," Butler said expansively as he rose from his chair. He extended his hand, which Cole and then Judy shook in turn. He provided them both a display of his formidable strength with his grasp. "Please sit down," Butler said, offering them seats in a pair of simple guest chairs in front of the desk. The cops sat down warily because of the effusiveness of the lawyer's greeting. They could only compare the experience to encountering a friendly shark in a shallow pond.

Cole didn't bring up the reason for their visit right away, but in the long run, he didn't have to.

"Chief Cole," the attorney began, "you have saved me the trouble of contacting your office. I wanted to arrange for the surrender of my client and also make arrangements for an immediate bond hearing for her in Criminal Court."

"Who is your client, Counselor?" Cole asked. Judy, seated beside him, appeared ready to explode with the answer.

Butler graced them with a cold, calculating smile. "You know her as Morgana Devoe, but I suggest that you amend your records because I have proof that her name is actually Morgana DeWitt. Margo and Neil DeWitt were her parents."

Cole turned to Judy. "I've got to give it to you, Sergeant Daniels, when you're right, you are very right."

10

Attorney Franklin Butler surrendered the wanted escapee that he identified as Morgana DeWitt (aka Morgana Devoe) to Chief Larry Cole and Judy Daniels; however, he attempted to do so with some degree of media fanfare. After making it known to the police that Morgana was in his office at De-Witt Plaza, Butler complied with everything that Cole demanded. Only the lawyer did it his way.

Cole sent Judy to get her unmarked police car, which was parked on the street at the north end of DeWitt Plaza, and drive it to the upper level of the commercial parking garage. Cole's plan was to bring Morgana down in an elevator to the parking garage level and then spirit her quietly to police headquarters. The chief called for a pair of uniformed officers—a female and a male—to assist in the transport in case of trouble. All was in place before Butler produced the wanted woman.

Cole looked at Butler. "Would you care to tell us what you know about how your client came to be here?"

"I will disclose that at Ms. DeWitt's bond hearing," Butler said in his best lawyer's voice. "I trust that upon her return to official custody you will expedite her processing so that she will arrive in bond court before nightfall?"

"Your client will be in court when you get there," Cole said.

Cole, Judy, and the uniformed officers from the Eighteenth District transported Morgana from Butler's office to the forty-eighth-floor elevator. As they walked along, the prisoner asked the chief of detectives, "How is your son?"

"He's doing just fine," Cole responded curtly.

"Please give him my regards when you see him," she said.

The chief appeared visibly uncomfortable, and it took him a moment to say, "I'll make sure that he gets your message."

Morgana was again handcuffed, and Judy had taken pains to make sure that the bracelets were not tight enough to bite into the flesh of her wrists. As they proceeded to the parking garage, Morgana was put into a protective box with Cole walking in front of her, Judy directly behind her, and the uniformed officers on either side. They rode down to the twenty-fifth floor without incident, but when the elevator doors opened, they were met by a throng of media types brandishing minicams equipped with bright strobe lights, still cameras with popping flashbulbs and clublike microphones. As soon as the cops and their prisoner were spotted, the reporters erupted with a barrage of questions that were uttered so close together, they became a babble of indecipherable noise.

Cole reacted instantly by physically shielding Morgana and the others with his body and forcing them back onto the elevator. Before any of the reporters could board, Cole punched the CLOSE DOOR and 48 buttons on the console, and the car rose to return to its point of origin.

"What are we going to do now?" Judy asked.

"We can use the private elevator from the penthouse directly to the garage," Cole said.

"Won't that require a special key to operate, boss?" Judy said.

Cole nodded. "We'll just have to ask Butler for it."

"But will he give it to us?"

"He'll give it to you," Morgana said quietly.

The attorney didn't like it, but he reluctantly gave them the key to operate the private elevator, and they managed to escape from De-Witt Plaza without further incident.

Shortly after Cole and Judy Daniels left Franklin Butler's office with Morgana once again in custody, Susanne York came out of the north entrance of DeWitt Plaza and walked west toward Rush Street. She was dressed in a black western-cut business suit, black shirt with a black string tie, black hand-tooled cowboy boots with silver stud or-namentation, and a black cowboy hat. The rain had slackened to a sporadic drizzle, and as noon approached, the sky brightened as the sun attempted to break through the cloud cover.

The Rush Street area is the central nightclub district of the Windy City and is always crowded with tourists come rain or shine, good weather or bad. There were quite a few bizarre sights on the street lined with bars and restaurants, which ran from Chicago Av-enue to Division Street, and the striking woman in black drew more than a small share of admiring, lascivious, and even simply curious glances. For her part, she proceeded to her destination with long pur-poseful strides.

She turned off Rush Street at Cedar and walked a quarter of a block to a metallic blue Lincoln Town Car. Susanne York opened the back door and got inside. Former Army Sergeant Major Gaskew was behind the wheel, and retired Brigadier General Goolsby occupied the front seat. They were clad in slacks and casual summerwear sports shirts, but their military backgrounds were evident from the creases in their trousers to the spit shine of their shoes.

"Good afternoon, boys," she said once she was settled. "Let's head up to Wrigleyville so I can tie up some loose ends."

As they pulled out into traffic and headed for Lake Shore Drive, Goolsby said, "The Cubs are playing the Mets at one thirty. The traffic is going to be heavy."

The woman in the black cowboy outfit gazed out the window at the passing traffic. She replied, "It'll make for better camouflage."

The three-story frame house was located on Wrightwood between Halsted and Sheffield. The building had been constructed during the Depression and had fallen into disrepair during the mid-fifties. Originally the structure had been a single-family dwelling, but following a bank foreclosure prior to World War II, the rooms were broken up into self-contained units often referred to as "kitchenettes." These units were rented out on a month-to-month basis, attracting the poor, the indigent, and the alcoholic, which had a debilitating effect on the entire neighborhood. In the mid-seventies, the entire area underwent a social and economic rejuvenation, which resulted in the structure being renovated for the young urban professionals that were flooding back into the Wrigleyville area.

The centerpiece of this near northside area of the Windy City was Wrigley Field at Clark and Addison Streets, which was the home of the Chicago Cubs. One of the oldest and most storied professional sports stadiums in the country, Wrigley was a brick structure with ivy-covered walls and a quaint, old world ambience, which attracted fans whether the National League Chicago baseball team was winning or not. "Not" was generally the state of affairs, as the Cubs hadn't won a pennant since 1945. Yet, on this overcast summer afternoon with a definite hint of rain in the air, close to forty thousand fans were headed for what Mr. Cub himself, Ernie Banks, had dubbed "the Friendly Confines."

Traffic from Montrose on the north to Fullerton on the south and Ashland on the west to Lake Shore Drive on the east was gridlocked prior to the 1:30 P.M. game time. As the Cubs and the New York Mets had flirted with the wild card spot the previous season, both teams were considered contenders, even though neither one of them had a record above the .500 mark. Yet the faithful still came out.

On this weekday afternoon, Blackie Silvestri and Manny Sherlock were inching along westbound on Fullerton, attempting to reach the address that magician's assistant and tiger handler Pamela Hoffman had listed with Actors' Equity. The humidity was high and the temperature had risen into the upper eighties, but as the cops fought the pre-game traffic, the squad car's air conditioner was off and all the windows were rolled down. Having doffed his suit jacket and loosened his tie, Blackie sat in the passenger seat, puffing contentedly on a twisted Parodi cigar. Manny, appearing totally unaffected by either the elements or the tobacco smoke, kept his eye on the traffic. Finally, when they had not moved for a full five minutes, the lieutenant said, "Quit screwing around, kid. We're on official police business."

With a shrug, the sergeant said, "Lights and siren coming up, Blackie." Activating the emergency equipment, Manny pulled onto the opposite side of the street and proceeded against traffic for the next few blocks. Within minutes, they were pulling into a bus stop less than a block from Pamela Hoffman's address.

Manny flipped down the Chicago Police Department official business placard behind the sun visor before locking the car and following Blackie to the remodeled four-story frame house. Game traffic was still thick with cars crawling along and pedestrians wearing Cubs caps and jerseys streaming by.

Blackie fieldstripped the stub of his cigar in the gutter as a young woman in a replica Cubs uniform consisting of a plunging halter top and very short shorts walked by. "Hi," she said seductively to the lieutenant. "Beat the Mets."

"I'm all for it," Blackie said. "The Second City runs it."

Manny was watching from the foot of the frame building steps. There was a frown on the sergeant's face.

"What?" Blackie asked.

"You should be ashamed of yourself. She's young enough to be your daughter."

Blackie began to climb the steps. "Actually, she's young enough to be my granddaughter, kid, but the department is into community policing, so my being nice to that young lady was just me doing my part for the 'city that works.'"

He had Manny there.

The three-story structure had been separated into three units. The first and second floor contained two three-room apartments. The top floor was a one-room attic apartment, which had been leased in April 2006 for one year by Pamela Hoffman. Each unit had an individual entrance off a stained wooden porch equipped with individual sundecks. When they reached the attic apartment entrance, Blackie was forced to stop to catch his breath.

"Are you okay?" Manny inquired.

"That was quite a climb," Blackie said, puffing hard.

"Can I ask you a question?"

The lieutenant shot the gangly sergeant a hard look. "That depends."

"Have you ever thought about giving up smoking?"

"No," Blackie snapped. "Cigars are part of my persona. Now let's find out if this Hoffman woman is home."

Opening their suit jackets to provide quick access to their guns, they flanked the attic apartment front door. Blackie rang the bell. There was no response. He followed this up with a hard knock on the center door panel. Still nothing.

"Hello, up there," came a woman's voice from the second-floor sun porch.

The cops looked over the railing to find a white-haired woman in a flower-print dress staring up at them. "Are you officers looking for the young lady who lives in the attic unit?"

"Yes, ma'am," Blackie said. "Have you seen her around lately?"

Despite there being no one in evidence to hear them, the woman whispered, "She's not home much, and I haven't seen her in over a week. Is she in trouble?"

"No, ma'am," Blackie said. "We just need to ask her a few questions."

"I see," the woman said, but there was a confused look on her face. "Are you going inside?"

"Yes we are," Blackie replied patiently. "We have a warrant."

"But how will you gain entry?" she asked, straining to see what they were doing but remaining firmly rooted to her sun porch.

"We have our ways," Blackie said, removing a set of lockpicks from his inside jacket pocket.

The attic apartment was fairly spacious with walls painted in a medium blue shade with white trim. The floors were covered with an inexpensive blue carpet, and there was virtually no furniture in evidence.

"This lady travels real light," Blackie said as they looked around.

The living room was furnished with only a scarred wooden table with a single wooden chair. The bathroom cabinet was empty, and there were no towels on the rack. Then there was the bedroom.

There was no bed or even a mattress on the floor; however, the walls were covered with pictures. Some of them were still photographs, a few were newspaper clippings, and the rest were pencil sketches, watercolor renderings and pastel drawings on canvas. The subject in each was equally recognizable. It was Margo DeWitt.

While Manny examined the pictures, Blackie checked out the rest of the apartment. The closets were empty, and there was no food, dishes, or silverware in the kitchen. But there was a covered stainless steel pot on the top of the gas range. Blackie was about to look inside this pot when Manny called to him from the bedroom.

Blackie found that Manny had discovered that the wall on which the pictures were displayed had a secret passage behind it. This passage could be accessed by way of a spring-operated mechanism concealed behind the frame of one of the watercolor portraits. A closer examination of the concealed area revealed that a fake wall had been constructed to hide one third of the already cramped sleeping area of the small apartment. And what the cops found inside the secret compartment was as fascinating as the pictorial shrine to serial killer Margo DeWitt.

They used pocket flashlights to illuminate the interior. There was a haphazard arrangement of items inside: various types of clothing; a theatrical makeup table littered with jars, vials, tubes of cosmetics, and a mannequin's head; and various styles and colors of fake hairpieces.

"Judy would love this," Manny said. "So what do you think is going on here, Blackie?"

"Beats me, kid," Blackie said, sniffing the air. "Do you smell something burning?"

The blue Lincoln Town Car, containing the former army career men Gaskew and Goolsby accompanying Susanne York, arrived at the Wrightwood frame structure just as Blackie and Manny entered the attic apartment.

"It looks like we're too late, Ms. York," Goolsby said. "The police are already here."

"That's really not a problem," she said casually. "Lieutenant Silvestri and Sergeant Sherlock are merely a minor annoyance. Pull in behind their black police car in the bus stop. I've arranged a little surprise for intruders to the magician assistant's lair."

Once they were parked, she removed a palm-sized black device resembling a cellular telephone from her pocket. She punched a series of numbers into the keypad on the face of the device before nonchalantly returning it to her pocket.

"Now what?" former Sergeant Major Gaskew asked.

She emitted a strangled laugh that came out sounding like the cackle of a witch and said, "We wait for the fireworks to start, gentlemen."

The lone pot on the stove of the attic apartment leased to Pamela Hoffman contained a substance developed by the military called thermite. It was in gelatinous form and by itself harmless. But a highly volatile catalytic agent in a test tube was suspended inside the pot. A tiny computer chip was contained in the top of the metal tube, and this chip was equipped to receive a signal that would activate the catalyst, which would in turn detonate the thermite.

The brewing chemical stew inside the metal pot began to cook slowly. The thermite was a highly volatile substance, and less than ninety seconds after the catalyst was armed, flames erupted from the pot with such force that it blew the top off. Then the fire began spreading.

The attic apartment became engulfed so rapidly that Blackie and Manny had little time to react. They made it out of the bedroom with the partitioned secret compartment into the living room to discover that the fire had expanded from the kitchen and was licking at the floors and ceiling. They rushed for the front door as a wave of intense heat slammed into them that was so powerful, it sucked all the oxygen out of the atmosphere. Manny was in the lead and, fighting the acrid smoke searing his eyes, lungs, and throat, it took him two tries to get the door open. He was about to dash outside when he realized that Blackie was not with him. Looking back into the apartment, Manny saw the lieutenant lying unconscious on the living room floor. The carpet was now on fire, and flames were licking at the downed man's clothing. Without a second's hesitation, Manny rushed back to get him.

From the Lincoln Town Car parked in the bus stop behind the chief of detectives' black command car, Susanne York and her escorts watched the attic apartment begin smoking before open flames shattered the windowpanes to seek the open air. It was obvious that the entire wood frame structure would soon be involved and subsequently destroyed.

"Our mission is completed, gentlemen," she said, leaning back in the comfortable leather seat and pulling her cowboy hat down low on her forehead. "Please take me back to DeWitt Plaza."

Without comment, Gaskew put the car in gear and, keeping his eyes cast stonily to the front as was the case with his companion Goolsby, headed out of Wrigleyville. They had traveled only a block when they heard the scream of sirens approaching the burning frame house.

11

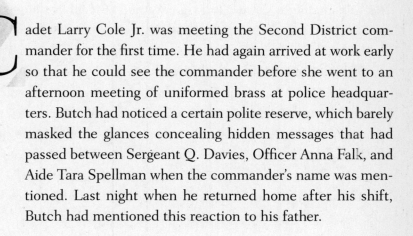

C adet Larry Cole Jr. was meeting the Second District commander for the first time. He had again arrived at work early
so that he could see the commander before she went to an
afternoon meeting of uniformed brass at police headquarters. Butch had noticed a certain polite reserve, which barely
masked the glances concealing hidden messages that had
passed between Sergeant Q. Davies, Officer Anna Falk, and
Aide Tara Spellman when the commander's name was mentioned. Last night when he returned home after his shift,
Butch had mentioned this reaction to his father.

Larry Cole Sr. had been oddly evasive. "Butch, Commander Stephanie Robinson-Smith is your boss, and the only way to get along with any boss on this job is to do what you're told. Are you following me, son?"

"Yes, sir," he replied. But the curiosity remained, and he decided to place a call to Judy Daniels late Sunday night.

So, when Cadet Cole walked into the commander's office that afternoon, he had some idea of what to expect. As always, the Mistress of Disguise and High Priestess of Mayhem had been dead-on accurate with her assessment of the cadet's new boss.

Commander Robinson-Smith was a fiftyish, attractive, medium-brown-complexioned black woman who wore her iron-gray hair in a short, somewhat severe hairstyle. She was of average height and weight and wore a smartly tailored uniform. When the cadet walked in, she was seated behind her desk and sized him up from over the tops of a pair of wire-frame glasses, which were pushed down on her nose. Her eyes remained on him for a long time as he stood at attention. Finally, she lowered her gaze and said, "At ease, Cadet."

He assumed a parade rest stance, but, as she had not offered him a seat, he did not take one. Judy had warned him about that. She had been known to explode into screaming tantrums at anyone who took liberties in her office. After he'd been standing for an additional thirty seconds, she said, "Sit down, Cadet."

He did so, but sat at attention, with his buttocks perched on the front of the chair and his back ramrod straight. They remained in their separate positions for the next two minutes as she turned her attention back to the paperwork on her desk. When she finally did speak, her words were far from those of a cordial greeting.

"You've hardly draped yourself in the mantle of glory since you've been assigned to the Second District, Cadet Cole."

"I beg your pardon, ma'am?" His tone held bewilderment; however, his posture remained erect.

Now she looked directly at him, but still over the tops of her glasses. "You were involved in that escape fiasco yesterday."

Under other circumstances and perhaps with someone else, he would have objected. But he had indeed been warned about Commander Robinson-Smith.

"Yes, ma'am," he responded to her comment about the escape.

She returned to her paperwork. During the brief period that the commander looked directly at him, Butch noticed that she was rather pretty, although advancing years had taken some of the bloom off the blush of her beauty. The cadet was also perceptive enough to notice something else about his first Chicago Police Department commander. Her fading looks were affected not only by her age, but also by a bitterness of spirit. Judy Daniels hadn't identified for him what could have caused such a thing to occur, but somehow Butch suspected that the Mistress of Disguise and High Priestess of Mayhem knew.

"Now, I know who your father is, Cadet Cole," the commander said, "and I really don't care." Her words were harsh to the point of accusation. "You will be treated just like anyone else in this command, and you've already started out under a cloud with me."

Butch made no effort to defend himself, because he knew that it wouldn't do any good. He remained seated in silent attention and waited.

The time stretched on through thirty seconds to a minute to ninety seconds. Finally, at the two-minute mark, Commander Stephanie Robinson-Smith snapped, "Dismissed."

The cadet got to his feet, rendered a sharp salute, which was acknowledged by a casual wave of the commander's hand, and let himself out of the office, closing the door softly behind him.

When he got to the front desk, the regular crew was present with the exception of Officer Perry Montoya, who was on his day off. Police Aide Tara Spellman was the first one to look up as the cadet took a seat at one of the computer terminals.

"How'd it go with the commander?" she whispered.

"Just like the last time," he whispered back.

She frowned. "You've met the commander before?"

Butch turned to her and smiled. "No, but I have had blood tests administered with blunt needles."

She managed to stifle a laugh.

Sergeant Q. Davies glanced up from his usual overflowing stack of arrest reports and said, "Look at it this way, Cole. Just another day in paradise."

The watch commander's door opened, and Captain Gary Harmon came out. Everyone noticed the tension surrounding him.

"Cole," Harmon called. "I need to talk to you."

As the captain ushered the cadet into his office, Q. Davies said, "Something sure as hell is wrong."

The Criminal Courts Building lobby at Twenty-sixth and California began filling up with reporters and the curious long before Morgana Devoe/DeWitt's scheduled arraignment and bond hearing at 3:00 P. M. Franklin Butler had pulled the rather lengthy and impressive strings that the DeWitt Corporation possessed to have the hearing scheduled on short notice. In fact, as soon as he reported on duty, Sergeant Q. Davies had received explicit instructions from the chief of detectives to have the escapee's paperwork expedited and hand-carried by uniformed police messenger to the Criminal Courts Building.

The cops and the defendant arrived first, and this time Cole made sure the media fanfare would be minimized until they got inside the courtroom. Still clad in her blue outfit and wearing handcuffs, Morgana was driven to court from police headquarters in a pastel-gray late-model unmarked Ford police vehicle. Keeping the operation as simple as possible, while maintaining an adequate security level, Cole drove the Ford with Judy, who was dressed in dark blue police coveralls displaying her badge and sergeant stripes, seated in the back with the prisoner. Cole was armed with a .45 Colt semiautomatic pistol with two extra eight-round magazines to supplement his shoulder-holstered Beretta nine-millimeter handgun. Judy carried a .45 Smith & Wesson stainless steel pistol in a belt holster with extra ammunition, a .380-caliber Colt Peacekeeper handgun equipped with a laser sight, and a six-inch-barrel Model 686 Smith & Wesson stainless steel revolver with two six-round speedloaders beneath the coveralls. She had changed from the dark-haired exotic look of this morning's visit to the Swissotel and DeWitt Plaza to a short-haired, scrubbed appearance in keeping with her well-armed profile. Although Morgana had escaped once, Cole did not think another attempt would be made to take her from custody. Actually, he'd been working on the motive behind yesterday's escape, and as with any other criminal case, the pieces began slowly falling into place.

While they were waiting for Morgana to be processed at headquarters, Cole had shared his thoughts with Judy.

"After they took her from the Second District, it would have been a simple matter for Butler or the DeWitt Corporation to spirit Morgana out of Chicago and have her on a private flight to Europe or Asia without us being able to do a lot about it," Cole said.

"But she would have remained a fugitive for the rest of her life, boss," Judy said. "Eventually someone would have discovered who she was, and despite the DeWitt Corporation's money, she would be right back where she started from."

"Agreed. Facilitating her escape was not meant to make her a fugitive. Someone, and I think we can agree that that someone is Franklin Butler, needed her for only a short period of time before he surrendered her back to us. The question is, what did he need her for?"

Judy thought about this for a moment before saying, "Beats me. Maybe he just wanted to make sure that she's who she says she is."

Cole sat up a bit straighter. "I had some thoughts along that same line. Let me make a couple of phone calls."

When Cole hung up, he said, "That was Sergeant Davies at the Second District. I had him pull her original incarceration form. There was nothing listed under marks, scars, bruises, or recent injuries."

This initially had no meaning to Judy. Then, "Morgana gave blood recently. There was a fresh Band-Aid in the crook of her arm when we took her into custody at DeWitt Plaza."

Cole leaned back in his desk chair and said, "Butler now probably has scientific DNA proof that Morgana Devoe is Margo and Neil De-Witt's daughter and the heir to the DeWitt fortune."

"That really doesn't make a lot of difference to us, does it, boss?" Judy said.

"I don't know," Cole responded. "I really don't know."

By prior arrangement with the Cook County Sheriff, Cole was allowed to drive the police car into a restricted area behind the Criminal Courts Building. From there, they spirited their prisoner into a rear entrance, where a freight elevator manned by a uniformed female deputy sheriff waited. A few minutes later, they were in a high-ceilinged courtroom with mahogany walls and spectators' benches. Cole and Judy, with Morgana between them, approached the prosecutor's table, where a petite Asian woman with straight black hair waited for them. Her name was Kim Wong, and around the Criminal Courts Building she was known as Poker Face for the cold, calculating manner in which she tried cases.

After Judy removed the handcuffs, the state's attorney extended her hand to Morgana. "Ms. Devoe, my name is Kim Wong. I am the Cook County state's attorney assigned to your case."

With an elegance that impressed the cops and the lawyer, Morgana said, "Even though you are the enemy, Ms. Wong, it's a pleasure to meet you."

Judy escorted Morgana to the defendant's table across the aisle to await Butler's arrival, while Cole and Kim Wong took seats at the prosecutor's table. "We've drawn Judge Pate for the arraignment," she said. "Butler has already submitted a motion for dismissal, which I am countering, but from what I've seen of your case, all we have is the weapons and escape charges against the defendant."

"What about the attempted murder of Richard Banacek?" Cole asked.

The state's attorney shook her head. "Looks good in a law book, Larry, but you've already established that someone else killed the actor, so Judge Pate won't even consider attempted murder at the arraignment. Butler's going to get a minimum bail on the other charges, and that young lady is going to walk right out of here."

Up until now there had been only a smattering of spectators in the courtroom, but that number increased dramatically with the arrival of the flamboyant Franklin Butler. A noisy contingent of media types followed in the high-profile attorney's wake. When he reached the defense table, Judge Angelica Pate, a no-nonsense female jurist clad in the black robes of her office, entered the courtroom from her private chambers. As she began banging her gavel to establish order in her domain, Larry Cole's beeper went off.

The Cubs lost to the Mets 11 to 10 in twelve innings. The rain returned at the conclusion of the regular nine-inning game, and most of the thirty-five thousand fans who had put in an appearance were long gone by the time the final pitch was thrown. A steady downpour fell on the city from midafternoon on, and as evening approached, lightning lanced across the heavens and thunder rumbled through the skyscraper canyons of the Loop, as if heralding a major cosmic disaster. With at least three full hours of daylight remaining, as the summer solstice approached, the heavy overcast forced drivers on the city's thoroughfares to turn their headlights on. Through this ghostly, twilight landscape, Butch Cole piloted his red Honda motorcycle toward Northwestern Memorial Hospital.

He pulled into the emergency room driveway and saw Judy's dark blue Chevy police car parked in a "reserved for official vehicles only" space. Chaining his helmet to the handlebars, Butch stripped off the rain-soaked Windbreaker he had worn, stuffed it in a saddlebag, and headed for the entrance. Just inside the sliding glass doors, he encountered a uniformed security guard who reminded him of the crusty old-timer on duty at the stage door of the Goodman Theater on the opening night of *Murder at the Opera*. Butch was about to go over and ask permission to leave the bike in the driveway, but the guard simply waved his hand and said, "I got you covered, Cadet. Your motorcycle will be okay where it is."

It was at this moment that Butch remembered he was wearing his Chicago Police uniform. The trousers were wet from the rain, but the short-sleeved shirt with the cadet badge and octagonal CPD patch was as crisply pressed as it had been when he put it on to go to work earlier today.

The emergency room was alive with nurses, doctors, orderlies, medical technicians, and cops. The cops came in all shapes and sizes, sexes and colors, and wore everything from the official spring field uniform of the patrol cop to the conservative business attire of the detective to the casual dress of the anti–street crime tactical unit. Their ranks also varied from the light blue of the patrol officer to the white of the supervisor. As Butch made his way through the throng, he was paid scant attention by the other CPD members present, which provided him with some degree of comfort. However, he didn't see any familiar faces and wasn't comfortable enough to ask a stranger, even if it was a cop, if they had seen Chief Larry Cole or knew where Lieutenant Silvestri or Sergeant Sherlock were being treated. Then a voice said from behind him, "Cadet Cole."

Butch turned around and came face-to-face with ADS Geno Bailey. The young cadet's inquisitor from the Morgana Devoe escape investigation did not come on with the same harsh attitude as had been the case the night before. In fact, Butch noticed an undeniable solemnity about him.

"Are you looking for your father?" Bailey asked.

"Yes, sir."

Bailey pointed to one of the curtained cubicles halfway down the west wing of the emergency room. "He's in there with Sergeant Sherlock."

When Bailey didn't say anything about Uncle Blackie, Butch felt a chill go through him. As if he were in a trance, Butch turned and walked over to the cubicle. With a glance back at ADS Bailey, the cadet stepped inside.

There he found his father, Judy, a uniformed nurse, and Manny Sherlock and Manny's wife, Lauren. Manny was lying in the lone bed, and Lauren, appearing tense but making a valiant effort to conceal it, sat in a chair. When Butch saw his old friend, he emitted an involuntary gasp of horror.

The young sergeant's hair had been nearly totally burned off, and every square inch of visible flesh was covered with ugly red blisters. There were IV tubes running from both his arms, and an oxygen tube in his nose. The patient was hooked up to an EKG machine, and the monitor bounded up and down like a runaway Ping-Pong ball. Despite his injuries, Manny was conscious, but only barely so. He was the first to spy the new arrival.

"Hey, kid," the patient rasped, "welcome to barbecue central."

"I'm sorry," the nurse said, "but Sergeant Sherlock has got to get some rest. We'll be moving him to a private room soon. You will have to wait until we transfer him, and then you can stay until visiting hours are over. Now, please go to the waiting room until we complete the transfer." Lauren was allowed to remain.

A few minutes later, Judy and the Coles took seats in the main waiting room on the first floor of Northwestern Memorial Hospital. When his father sat down on one of the red plastic sofas, Butch noticed that the elder Cole appeared more fatigued than he'd ever seen him before.

"Dad," Butch said in such a low tone of voice that his father barely heard him, "how is Uncle Blackie?"

Cole let a slow whistle escape from between his front teeth, took in a deep breath, and responded, "About like Manny, Butch, as far as the burns go, but they placed Blackie in intensive care because he suffered a heart attack while they were trapped in the fire. Maria's with him, and he's resting comfortably, but they're waiting for a cardiologist to give him a thorough evaluation. All that we can do now is wait."

Seated together in the drab hospital waiting room, that is what the three cops did.

The bond hearing went exactly as Franklin Butler had anticipated. Judge Angelica Pate, a no-nonsense jurist from the old school, took a dim view of Morgana's story that she knew nothing about the men who had spirited her away from the police. The judge had even been guardedly critical of the defense attorney when he also professed ignorance of his client's whereabouts during the twenty-four-hour period that she was a fugitive from justice. However, a great deal of steam went out of the State's case when Larry Cole and Judy Daniels were forced to leave the courtroom because of an emergency.

Prosecutor Kim Wong had carried on, and Morgana's bond had been set at a high—but hardly unreachable for the DeWitt Corporation CEO—half a million dollars. A brief moment of bedlam erupted in the so-far-orderly courtroom when Butler requested that the complaints be amended to reflect the defendant's name as Morgana De-Witt. Judge Pate had quickly taken back control of the courtroom with a few bangs of her gavel and threats to have anyone ejected who continued to behave in a disorderly fashion. The judge then informed the defense that she would take the name-change issue under advisement before adjourning the proceeding.

In the corridor outside the courtroom, Butler issued a statement to the press: "My client's trial date has been set for September fifteenth, at which time I promise that she will be proven innocent of all charges, including the onstage murder of Richard Banacek and the escape from custody charges."

"Attorney Butler," asked Randy Salerno, a tall handsome reporter from WGN TV News, "you made a motion for your client's surname to be changed from Devoe to DeWitt on the court complaints?"

"That's correct," Butler responded, staring deadpan into the bank of cameras facing him.

Salerno quickly asked a follow-up question. "Is your client the daughter of Margo and Neil DeWitt?"

"She is," Butler responded, before using his formidable strength to forge a way through the media throng, which had erupted with questions. As Butler and his chauffeur ushered Morgana toward the exit, the attorney called back to them, "I have no further comment at this time."

Morgana remained mute during the bond hearing and the impromptu Criminal Courts Building press conference. Later, that pose, caught by the still and television cameras, would draw comparisons between the young woman and the notorious serial killer who was alleged to be her mother, Margo DeWitt.

On the ride back from the courthouse, Morgana said very little despite Butler's attempts to make small talk in the wake of the successful legal proceeding and appearance before the media. The attorney attempted to gauge her mood, and he initially believed that she was sullen, as if she were pouting. Then he realized that there was something less emotional and a great deal more calculating about her. Ms. Morgana DeWitt, as Butler thought of her now, was deep in thought.

When they arrived at DeWitt Plaza, Morgana hesitated before getting out of the limousine. "I am staying at the Swissotel on Wacker Drive."

Butler was ready for this. "When you agreed to have me represent you, Morgana, I took the liberty of checking you out of the hotel. Your bill has been paid and your belongings collected. They have been moved to your accommodations here at DeWitt Plaza."

Morgana took this in for a moment before saying, "I see you think of everything, Mr. Butler."

"Please call me Franklin."

As they ascended to the penthouse in the elevator, she said, "I'm not really comfortable staying here. Tomorrow I plan to make other arrangements."

He started to argue, but decided against it. "If that is what you wish, I see no problem as long as we keep the court apprised of your whereabouts. That is a condition of your bond."

Despite the controlled temperature maintained throughout DeWitt Plaza, Morgana shivered, which the attorney took for the realization of her status as an accused felon.

When they reached the forty-ninth floor, Butler said, "Can I have something prepared for you by the kitchen staff? It has been a long day and you're probably hungry."

"Thank you, but no," she responded. "I'm fine right now. I'd like to take a look around the penthouse and see where my—" She hesitated. "—parents lived."

Something about her tone of voice made Butler study her more closely. He had noticed a certain degree of bitterness now that had not been present before. But when he looked at her, she gave no indication of what she was feeling or thinking.

"The place is yours, Morgana," he said. "Literally and figuratively. If you require any assistance, I will be in my office on forty-eight."

Franklin Butler worked in his office for the next two hours. When he was finished, he went in search of his new, most prized client. He found her on the top floor of the penthouse, staring out the floor-to-ceiling windows that provided a view of Lake Michigan. The cloud cover was still low, bolts of lightning illuminated the heavens from horizon to horizon, and heavy rain continued to fall. Morgana, her arms folded around her upper body, stared out at the elements through the protective glass. Butler recalled stories that were told by some of the old staff, which had been employed at the plaza when Margo and Neil were alive. Reportedly, Margo liked to walk nude on the roof of the fifty-story building during violent thunderstorms. Butler didn't know if Morgana was as foolhardy as her mother had been, but it was obvious she was not afraid of the elements. As if nature were providing a verification of that thought, a lightning bolt struck close enough to Dewitt Plaza to cause the entire building to shake. Even the physically powerful Franklin Butler jumped at the close proximity of the thunderclap. Morgana didn't move a muscle.

Then, standing in the shadows of the fiftieth-floor corridor, Butler realized that he was not alone. Susanne York stepped up behind him and whispered, "She is exactly like her mother, isn't she?"

Butler turned to grace his nefarious assistant with a disapproving glare before walking off down the corridor toward his living quarters. Susanne remained standing in the shadows, watching Morgana De-Witt stare down a thunderstorm.

PART 2

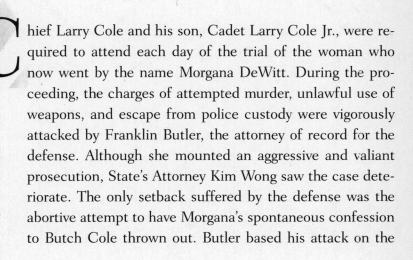

12

October 5, 2006
9:45 A.M.

C hief Larry Cole and his son, Cadet Larry Cole Jr., were required to attend each day of the trial of the woman who now went by the name Morgana DeWitt. During the proceeding, the charges of attempted murder, unlawful use of weapons, and escape from police custody were vigorously attacked by Franklin Butler, the attorney of record for the defense. Although she mounted an aggressive and valiant prosecution, State's Attorney Kim Wong saw the case deteriorate. The only setback suffered by the defense was the abortive attempt to have Morgana's spontaneous confession to Butch Cole thrown out. Butler based his attack on the young cadet's failure to advise the defendant of her Constitutional rights.

The trial was a newsworthy event, and despite the state's attorney's attempt to keep cameras out of the courtroom, Franklin Butler again carried the day. The trial of the infamous daughter of Margo and Neil DeWitt was carried on the cable Court TV channel. Although a limited audience viewed the gavel-to-gavel proceedings presided over by Judge Angelica Pate, highlights from the trial were carried on the nightly local network newscasts. On the day that Cadet Cole testified concerning the events of June 16, the coverage was fairly extensive on all channels.

The young cadet was a prosecution witness called by Kim Wong to establish the circumstances of the arrest and uphold Morgana's confession that she believed she had murdered Richard Banacek while he was performing onstage. Initially, when the cadet took the stand, Butch appeared nervous. But as the state's attorney guided him through the events of the night the stage play *Murder at the Opera* premiered, the witness relaxed and answered each question in a clear, strong voice. When Kim Wong was through with the direct examination, it was Franklin Butler's turn.

"Tell me, Cadet Cole," the defense attorney's deep voice reverberated through the packed courtroom, "how long have you been a member of the Chicago Police Department?"

"Since May first of this year."

Butler turned to the nearest television camera before asking his next question. "In your Chicago Police Academy training were you given instructions on the provisions of the United States Constitution?"

"Yes, sir."

Butler continued to face the camera with his profile to the witness box. An alert cameraman shifted the shot from the defense attorney to

Larry Cole, who was seated on a bench behind the prosecutor's table. The elder Cole's gaze displayed concerned intensity.

"Specifically, Cadet Cole," Butler questioned, "were you instructed on the requirements for giving Miranda warnings to all persons taken into custody by law enforcement officers in this country?"

"Yes, sir," Butch replied.

"Did you notify the defendant of her rights at the time you arrested her?"

"No, but—"

"That's all, Cadet Cole. I have no further questions." With that, Butler returned to the defense table.

Kim Wong rose, and on redirect cross-examination made it clear that Butch had no intention of arresting Morgana when he approached her and that she confessed to the murder spontaneously. The confession was upheld. The next prosecution witness was Chief Larry Cole. To the surprise of trial participants and spectators, Butler had no questions for the high-ranking cop.

Kim Wong presented the prosecution's case over a period of three days. It took Butler two weeks to present the case for the defense.

Butler's list of witnesses included the housekeeper and cook who had served Morgana and Isaac Weiss in Paris when she was a child; the Geneva police detective, now retired, who had investigated Weiss's murder in Geneva in October 1998; and an official from Interpol, also retired, who was an expert on the deceased Carlos Perfido, aka Richard Banacek. Butler followed that with a series of character witnesses consisting of Swiss bankers, businessmen, and prominent citizens transported to the United States at the DeWitt Corporation's expense. Finally, he called Morgana DeWitt to the stand.

Larry Cole watched Morgana cross the courtroom and enter the witness box. She remained standing while the clerk came forward and swore her in. The oath concluded, she took a seat. Throughout the trial, the young defendant had worn tailored conservative clothing in tastefully subdued colors. Her dark hair was professionally styled before each court appearance, and only a slight touch of makeup was applied to her face. Cole was forced to admit that she was a stunningly beautiful woman, but her looks failed to conceal a flaw. She was haunted, and there was a sadness of spirit about her that was so pronounced, it was nearly physical.

As Cole watched her from across the courtroom, he attempted to find some shred of resemblance between the defendant and her mother and father. Initially, he was unable to find anything even remotely in common about the super-rich couple he had investigated years ago and this woman now. But as he had done with criminal investigations in the past, he decided to approach the comparison between Morgana and her parents from a different perspective. Cole began to examine what was different about them. It was then that it came to him.

It was as if Morgana were a caricature of Margo and Neil. An image in reverse. Where the serial killing couple had been arrogant and haughty, the young defendant was reserved. Where Margo had been pretentious, Morgana appeared shy to the point of reticence. Neil DeWitt had been a violent human predator; Morgana, despite her attempt to murder Richard Banacek, was more of a victim. But Cole was also aware that the young woman was someone whom it would be fatal to underestimate, which was evidenced by the events surrounding her arrest. Larry Cole was also very much aware that during the three-week trial, Morgana and Butch had found it difficult to keep their eyes off each other. Cole had not mentioned this to his son, but it was quite obvious to everyone in the courtroom. Luckily, the Court TV cameras failed to pick up the attraction between them.

With consummate skill, Franklin Butler led Morgana through the events of her early life living with Isaac Weiss in Paris and Geneva up until the afternoon in the fall of 1998 when she returned home and found Carlos Perfido standing over her uncle's dead body.

"Did you recognize the man who murdered your uncle?"

"Yes," Morgana responded. "It was Carlos Perfido. He'd done business with my uncle in the past."

"Do you know why he murdered Isaac Weiss?"

"Objection," Kim Wong called from the prosecution table.

"Sustained," the judge said.

Butler continued without hesitation. "What happened after Perfido saw you?"

"He chased me from the apartment."

"Did he catch you?"

"No. I managed to elude him."

"How?"

"He pursued me to the Rhône River, which was a short distance from the apartment building where I lived. There was no other way for me to escape, so I jumped into the water."

"According to the Geneva police detective who investigated your uncle's death, you nearly drowned," Butler stated.

"That's correct," Morgana said.

"After you recovered from Perfido almost killing you as well, what did you do?"

"I began searching for him."

It was subtle, but Cole noticed a change in the young woman's demeanor. Something about her manner hardened, and he was able to glimpse a brief likeness between Morgana and her mother. When Cole was investigating Margo DeWitt for a series of child murders, he had crashed a dinner party she was hosting at DeWitt Plaza. Cole had intentionally baited her until she became angry. On the witness stand now, he saw a bit of that same homicidal anger flare in her daughter.

"What did you intend to do when you caught up with him, Ms. DeWitt?" Butler asked.

Without batting an eyelash, she responded, "I planned to kill him."

Butler waited for the reaction from the jury and spectators in the courtroom. It was not very pronounced, amounting to no more than a few audible intakes of breath and some foot shuffling, but was there nonetheless.

"How did you succeed in locating Perfido?"

"I employed a private detective firm based in England that employed operatives worldwide. They mounted a search, which took eight years."

"And they eventually located him for you?"

"In a matter of speaking," Morgana responded.

"Would you please explain that to the court?"

"I put up a ten-thousand-dollar reward for any information leading to Perfido's whereabouts. There were a number of false leads over the years, which did not pan out. Then in April of this year, an envelope was received by the detective agency containing an extensive dossier on the man now known as Richard Banacek. That dossier also contained photographs and composite drawings of Perfido, which revealed quite convincingly that he had molted into the American actor."

Butler spun away from the witness box and crossed to the defense table. He picked up a two-inch-thick folder, which he raised above his head and said, "Your Honor, I would like to submit the file compiled by the Stratford/Smythe private investigations firm of London on Carlos Perfido, aka Richard Banacek, as Defense Exhibit D."

"Has the State been given a copy of that file?" the judge asked.

"We have, Your Honor," Kim Wong replied.

Butler resumed the questioning. "Ms. DeWitt, do you know who gathered the information identifying the criminal wanted in Europe as Carlos Perfido as American stage actor Richard Banacek?"

"No, I do not," she responded. "The author of the document was never identified, and there was no attempt made to claim the reward."

"Did you have the information contained in the dossier verified?"

"Yes, I did."

"By whom?"

"The London detective firm."

"Tell me, Ms. DeWitt," Butler said, "over the years that you employed Stratford/Smythe, how much did you pay them?"

"Close to a hundred thousand pounds."

At that moment, Butler struck a pose with one hand in the trouser pocket of his tailored black suit and the other raised to grasp his closely shaven chin between thumb and forefinger. After a dramatic pause, he continued. "After you were certain that Banacek was indeed Perfido, what did you do?"

"I came to the United States to kill him."

"How did you plan to accomplish this?"

"I was going to shoot him from the audience of the Goodman Theater while he was performing onstage in the play *Murder at the Opera*."

Butler snatched a sheet of paper from the surface of the defense table. "If it pleases the court, I would like to refer to the Chicago Police Department Forensic Services Unit report on the weapon seized from the defendant at the time of her arrest."

"Ms. Wong?" Judge Pate queried the State's Attorney.

"I have no objection, Your Honor," Wong said.

"Proceed, Mr. Butler."

"Thank you, Your Honor," Butler said. Raising the report, he read, "'The weapon in question is a nine-millimeter firing mechanism with a four-round capacity, which was concealed within the housing of a pair of Zeiss binoculars. It is equipped with a telescopic sight calibrated to zero accuracy.' This report is signed by Captain Michael Zefeldt, the commanding officer of the Forensic Services Unit. If it pleases the court, from my own experience, as a graduate of the United States Military Academy at West Point, I can clarify for the court that zero accuracy means that whatever the weapon is sighted in on, it will hit."

"Ms. Wong," the judge said, "will you accept Mr. Butler as an expert in regards to that part of the Forensic Services report?"

Stony-faced as ever, Kim Wong responded, "I have no objection, but for the record, the State is also aware of the properties of zero windage and zero elevation on the accuracy of a sighting mechanism."

"Touché, Ms. Wong," Butler mumbled before turning back to his witness. "Ms. DeWitt, what was the maximum effective range of the weapon you used to shoot Richard Banacek?"

"One hundred feet."

"Again I refer to the Forensic Services Unit document," Butler said. "You were in seat 9M of the Goodman Theater, which placed you exactly forty-eight feet four inches from Banacek's position on the stage at the time he was shot."

"Your Honor," Kim Wong intoned, "is there a question somewhere within the defense attorney's ballistics lecture?"

"My question to the witness," Butler said, "is, how did you fail to fatally wound Richard Banacek at such close range with such an accurate weapon?"

"Objection, Your Honor!" Kim Wong said, leaping to her feet. "The question is irrelevant and immaterial. The fact that the defendant fired a deadly weapon in the direction of the victim is a clear indication of her intent to either kill him or cause him great bodily harm."

"My question goes to motive, Your Honor," Butler said.

Judge Pate hesitated before saying, "I'm going to allow the response, Ms. Wong. Objection overruled."

It was then that Morgana answered, "I had second thoughts about killing him before I pulled the trigger, which affected my aim."

Larry Cole was forced to admire the skill with which Butler wove the fabric of the defense case. He had taken the facts uncovered by the police investigation and presented them in such a manner as to make Morgana DeWitt appear to be the victim of the man she had shot on the stage of the Goodman Theater. Yes, Banacek, when he was Perfido, had murdered her uncle. But it went to the heart of premeditation for her to spend hundreds of thousands of dollars and post a reward so that she could first locate him and then kill him. In a perfect world, Morgana would have been convicted hands down, but Cole had been a cop for too long not to realize that the criminal justice system did not operate in a perfect world.

As Butler concluded his questioning of the defendant, Cole examined the jury. The majority of the assembled group of Morgana's peers were young, and their attire indicated that they were middle class with a smattering of young professionals, who probably had some college, if not a degree. If they were sitting in judgment of a gangbanger or violent street criminal, their decision to convict would be swift and decisive. But Morgana was a young well-to-do woman who had been victimized by a dangerous, despicable man. It had also been made quite clear to them that the defendant had not been responsible for Banacek's death.

Kim Wong went after Morgana DeWitt, but it was apparent that Butler had prepared his client well. The state's attorney attacked every facet of the defense case and made some telling points. However, it was obvious to Cole that the prosecution was going down fast in the case of the State of Illinois v. DeWitt.

The closing summations were anticlimactic, and the jury went out late on a Wednesday afternoon. On Thursday, October 5, they rendered their verdict. Morgana DeWitt was found not guilty on all charges. A rumbling swept through the packed courtroom, and there was even some scattered applause, which was quickly silenced by the judge's gavel. With that, Morgana became a free woman.

This was not a case Larry Cole felt bad about losing, but it was definitely one of the most unusual he'd ever been involved with. Rising with his father to leave the courtroom, Butch said, "Excuse me a minute, Dad."

Cole watched his son cross the courtroom to the defense table. Morgana was surrounded by reporters and flanked by the formidable Franklin Butler when Butch walked up. It looked as if he was going to be shut out by the press crowd, but she spied him and stopped the impromptu interview. With the media and the chief of detectives looking on, the former defendant walked over to the cadet.

"Congratulations," he said awkwardly, extending his hand.

Taking the hand, she replied quietly, "Thank you."

That was all, but the simple greeting conveyed a great deal more to those observing it.

When Butch returned to his father's side, Cole said, "We don't usually congratulate defendants in cases we lose, son."

The young man frowned and said, "But wasn't justice done?"

There wasn't a great deal Cole could say to that.

When they reached the police car in the garage across the street from the courthouse, Cole said, "What have you got planned for the rest of your day off?"

"I'm going to help Uncle Blackie and Manny with their rehab. Then I've got a Sociology quiz to study for."

"This evening why don't we take in a movie or something?"

Butch shrugged. "Thanks, but I think I'll just hang out tonight."

Once more it came back to Cole that his son was rapidly becoming an adult.

13

October 8, 2006
11:02 A.M.

Lauren Sherlock applied the burn salve to her husband's back. She did so carefully, despite being amazed at the rapid recovery he'd made. The lotion was a combination of aloe vera and vitamins A and E, which, following a twice-daily application, had succeeded in nearly completing obliterating the burn marks.

"Now that feels real good, babe," Manny said, purring like a big cat.

She looked at the flab that had been added to his lank frame since his injury. Although he was far from what could be considered overweight, he was still heavier than he had ever been since the day they'd met.

"When you go to rehab, Manny, what do you really do? Sit in Blackie's basement and drink beer?"

In a drowsy voice, he responded, "Butch works us like dogs. He's even got Blackie up to actually running a mile and a half."

"Then you drink beer."

"Only a couple," he confessed, sitting up on one elbow and turning to look at her. "Since Blackie's stopped smoking, he's down to four beers a day. He's lost twenty pounds."

She slapped him on the behind. "It looks like you've gained the weight that he lost, Manny."

"Complaints, complaints," he said, collapsing back on the couch, closing his eyes, and emitting a deep sigh.

"You'd better get your tail in gear, Sergeant Manfred Wolfgang Sherlock. It's after eleven."

Jerking upright, Manny glanced at the wall clock before leaping to his feet. Now she was able to see that her husband had actually gained very little weight and was as lean and lanky as ever. Over the years, he had developed the muscles of his shoulders and chest with weightlifting, but he still looked more like Ichabod Crane than like Arnold Schwarzenegger.

"Gotta run," he said, dashing to put on his sweatsuit.

She had applied the anti-burn salve in the den of their southwest-side eight-room, ranch-style home. The brick structure was less than twenty years old and had been meticulously maintained by the previous owner. It had two and a half baths, a finished basement equipped with a built-in hot tub, and a three-car heated garage. The washer, dryer, stove, and refrigerator were less than a year old when they moved in. Their mortgage rate was low due to Manny's having gotten a special deal through the Chicago Police Department's Employees'

Credit Union. The Sherlocks lived only three blocks from Blackie and Maria Silvestri in a neighborhood with rising property values and good schools for the family that she and Manny planned to start soon. But despite Lauren living in her dream house with a man that she loved more than life itself, she was troubled. The reason: She was worried about Manny.

This was the third time he had been hospitalized with a line-of-duty injury since they had been married. The first time, Manny had been shot repeatedly by a Mafia hit man in the employ of the notorious Tuxedo Tony DeLisa. Manny had come so close to death that they were not only forced to replace all his blood, but he'd also been given the last rites. The next time was not so serious, as he and Blackie had spent the night in University Hospital after they were exposed to a canister that had contained an atomic bomb. Then there was this last time.

Although the burns were almost healed and he'd passed through the trauma with his usually garrulous, crazy sense of humor in place, Lauren had been more deeply affected than was the case with the other incidents. Perhaps that was because Manny and Blackie had been burned. Lauren was pathologically terrified of fire due to an incident she had experienced as a child. Also, the newscasts had shown the flaming Wrigleyville building they had been trapped in. Lauren marveled that anyone had been able to escape from that inferno. Had Manny become incapacitated before he pulled the unconscious Blackie out of the building, they would both have died. What it all came down to was Manny and the other members of Larry Cole's crew being human and working in an extremely dangerous occupation.

Lauren Sherlock was neither a weak nor timid woman. Prior to meeting and subsequently marrying Manny, she managed four-star restaurants and even now occasionally took part-time employment supervising catering crews for high-profile weddings and receptions.

However, she had come from a police family. Her uncle, Lieutenant Edgar "Doc" Holmes, was a legendary cop who had retired as the supervisor of the citywide burglary unit. She understood the hazards of police work better than most cops' wives did. Yet that still didn't make it any easier. She loved her husband too much. But she would never voice her concerns to him. Never attempt to make it a choice between her and the job. And although she knew Manny loved her, Lauren was not certain that if she did present him with an ultimatum whether or not he would choose her over the Chicago Police Department.

Dressed in a yellow sweatsuit, white gym shoes, and a white knit cap, Manny came bounding out of the bedroom. Coming over to where she was still seated on the couch, he planted a wet kiss on her mouth and said, "Be back soon, babe. This afternoon we'll go to the mall."

"Sure thing, Manny," she said.

Then he was out the door on his way to rehab with Blackie and Butch Cole.

The first time Blackie traversed the mile circumference around Pushkin Park, he thought he was going to have another heart attack. It was two weeks after his release from the hospital, and he'd been lying around watching a lot of television and sleeping up to fourteen hours a day when Larry Cole paid him a visit. Although Cole was Blackie's best friend and they had worked together for over thirty years, the recovering cop wasn't prepared for the visit. He was clad in his pajamas, lying in the recliner in his basement. He was unshaved, his wife, Maria, had smeared burn ointment all over him, and he looked a mess. Cole appeared not to notice his sorry state.

Cole took a seat on a barstool in front of the fully stocked bar. "How are you feeling, Blackie?"

With a shrug, he responded, "The medication they're giving me saps all my energy, but the burns are healing up pretty good."

"Maria told me your cardiologist has recommended that you get some exercise. Working out will not only make you feel better, but strengthen your heart."

Blackie managed a weak laugh. "The way I feel right now, I can barely stand up."

"So we'll have to take it a little bit at a time," Cole said with a grin. "That way you'll be back to work before the New Year, and I can get you out of Maria's hair."

At the time, Blackie thought that his old friend was kidding. He was not.

Blackie thought for a moment. "Isn't six and a half minutes kind of slow for half a mile?"

"A bit," Cole said. "But we'll fix that tomorrow."

Although he was afraid to ask, Blackie said, "How?"

Cole's eyes twinkled as he responded, "You're going to start jogging."

Blackie Silvestri had never been much for physical exercise. He wasn't into sports during his school years, and once he became a cop, he had cultivated a somewhat sedentary lifestyle. In fact, he was proud of his affinity for good food, a few beers now and then, and, of course, those little black Parodi cigars he was so fond of. But what occurred in that Wrigleyville apartment back in June frightened Blackie, which was something that had seldom happened to him during his fifty-plus years of life. So he gave up the cigars, went to weekly checkups with a cardiologist, took a lot of pills, and submitted to what he considered marathon exercise sessions at the hands of his taskmaster, Larry Cole.

Blackie progressed to the point that Cole gave way to Manny and Butch accompanying the lieutenant on his daily exercise rounds.

Although the younger men would never dare attempt to order Blackie to do anything. At least not more than once.

But as the summer gave way to fall and the leaves began to change to various shades of gold, amber, and red, Blackie Silvestri experienced a physical rejuvenation. He began waking up in the morning looking forward to his workouts. By the first week in September, he was able to jog the mile distance around Pushkin Park in thirteen minutes. Within a week, he had brought the time down to slightly below twelve minutes. With Cole pacing him, he did a ten-minute mile in mid-September. Then Blackie began going for distance.

On the last day Cole worked out with him, before deferring to Butch and Manny, the two cops completed a lap of the park. At the conclusion of the mile, Cole began slowing down, but Blackie kept going. When Cole caught up, he asked, "What are you doing?"

Although he was puffing a bit, Blackie said, "I feel great. Let's go around again."

"Don't overdo it. A mile and a quarter will suffice right now for you. Then you can ease into two miles. I don't want to see you back in the hospital."

In addition to the running, Blackie began doing fifty push-ups and one hundred sit-ups a day. He made plans to buy some weights and an exercise bench as soon as he got stronger and the changes in his physique became obvious as he shed twenty-five pounds. He also found that his clarity of thought and reflexes had improved, and he began shutting off the television set in favor of reading novels.

Maria Silvestri watched her husband's transformation and was pleased. She had been worried for years about his hectic lifestyle, which included long hours on the job and smoking as many as ten Parodi cigars a day. Now, as his exercise program progressed toward the Olympic training stage on this October afternoon, she was preparing a post-workout snack. Ham sandwiches on French bread rolls with provolone cheese, potato salad, and soft drinks would be waiting for Blackie, Manny, and Butch when they returned from their sojourn to Pushkin Park. She also had fresh coffee and hot chocolate if they got cold. The temperature outside was in the mid-forties and was not expected to go above fifty degrees all day.

Placing the cold cuts in the refrigerator, Maria poured herself a cup of coffee and took a seat at the kitchen table. Blackie would be down soon to drink a cup of herbal tea sweetened with honey, which enhanced his energy during the workout. Before he was injured in June, this had been Maria's quiet time of the day. With him recuperating at home, she did not have so much free time to herself as before, but that was okay. She liked having him around, even if he did get underfoot from time to time.

The doorbell rang, and before Maria could make a move to answer it, she heard Blackie bounding down the stairs like a teenager, calling out, "I'll get it, honey. It's Butch."

A few minutes later, the young man, whom Maria had known all his life, came into the kitchen. He was dressed in a sweatsuit with a top that bore the logo, CHICAGO POLICE HOMICIDE SQUAD — OUR DAY BEGINS WHEN YOURS ENDS. Coming over to where she was seated, Butch kissed her gently on the cheek. "Hello, Aunt Maria. How are you today?"

"I'm fine, Butchie," she said, as always marveling at how tall and broad-shouldered he was. Then her eye turned critical. "Are you dressed warm enough?"

"Yes, ma'am," he said sheepishly.

She got up and left the kitchen to return with a scarf, knit cap, and gloves. "It's cold outside, and when you start exercising, your pores will open. If you're not bundled up, you'll catch your death of cold."

Butch looked far from happy over the items the woman he called Aunt Maria had selected for him—the cap had blue and white stripes, the scarf was Kelly green, and the gloves were brown—but it was indeed a raw day outside. He had ridden his motorcycle to the Silvestris' house, and he'd been dressed warm enough along the way. But he wasn't about to work out clad in his motorcycle helmet and the three-quarter-length black leather jacket his father had given him as protection against unpredictable Chicago weather.

A couple of minutes later, Manny arrived, and the joggers paused a moment to stretch in front of the brownstone before heading for Pushkin Park.

The three men had vastly different jogging styles: Manny possessed a high knee kick with his long legs and rigidly upright posture, which resembled a goosestep. Butch was more conventional, with a hunched-over-at-the-shoulders boxer's style of running, which made the exertion appear effortless. Blackie's style, like everything else about him, was unique. The lieutenant ran with a jerky, side-to-side motion that resembled the waddle of a pregnant duck. They were an odd group to behold, but they covered the distance at a good clip. Manny and Butch were capable of running a vastly greater distance than a mile and a half, but they were under strict orders from Cole not to push the recovering cardiac patient too hard.

They completed the run and slowed to a walk. Butch and Manny noticed that Blackie's breathing was barely labored.

"How are you feeling?" Manny asked.

"Like a million bucks," Blackie responded, sucking in the cold October air. "I should have started doing this years ago. There really is something to be said for exercise."

"What did the doctor say about what happened to you?" Butch inquired.

Blackie hadn't discussed his heart attack with anyone except Maria and Larry Cole. Now, because he was feeling so good, he responded, "In layman's parlance, I had what is known as a mild myocardial infarction. I had partial blockages in all my arteries, and my smoking and sedentary lifestyle would have eventually caught up with me; maybe even have killed me." Blackie went momentarily silent. "When we were caught in that booby-trapped apartment, a combination of exertion and smoke inhalation triggered a coronary." He unzipped his Windbreaker and reached a gloved hand inside before he realized what he was doing. It was a purely reflex action. Blackie Silvestri was reaching for a cigar. Quickly closing his jacket, he said, "If it hadn't been for Manny pulling me out of there, I'd be pushing up daisies right now."

In a fair imitation of *Star Trek*'s Mr. Data, Manny replied, "Captain Picard, I did no more than preserve a police department resource so that it could continue to serve the citizens of this great city."

They all smiled, but the mood was far from lighthearted. Then Blackie said, "Look, guys, I'm going to do another half mile or so."

"C'mon, Uncle Blackie," Butch protested. "Dad said—"

Blackie held up his hand. "Don't worry, kid. I'll survive, and there's no need for us to tell your father."

"We'll go with you," Manny said.

"No, you won't," Blackie snapped with finality. "It's high time I started doing things on my own again." He took off with his duck-waddle gait.

Manny was crestfallen. "Did I say something wrong?"

"Naw, Manny. Dad told me that Blackie's restless. He needs to get back to work. Then he'll be his usual cantankerous self again."

Manny gave Butch a disbelieving look. "What was that supposed to be, his Jolly Old St. Nick imitation?"

Butch didn't hear him. He was looking off across the park, focusing on nothing in particular.

Cupping his hands around his mouth to produce a megaphone effect, Manny boomed, "Earth to Cadet Cole! Do you read me? Come in, please!"

Butch snapped out of his trance and even managed a weak smile. "Did I space out again? Tara Spellman, the detention aide on my watch in the Second District, said I have a tendency to do that lately."

"Well, you were spaced," Manny said, looking off in the distance at Blackie making his way around the far side of the park. "You want to talk about what's bothering you?"

Butch took a moment to also glance at the jogging man. Then, with a shrug and a sigh, he asked, "What can you tell me about the department's prohibition against cops associating with people who have police records?"

14

T he board of directors of the DeWitt Corporation met in an emergency session, which was called by C. J. Cantrell. Since Franklin Butler had assumed the position of acting chairman of the board, this was the first such meeting that had been convened. Under the provisions of the corporate bylaws, which had been written by Butler's predecessor, Seymour Winbush, any board member could call an emergency meeting with forty-eight hours' notice. It was also stipulated in the bylaws that the reason for the meeting had to be stated in writing. In the notice that C. J. Cantrell had hand-carried to each board member, the reason for the emergency meeting was stated as, "The removal of the acting chairman from office due to gross mismanagement of the DeWitt Corporation and criminal negligence." Of the eight board members, five acknowledged the meeting notice and confirmed that they would be present. The three absentees, of whom two were loyal to Butler, were out of the country. This gave C. J. Cantrell three votes, including his own, to Butler's two votes. Again in compliance with the corporation's bylaws, if the vote went against Butler, Cantrell was in an excellent position to take the arrogant attorney's place as acting chairman.

The meeting was scheduled for 2 P. M., and Cantrell arrived fifteen minutes early. The rest of the board members drifted in over the next thirty minutes. There was a definite tension in the air, and the four men mingled around the room, speaking to each other in hushed tones. But for the most part, they remained silent. A coffee service, soft drinks, and a snack tray had been set up on a table adjacent to the conference table. Not one of them made a move toward it.

After the responding board members were allowed to stew for a select few tension-building moments, Franklin Butler and Morgana DeWitt entered. As usual, the recently acquitted young heiress was dressed in dark clothing, which made her appear older than her years. Butler was clad in a charcoal-gray pin-striped suit and a black turtle-neck sweater. With his massive shoulders and shaven head, he looked more like a Mafia hit man than the CEO of a multinational corporation. To say the least, his appearance was menacing. That was by design.

Butler escorted Morgana to a seat at the head of the conference table. He held one of the high-back black leather-and-chrome chairs for her before taking a position on her left. The rest of the board members were scattered around the table. It was obvious from the looks on their faces that they would rather be someplace far, far away from De-Witt Plaza at that moment.

Despite the air-conditioning, C. J. Cantrell was sweating. When he conceived this confrontation, he had envisioned it being a great deal different from how it was proving to be in actual fact. Although Butler appeared physically imposing, Cantrell wasn't afraid of him. If the big black attorney ever laid a hand on him, the smaller man would sue him for every penny he was worth. In fact, the theatrical producer felt such a high degree of animosity toward the attorney that Cantrell often mused, after he'd had a few drinks, that he would have no compunctions at all about getting a gun and killing Butler. But now there was another element in the equation: Morgana DeWitt.

Cantrell had never seen this woman before in the flesh. When he saw her on television after her arrest at the Goodman Theater and during her trial, he had considered her no more than another criminal who would soon be on her way to prison. Butler getting her off was no great surprise, as C. J. had never disputed that he was a good attorney. Now that Cantrell was viewing Morgana in person, he felt an odd uneasiness, the source of which he couldn't identify. Physically, she was thin to the point of being spare. She was attractive in a dark Mediterranean way, but he preferred the Nordic blond look. He was unable to see anything of her mother—whom he had worked for briefly before that cop, Larry Cole, killed her—or her father in this Morgana DeWitt. Back in late September, Butler had sent each board member a memo containing the results of a DNA test, which was reputedly scientific proof that she was the heir to the DeWitt fortune. Such technical mumbo jumbo didn't mean anything to C. J. Cantrell, and he planned not only to prevent this young woman from taking over the corporation, but to dispose of Franklin Butler in the bargain.

In his capacity as acting chairman of the board, Butler opened the proceedings by saying, "This emergency meeting is hereby called to order. Because we don't have a secretary present to take the minutes, we will dispense with a calling of the roll, as not all board members are in attendance." With that out of the way, he cast a cold glance at Cantrell, who was seated halfway down on the opposite side of the conference table and said, "Okay, C. J., this is your show. You have the floor."

Removing a handkerchief from the inside pocket of his houndstooth jacket, Cantrell mopped his brow, got to his feet, and began. "At three o'clock this afternoon, the DeWitt Corporation will be served with a court order barring the acting chairman from expending any further corporate resources or funds on behalf of the woman alleged to be the heir of Margo and Neil DeWitt. The legal document will also require the acting chairman and Ms. DeWitt, whose United States passport bears the name Morgana Devoe, to appear in Cook County Circuit Court to show cause for the fraudulent use of DeWitt Corporation corporate funds to pay the legal fees and expenses of Morgana Devoe during her recent criminal trial."

Cantrell paused to pour a glass of water from a carafe on the table. He gulped it down, stifled a belch, and continued. "As the acting chairman of the board will be unable to continue performing the duties required to administer the corporation due to the ensuing litigation, I have called this meeting so that the available board members can vote on a new acting chairman." With that said, Cantrell sat down.

A long awkward silence ensued, during which no one at the conference table moved. Finally, Butler spoke, "Are you sure you want to get into this, C. J.? Corporate legal battles can be very, very messy."

Without looking up from the conference table surface, Cantrell responded, "You're the one making a mess, Butler."

"Then I have to advise you that a pending court order is one thing, C. J.," Butler said, "but the existence of a previously issued injunction by a higher court is something else."

The attorney opened a leather portfolio that he had brought with him and removed a stack of papers from it. With a flick of his wrist, Butler shoved the papers across the varnished surface of the conference table. Cantrell and the other board members reluctantly picked up copies of the document.

Butler explained, "What that is, gentlemen, is an injunction issued by the Probate Judge Timothy J. Kennedy on the first of October. It was issued based on documentation reviewed by Judge Kennedy, which irrefutably verifies that Ms. DeWitt is the heir to this corporation. The injunction itself prohibits this board, and I quote the provisions set forth on page three, paragraph two, '. . . from interfering, obstructing, or countermanding any action by said heir without a prior hearing of the issuing authority.'"

To say the least, the assembled board of directors of the DeWitt Corporation was stunned. A few worried eyes flicked in C. J. Cantrell's direction, but he was as much at a loss for words as they were.

Throughout, Morgana had remained silent. Now, without saying a word, she got to her feet, turned, and walked toward the exit. Franklin Butler was right behind her.

Defiant to the last, C. J. Cantrell called after them, "The two of you haven't heard the last of this."

Before he left the conference room, Butler said, "Neither have you, C. J."

Judy Daniels was responding to a homicide. She drove her unmarked midnight-blue police car north on Lake Shore Drive. Crossing the Chicago River Bridge adjacent to Navy Pier, she continued to the North Avenue exit and entered Lincoln Park. She proceeded to the first cross street and made a right turn. Immediately, the cluster of police vehicles and officers in and out of uniform became visible.

Parking her car in the bus stop so she wouldn't block traffic, she strolled back to the crime scene.

The woman who walked through Lincoln Park south of the zoo toward the crime scene had lank blond hair, a full face, and she carried what appeared to be two hundred pounds on a five-foot-three-inch frame. She wore a baggy, light blue denim pantsuit and a red turtleneck sweater. There was a metal chain around her neck with a leather badge holder attached, which displayed a Chicago Police sergeant's badge. Beneath the denim jacket, she carried a Beretta semiautomatic handgun in a holster attached to a belt, which also held handcuffs, a canister of pepper spray, extra bullet clips, and a cellular phone. There was nothing in the least bit remarkable about this woman, so far as appearances went. But, in fact, Judy Daniels's current disguise was a genuine masterpiece.

It had been reported from the field units already on the scene that a homeless person had discovered the body of a white male in the park. Black-and-yellow barrier tape was strung around a grotto of trees at the bottom of an incline just off the bicycle path. Uniformed officers were stationed at strategic locations encircling the crime scene perimeter to keep out curious civilians and the media, who had yet to put in an appearance. At this point in the investigation, only a small number of onlookers were standing around, trying to get a glimpse of what was going on, but from their vantage point, there was nothing to see. The notification to police headquarters had explained that keeping the public units on the scene was by design.

Recognizing the cased silver star around Judy's neck, one of the cops guarding the perimeter lifted the barrier tape and said, "The body is right down this path, Sergeant."

Judy entered the grotto, which was overgrown with bushes. The park floor was covered with falling leaves, which crunched under her feet. Overhead tree branches shrouded the area in shadow and also effectively concealed the area from high-rise apartment buildings surrounding the park. Whoever committed this murder had hidden the corpse well, Judy thought. Then she came to the end of the path and stepped into a clearing. Now she could clearly see why the crime scene was so carefully guarded.

The body of a nude male was lying in the clearing. The corpse was spread-eagled with his arms and legs securely anchored with coat hanger wire attached to metal stakes that had been driven into the ground. The body had been charred to a cinder, and it appeared that the homicide victim had been burned alive.

A balding lieutenant from Area Three detectives, headquartered at Belmont and Western, and a young redheaded detective were standing at the edge of the clearing. The lieutenant, clad in shirtsleeves in spite of the cool autumn temperatures, and the detective exhibited a mixture of horror and awe at the fire-blackened condition of the corpse. A trio of Crime Lab technicians was finishing up collecting evidence around the body, and the supervisor came over to give his report to the lieutenant. Judy joined them, resulting in curious stares being directed at her due to the effectiveness of her disguise. In defense, she said, "I'm from the chief of detectives' office."

The lieutenant's eyes narrowed momentarily in a questioning squint before he turned to listen to the lab tech's report.

"The guy was staked out and then set on fire while he was still alive. My guess is that he was unconscious when he was tied up, but alive when the fire started. We found what was left of a cloth gag, which was apparently stuffed into his mouth and swallowed during the conflagration. There were also traces of a residue of what appears to be an igniting fuel, such as charcoal starter or lighter fluid around the body." The technician turned to look back at the victim. "He must have been soaked with it, because he's been literally burned to a crisp."

Judy spoke up. "You'd need an awful lot of lighter fluid to burn a human body to that extent."

The three men stared at her.

She stood her ground. "The lab analysis will probably turn up a more volatile substance in addition to the fire starter. Something that will burn hot for a long time."

The Crime Lab technician nodded his head in silent agreement, the lieutenant continued to stare quizzically at the female sergeant, and the young detective simply appeared confused. Before she was forced to answer any time-consuming questions about her identity, Judy asked, "Do we have any idea who the victim is?"

The lieutenant responded, "He had on a metal identification bracelet that was pretty badly scorched, but we were able to make out the name on the face plate." He checked the notebook stuffed in his shirt pocket. "His name was Juan Campos. The canvassing beat car discovered an old Caddie parked in a bus stop on Lincoln Park West, not far from here. It's registered to the same name as the one on the bracelet with an address in Humboldt Park."

The technician added, "The car's unlocked, and we've already been through the passenger compartment. We didn't come up with anything we can connect to the homicide at this point. We couldn't locate the keys, so we'll have to wait until it's towed to the pound so we can take a peek in the trunk."

"What year is the Cadillac?" Judy asked.

The technician shrugged. "Late seventies, early eighties. A real rust bucket."

"I can open the trunk for you," she said.

They exchanged questioning looks. Then the lieutenant said, "Right this way, Sergeant—?"

"Daniels," she said.

The technician appeared shocked, because he had seen the Mistress of Disguise and High Priestess of Mayhem before. At least, he thought that he had. Finally revelation dawned.

"Ryan," the lieutenant said to the young detective, who hadn't a clue as to what was going on, "escort Sergeant Daniels to our murder victim's vehicle."

The 1981 powder blue, four-door Cadillac had also been cordoned off with barrier tape. This forced Chicago Transit Authority buses to double-park in order to pick up fares on the exclusive Lincoln Park West thoroughfare. A pair of uniformed officers were sitting in a beat car parked behind the suspect vehicle. When Judy saw them, she guessed that they were more or less standing guard. When the lieutenant approached with Judy, the young detective, and the Crime Lab supervisor, the cops—who looked like they spent more time eating doughnuts than they did working out—grudgingly hefted themselves out of the police car. They stood at the back of the Cadillac, assuming slouched positions of semialertness.

The front windows of the Cadillac were down, and moisture had accumulated on the worn seats, indicating that the car had been parked at this location sometime during the night. Fingerprint powder was visible coating the surfaces of the filthy interior and the accumulated beer bottles littering the backseat. It would be a simple matter for Judy to open the trunk by utilizing the automatic release button in the glove compartment. The button would not work when the ignition was off; however, Judy had learned a method of circumventing the automatic trunk mechanism from Blackie.

By removing the courtesy lightbulb in the glove compartment and the trunk button, it was possible to hotwire the trunk lock by using a pair of metal keys to serve as a conduit for the electrical current. The procedure was an old car thief's trick, and Judy had jokingly questioned Blackie about where he picked it up. He had merely smiled and said, "A good cop's got to know how criminals work, Judy."

Now, as Judy opened the door and climbed into the passenger front seat, she repeated what Blackie said when he taught her the trick. The balding detective lieutenant was standing nearby and over-heard her. He smiled. "I guess you learned a thing or two from Blackie Silvestri, Sergeant Daniels, just like I did."

Judy smiled, too, and, removing a small screwdriver from a minia-ture tool kit she carried, went to work on the glove compartment au-tomatic release button. The courtesy light in the old car was burned out, but after removing the bulb, she found that the current was still flowing. That would give her the twelve volts she needed. She was just about to touch a pair of keys from her key ring to the orange wire be-hind the courtesy light and the black wire behind the trunk release button when the sharp autumn wind shifted. Judy caught a whiff of what she initially thought was kerosene. She recalled reading some-thing in a novel about a burned man and a car with a locked trunk, which was booby-trapped. Slowly, she got out of the car.

"What's wrong, Sarge?" the lieutenant asked. "Your car thief trick didn't work?"

"I think that this car is rigged to explode when the trunk is opened," she said.

"What are you talking about?" the Crime Lab supervisor argued. "My guys went through that thing and didn't find anything more ex-plosive than a book of old matches."

"Do you know what thermite smells like?" she said.

At the mention of the chemical, the supervisor took a step back-wards. Seeing that, the detective lieutenant and the detective also backed away, which caused the overweight uniformed cops to follow suit.

"We need Bomb and Arson down here right now," Judy said. "Use a landline to contact them in case this thing is rigged to go off from a radio signal."

"Do it," the lieutenant said to the young detective, who stood on the sidewalk as motionless as a statue, continuing to stare at the Cadillac.

Grabbing the detective by the arm, the lieutenant whispered urgently, "Go find a pay telephone and call Bomb and Arson!"

Galvanized into action, the detective ran off down the sidewalk. The remaining cops continued stare at the ragged blue car.

Larry Cole found himself ensnared in one of the busiest and most hectic periods of his police career. He commanded a force of a thousand detectives who were charged with follow-up investigations of all unsolved crimes committed in a jurisdiction with a population of close to four million people spread out over 224 square miles. The overall crime rate was comparatively low and had been dropping steadily for the past five years despite the scourge of illegal drugs, gang violence, and unlimited access to powerful illegal weapons. Yet there were still the periodic high-profile cases requiring the chief of detectives' personal touch to solve. Lately those high-profile cases had come fast and furious.

Beginning in late August through that past Tuesday in early October, there had been a series of jewel robberies plaguing the city. The victims were traveling salesmen who were robbed either shortly after they arrived in Chicago or just as they were about to leave. The points of entry and exit were the city's two major airports—O'Hare and Midway. Two men wearing ski masks and who displayed large-caliber handguns robbed them in airport washrooms, Loop hotel rooms, and taxicabs. To date, the robbers had taken four and a half million dollars' worth of fine cut gems and valuable watches. The detectives assigned to the cases had examined every clue they could find, but still no leads to the identity of the offenders had been discovered. Cole checked the reports himself and had also sat in on interviews with two of the six

victims, but they still came up with nothing. He had considered initi-
ating a decoy operation, but there were literally hundreds of salesmen
carrying millions of dollars in valuable merchandise coming into the city
by air each day. It would be pure luck for the robbers to select the police decoy, so before Cole decided on this course of action, he planned
to wait for a while. Experience had taught him that the crooks couldn't
stay lucky forever. At least the chief of detectives hoped not.

There were a number of other crimes that also called out for his
attention, from high-profile murders to a residential home-invasion
ring working the Gold Coast. A day didn't go by when a hot case wasn't
breaking. And Cole tried to handle as much of it as he could, but it
was becoming overwhelming. Blackie and Manny being on medical
leave didn't help, and Judy was trying her best to take up the slack.
Hopefully, Cole's administrative lieutenant and sergeant would be
back on the job by Thanksgiving.

To help him keep abreast of breaking cases, Cole carried a pocket
computer programmed to emit an audible beeping signal when serious offenses were reported. The device went off so much that while
he and Butch were having dinner the previous night, Cole shut it off.
The next afternoon, he was at his desk having a turkey sandwich on
an onion roll with mayo with a cup of black coffee for lunch when the
computer again beeped. Swallowing a bite of sandwich and chasing it
with coffee, Cole checked the display.

The report was of a homicide/arson in Lincoln Park. He noticed
that Car Fifty David, Judy's call number, was on the scene. When he
read on the LED screen that the Bomb and Arson Unit had been
called to defuse a thermite device, he headed for the door.

Larry Cole and Judy Daniels stood at a safe distance down the block
behind a barricade of blue wooden POLICE LINE horses. They watched

a bomb technician, clad in a metal helmet and a heavily padded flame-retardant suit, remove a metal canister from the trunk of the dilapidated blue Cadillac. The previously quiet homicide investigation had taken on the dimensions of a three-ring circus, replete with lions, tigers, bears, clowns, and a Ferris wheel.

"If I had opened the trunk, that car would have gone up like an Atlas booster rocket with me as the payload," Judy said.

Cole's expression was grim as he watched the bomb technician place the canister of thermite in a bombproof chamber mounted on a tractor towed behind a police SUV. "That's the same type of device that set the fire that trapped Blackie and Manny in the bogus tiger handler's apartment."

"Well, whoever's playing around with thermite not only knows what they're doing, they also followed the storyline from an old mystery novel in setting up the crime scene."

"I'm not following you."

"The victim was staked to the ground and burned alive in a public park, and his car was booby-trapped as a nasty little surprise for the police. That is the same scenario that unfolded in chapter one of the novel *The Burned Man* by Debbie Bass."

Cole stiffened. "That book came out a long time ago. Debbie Bass was one of Margo DeWitt's last victims. The DeWitts also used mystery novels as blueprints to kill."

"Déjà vu, boss?"

The helmeted bomb technician signaled an "all clear" as Cole responded, "I sure hope not."

Over two hundred spectators had gathered on Lincoln Park West to watch the police operation. Standing in the crowd south of the rusty light-blue Cadillac, Morgana DeWitt stared at Larry Cole and the stout blond woman he had been talking to. For the first time since her trial ended, Morgana had a reason to smile. That was because she saw a familiar face, one was not connected to the DeWitt Corporation or her heritage as the daughter of a pair of serial killers. When she looked at Larry Cole, she saw his son Butch in him, and that gave her a seldom-experienced feeling of joy.

As the crowd dispersed, Morgana turned and walked off in the direction of North Avenue. After she had traveled a quarter of a block, a tall woman wearing a wide-brimmed floppy hat and sunglasses crossed the street and followed her. Susanne York was tailing Morgana DeWitt.

15

C hicago weather is unpredictable. From the chill of early October, which produced snow in the predawn hours of October 10, a warm front blew in from the southwest, and November came in with a record high temperature of eighty-two degrees. After his morning workout with Blackie and Manny, Butch returned to the lakefront condo he shared with his father and took a shower before dressing in his police uniform. A couple of slices of cold pepperoni pizza and a Coke served as lunch, despite Maria Silvestri having fed them Italian beef sandwiches and lemonade after their workout.

The midday traffic was light as Butch rode to the station

and parked his motorcycle beneath the paved overhang leading to the east entrance. There were three other motorcycles in the area, which was generally utilized for the storage of bulk items confiscated from arrestees. The young cadet figured that the warm Indian summer weather had brought out some hibernating motorcycle enthusiasts. Walking into the station, Butch Cole was whistling.

He entered the same corridor that the phony lieutenant had come through on the day Morgana DeWitt had escaped from custody. Leading off this corridor were six doors. One led to the Second District lockup, three led to prisoner visitation cubicles, another to a small interview room, and the last was a padlocked storage facility for walkie-talkies and shotguns. Walking along wearing a lightweight black cotton shirt over his police uniform, Butch was on his way to the station desk when a uniformed officer named Rodriguez came out of the interview room. The cop was a thin middle-aged man who was not very popular with Sergeant Q. Davies's desk crew, because he specialized in traffic enforcement to the exclusion of everything else. Butch had also heard that Rodriguez was lazy to the point of gross negligence. But as his father had taught him, the cadet reserved passing judgment on anyone until he had gathered the facts for himself. Butch Cole was about to learn a great deal.

There was a thin dirty-looking man accompanying Rodriguez. Butch noticed that this man was not only walking too close to the cop, but was also behind him, which was a procedural error. Then the cadet noticed the man was holding a small-caliber automatic pistol.

Butch had been in danger many times before in his life. He had faced perilous situations with a quiet calm and had acted decisively, although at times his father termed his actions reckless. Now the cadet moved directly toward the armed man, who had yet to look in his direction.

Butch's objective was to simultaneously confiscate the suspect's weapon and immobilize him. He wasn't quite certain how he was going to do this, but he had taken classes in defensive tactics—a modified form of judo for cops—at the police academy. The instructor had taught the cadet class a come-along hold, which might work effectively against the man holding the gun.

The cadet had closed the distance to less than six feet when the captured policeman turned and looked right at Butch. The shocked expression on the cop's face made the gunman turn around as well. When he spied the cadet, he pointed the gun at him and pulled the trigger.

For a horrible instant, the captive cop, the hostage-taking criminal, and the cadet were frozen in time. The hammer of the small automatic pistol fell, and the firing pin struck the primer of the chambered round. The lead bullet should have been propelled out of the barrel of the gun to penetrate the chest of Cadet Larry Cole Jr. Later the Crime Laboratory would find that the weapon worked perfectly and that the ammunition was serviceable. St. Michael, the patron saint of police officers, was looking out for the young cadet, because the gun misfired with a sharp, audible click.

The man dropped the gun and ran for the door leading out to the parking lot. At that moment, four uniformed officers entered the station. Spying them, the man, who had just attempted to kill a cop, raised his hands and surrendered.

Butch and Rodriguez looked from the suspect, back at each other, and then down to the gun on the floor.

"All I had him for was a minor traffic violation," Rodriguez said. "He didn't have a driver's license, so I brought him in."

One of the officers who had come in from the parking lot, handcuffed the suspect.

"Aren't you supposed to search your prisoners?" Butch said in a less-than-cordial voice.

Rodriguez shrugged. "Everybody's entitled to one mistake, kid."

All Butch could do was stare at him.

C. J. Cantrell had begun drinking heavily since his failed attempt to seize the acting chairman of the board post from Franklin Butler. C. J. had always been a substance abuser, from marijuana cigarettes washed down with six packs of beer in college to cocaine and martinis when he became a member of the Rush Street jet set.

He lived on the thirty-fourth floor of the Siebert Towers apartment building on Michigan Avenue across the street from the Chicago Cultural Center, which had once housed the main branch of the Chicago Public Library. The seventy-five-year-old, forty-story apartment building was named after Phineas Aloysius Siebert, who had been C. J.'s grandfather's business partner. P. A. Siebert, as he had been called, committed suicide by jumping off the roof of the building after he lost his fortune in the 1929 stock market crash.

Siebert Towers was originally constructed as an office building and had done quite well since it opened its doors in 1924. However, a building boom in the Loop, age, and the failure to maintain an acceptable infrastructure had succeeded in reducing the business occupancy to less than 50 percent by the mid-eighties. A number of times over the years, the building had come perilously close to being shut down, but had somehow managed to stay afloat. In 1996, C. J. obtained a high-interest building-improvement loan through a LaSalle Street bank and had the building converted to residential living. An influx of new housing in the downtown area caused the occupancy rate of the building, now renamed the Siebert Towers, to soar above the 75 percent mark. But during the first two years of the twenty-first century, the downtown housing boom peaked and cheaper properties becoming available caused the Siebert Towers to suffer a high vacancy rate. As was the case with all the rest of C. J. Cantrell's financial ventures, the building began losing money.

The businessman lived in a corner apartment with a view of the south side of the city. C. J. seldom looked out the windows, because he suffered periodic bouts of vertigo. He kept his drapes closed, which made it necessary for him to keep lights burning inside the apartment twenty-four hours a day. He employed a cleaning crew to come in twice a month to clean the place, which was a difficult task because C. J. kept it so cluttered. It appeared as if every square inch of space was covered with papers, books, and miscellaneous items, ranging from discarded clothing to golf and tennis accessories. He occasionally dabbled in various sports in an effort to lose weight, but he never stuck with anything for long. Then there was the bar.

C. J. liked to drink in the living room, which looked more like a basement storage bin than living quarters in a downtown high-rise. A fifty-two-inch wide-screen television dominated the center of the room. There was a stained beige brocade couch in front of it. Next to the couch was a sturdy, scarred oak table that had once belonged to C. J.'s great-grandfather. On top of this table there was an array of liquor bottles containing scotch, vodka, gin, and vermouth. In a space beneath the table was a small refrigerator, which was kept fully stocked with beer, wine, and various mixers. It was C. J.'s habit to plunk himself down on the sofa with a glass and a bucket of ice. He would then proceed to drink himself into a stupor while watching whatever happened to be on television. With the assistance of a remote control device, C. J. went through the one-hundred-plus channels on the local cable system. He was particularly fond of World War II documentaries and John Wayne Westerns.

After lunch that day, C. J. decided not to go back to his Clark Street office and instead went to his apartment. Stretching out in front of the TV, he flicked on a documentary channel broadcasting a

World at War marathon. As the Nazis marched across the screen in old black-and-white films, C. J. drank two sixteen-ounce six-packs of Budweiser. As the plastic trash container beside the couch filled to the overflowing point with empty cans, he took a break from his television watching and ordered a bratwurst with grilled onions and hot mustard from a delicatessen on Wabash Avenue that provided delivery service. After consuming the brat and chasing it with the last beer in the twelve-pack, he returned to the couch with a terrible case of acid indigestion and gas. He stumbled around the apartment to toss the empties down the garbage disposal and pop a half dozen antacid pills. When he returned to the couch, he poured himself an eight-ounce glass of scotch and soda, which was intended to calm his queasy stomach.

He switched to the Western channel, finding to his disappointment that a Clint Eastwood spaghetti Western was being broadcast. For want of anything better to do, C. J. watched the movie but turned the sound low so he wouldn't have to hear the irritating guitar music soundtrack. His now booze-soaked brain drifted to his situation on the board of directors for the DeWitt Corporation. C. J. found that he'd been totally outfoxed by Franklin Butler. Morgana DeWitt would soon be irrevocably installed as the heir to holdings worth billions of dollars worldwide. A depression settled on C. J. Cantrell at the same time that a drunken solution to his problems occurred to him. He could kill Morgana DeWitt and Franklin Butler!

Even though he was drunk, C. J. realized he could not do the deed himself. He did have a gun: a nickel-plated .38-caliber snub-nosed Detective Special revolver that had belonged to his father. C. J. kept it on a shelf in his bedroom, and the last time he picked it up, about a year ago, the gun was covered with a thick coating of dust. It probably wouldn't work, and even if it did, he wasn't gutsy enough or smart enough to pull off the murders without getting caught. So he would have to hire somebody to do it. He wondered how much a professional hit man would cost him. He was currently having problems with his cash flow, but after DeWitt and Butler were dead, he could easily take over the board of directors, giving him access to millions.

C. J. considered the hit man's fee a business expense, although it would never appear on his income tax return. The thought made him laugh. To celebrate the formulation of a plan to deal with his enemies, he turned to the drink table for a scotch refill. He was initially shocked, which quickly turned to horror, when he discovered an intruder standing beside the couch. An intruder he recognized.

The Siebert Towers employed doormen who worked from 7 A.M. to 11 P.M. They were paid little more than minimum wage and were expected to make up the lack of salary with tips for summoning taxis, opening car doors, and helping residents with packages in and out of the building. However, since the Siebert Towers' occupancy rate had fallen, tips were rare, and it became more and more difficult for the doormen to make ends meet.

The doorman assigned to the front lobby on this November afternoon was a moonlighting Northwestern University student. A thin young man with protruding eyes and curly hair, he had taken the job to help defray the expense of his education. He was forced to provide his own white shirt, black tie, and dark trousers to go along with the management-issued gray uniformed doorman's jacket and cap. Because the jacket was too small for him, he wore it only when a suit from the front office forced him to. As far as hustling tips went, he'd found it far more profitable to remain at the security desk in the narrow lobby and study his textbooks than dashing outside every time a car pulled up out front. The main office received complaints about his lack of interest in the job, and he'd been called on the carpet twice. But he didn't care. If he got fired, it would be easy enough for him to find another mindless, menial job like this one.

The only duty that he was fairly diligent about performing was ensuring that no unauthorized people, such as peddlers, drunks, or the homeless got into the building. That wasn't due to any sense of duty on the doorman/student's part, but rather personal prejudice. He was studying accounting at NU so that he would never be considered on the same low social plane as such human vermin. So he kept half an eye on the closed-circuit monitors set into the console of his lobby desk while he was more or less on duty.

He was studying one of his textbooks when he noticed on the rear entrance monitor that the alley door was standing open. There were no deliveries scheduled for this afternoon, so the door should have been closed. Going to investigate, he crossed the lobby and entered a corridor next to the elevator bank, which led to the rear of the Siebert Towers.

The back door was equipped with a dead bolt lock that required keys to open from the inside as well as the outside. Now, besides standing wide open, the door was unlocked. This made it necessary for the doorman/student to return to the front lobby and retrieve the building passkeys from his desk drawer. He made the round trip in less than two minutes. To his surprise, when he got back to the rear entrance, the door was closed and locked. Puzzled, he pulled on the door and, finding it secure, returned to the lobby. A pair of uniformed cops were waiting for him.

"You the doorman?" a rather pretty female cop said in a voice that would do justice to a longshoreman.

"Yeah," he replied.

"I think you'd better have a look outside, pal," the lady cop's partner said with the same snarl.

The student/doorman accompanied them out onto Randolph Street without protest.

The streetlights were on, and the weather was still warm enough for hundreds of pedestrians to have gathered in front of the Siebert Towers. There were also three marked police cars parked at the curb and another one pulling up. The confused doorman asked the cops, "What's going on?"

The female cop pointed toward the facade of the building. "Looks like you got a problem, pal."

He looked up at the Siebert Towers, but initially he couldn't see what she was talking about. A squad car spotlight was switched on, illuminating the upper floors of the apartment building. It was then that he saw the body of a nude man hanging by a rope from the upper floors of the building. The body was that of C. J. Cantrell.

16

A ssistant Deputy Superintendent Geno Bailey investigated
the attempted escape of Officer Rodriguez's prisoner. Commander Stephanie Robinson-Smith sat in on the proceedings but said little. Butch found the investigative procedure
to be a carbon copy of the one that had taken place the
night Morgana escaped. However, there was one obvious
difference. The young cadet found that he was now a hero.

The interviews took place in the same second-floor detective division interrogation room where Bailey had questioned Butch before.

"When you approached the offender, did you know that he was armed, Cadet Cole?"

"Yes, sir. I saw that he had a small-caliber pistol pointed at Officer Rodriguez."

"What did you plan to do when you reached the offender?"

Butch shrugged. "Disarm him with a front come-along hold I learned in the police academy."

Bailey and Robinson-Smith exchanged glances of amusement tinged with no little degree of awe at the young man's audacity.

"But before you reached him, he became aware of your presence," Bailey said. "Then what happened?"

Matter-of-factly, the cadet replied, "He pointed the gun at me and pulled the trigger, but the weapon misfired."

The commander could no longer remain silent. "It misfired?" she repeated.

"Yes, ma'am. Sergeant Davies examined the .25 automatic, and the ammunition in it and everything appeared to be working within normal parameters. The gun is on its way to the Crime Lab, where I'm sure we'll find out why it didn't go off."

Initially, the ADS and the district commander thought that young Mr. Cole was displaying a bit of arrogance in his pronouncement about the Crime Lab. Then they quickly came to the realization that he was merely giving them an honest oral report of what had occurred and its aftermath to the best of his ability. They could also see quite clearly that he was showing no ill effects from having been placed in such deadly peril.

"How are you feeling now, Cadet?" the commander asked.

The question surprised him. "I'm fine, ma'am."

"Would you like us to call your father?" Bailey asked.

"No, sir. I'll tell him about it when I get home tonight."

Bailey turned to the commander. "I am going to advise Cadet Cole of the CPD's Employee Assistance Unit's Traumatic Incident Program and recommend that he contact them tomorrow. With your permission, I would like to excuse him for the rest of the day."

Butch appeared about to protest, because Sergeant Q. Davies's desk crew was shorthanded. The commander silenced him with one of her patented glares. "As soon as our investigation is completed here, you are excused, Cadet Cole," she said.

So at six o'clock that evening, Butch found himself on his motorcycle riding north under the McCormick Place complex on Lake Shore Drive. It was four hours before his usual quitting time, and he didn't have the slightest idea what he was going to do with himself. His motorcycle helmet was equipped with an AM/FM radio that blasted music from a local rock station through his head. He had his visor up and was enjoying the summerlike fall weather of this November day when the rock DJ interrupted with a newsbreak.

"The weather is mellow in the Windy City, but we can expect snow by early next week, boys and girls. On the crime front, there's a body hanging from the side of a building at Randolph and Michigan Avenue. The police are at the scene investigating. Stand by for more on WROCK 110 FM Chicago."

Another tune began playing as Butch turned off Lake Shore Drive and sped west toward Michigan Avenue. He found Randolph Street cordoned off and the crowd of onlookers numbering easily over a thousand. Traffic had slowed to a crawl. Finding a parking spot up the street, he parallel-parked and got out.

Butch slipped through the crowd until he was standing at her side. "Hello, Morgana."

She turned to look at him with a blank expression totally devoid of recognition. For a moment, he was confused by her lack of response. Then, as if she were snapping out of a trance, she smiled and said, "Hello, Butch. It's good to see you again."

An awkward moment of silence ensued. He searched for something to say to this beautiful young woman, but words deserted him. Suddenly, the crowd became agitated and everyone looked up at the hanging man. They were pulling the corpse back into the thirty-fourth-floor window.

Chief Larry Cole stood in C. J. Cantrell's living room and supervised the corpse-recovery operation. The cluttered apartment was teeming with police officers and firefighters. The number of Emergency Service personnel was unusual, because the operation was extremely delicate. This was not due solely to the body hanging from the exterior of a building in the heart of the Chicago Loop. There was also a strong possibility that the scene of this crime was booby-trapped.

In the months since Blackie and Manny had been trapped in the fire at the murderess tiger handler's apartment in Wrigleyville, a pattern of arson-related homicides had formed in which fiery traps were rigged with the express objective of killing the investigating officers. What troubled Cole was that the pattern was damnably familiar. He had seen something very similar to this happen before when Margo and Neil DeWitt used mystery novels as instruction manuals to commit crimes. Margo had adopted the novel *Bless the Children* by author Harry McGhee as her personal blueprint to murder young children and even the attempted murder of Cole's son. Now a series of novels were being used in the same fashion.

C. J. Cantrell's body was suspended outside the thirty-fourth-floor window of the Siebert Towers by a twenty-five-foot length of one-half-inch-in-diameter hemp rope. The rope was tied to the leg of the couch, which was sturdy enough to support the weight of the corpse. The hands and feet were bound with wire, and only an autopsy would be able to determine whether he died before or after he went out that window. But they couldn't pull the body back inside until any possible booby-traps were located and eliminated.

Cole walked over to the makeshift bar next to the sofa. Some of the bottles had been overturned, there were a few minuscule bloodstains on the sofa cushions, and there were signs of fresh scuffmarks on the floor. Crime Lab technicians were busy collecting all available evidence in the apartment, and the Bomb and Arson Unit was wrapping up the search for any explosives. So far the police had come up empty.

A broad-shouldered fire department captain, sporting a prickly crew cut, came over to Cole. In a deep, raspy voice he said, "We've got everything in place, Chief. We can move the body anytime you give us the word."

A rotund balding lieutenant from Bomb and Arson was right behind the fireman. Cole noticed that the cop was sweating profusely. "We've checked everything in this apartment, boss. It's clean as far as we can tell."

Cole stared at the open window. "There is only one remaining place where an incendiary device could be hidden." He paused for a moment, lost in silent contemplation before adding, "It could be somewhere on the body we're about to pull back up through that window, but we have no choice. We've got to do this right now and very carefully, Captain. Lieutenant, have your people keep a very watchful eye on the operation."

With that, the two officials hurried away to conduct the grisly retrieval operation.

Morgana DeWitt and Butch Cole watched the body of C. J. Cantrell inch its way slowly upward toward the open window on the thirty-fourth floor of Siebert Towers. Morgana studied the event with the same rapt attention she had displayed when Butch first saw her. As a collective tension gripped the crowd, she stepped closer to him until her shoulder made contact with his chest. Without either one of them taking their eyes away from the spectacle unfolding far above them, he put his arms around her, and she snuggled protectively against him.

The Bomb and Arson Unit lieutenant had taken up a post in an apartment on the thirty-second floor. He was studying the body through a pair of binoculars equipped with night-vision lenses. The lieutenant was fifty-four years old and had been defusing bombs since his days as a combat soldier in the jungles of South Vietnam. He was very good at what he did, but after thirty years on the force, he was tired. Very tired. He planned to retire on January 15, 2007. He could have taken a desk job to ride out his remaining days in peace. However, he was the ace of the Bomb and Arson Unit, and there was no one better qualified at detecting and defusing sophisticated incendiary devices.

The sweat was flowing freely down his forehead and across his cheeks. It was difficult for him to hold the binoculars steady, because he was trembling so violently. He ignored his physical problems and concentrated on the task at hand, searching for any indication of a booby trap. For long minutes, as the corpse inched upward, he could see nothing amiss. The operation was nearly over and the emergency service personnel were about to pull the body back in the window when the lieutenant detected a thin wire protruding from the dead man's back.

Snatching a walkie-talkie from his jacket pocket, he depressed the transmit key and shouted, "Stop, stop, stop! Hold the body right where it is. I'll be right there."

His heart pounding furiously and his breathing coming in sharp rasps, the Bomb and Arson lieutenant sprinted up the two flights of stairs and down the corridor to the open door of C. J. Cantrell's apartment. In the living room, he raced past Chief Cole and dashed to the window. The head and shoulders of the hanged man were visible above the edge of the windowsill. Leaning out the window, the lieutenant studied the dead man's back. The device was taped to his torso and partially concealed by his shirt.

The trigger wire led from the device to the rope. Had the ESU people pulled it back through the window, the explosive would have detonated. A subsequent examination of the device revealed that it contained a nasty concentration of thermite and C4 plastic explosive. When detonated, it would have ignited every combustible surface within fifty feet, producing an inferno in which a number of cops, including Chief Larry Cole, would have been trapped.

The lieutenant leaned out the window until his upper body was exposed above the street below. Using a pair of wire cutters borrowed from one of the ESU people, he snipped the wire. All the eyes in the apartment were on him when he straightened up and turned around. Mopping his face with a handkerchief, he spied Cole and said with a fatigued smile, "You can pull him in now, boss. I'll remove that nasty little package from his back when they get him inside."

A short time later, Larry Cole rode down on the elevator to the Siebert Towers lobby. This was the sixth murder that had occurred following a pattern that indicated the killer was imitating previously published mystery novels. From *The Burned Man* by Debbie Bass to *The Tale of the Hanged Man* by Jamal Garth, which detailed a crime almost exactly like the murder of C. J. Cantrell outside the Siebert Towers, each real-life murder went one better than its fictional counterpart. An incendiary had been rigged at each crime scene in an attempt to trap and kill the investigating officers.

Cole had asked authors Barbara Zorin and Jamal Garth to examine each of the murders and see if they could form a definite connection to specific works of mystery fiction. Cole was doing this merely to be thorough, because he was fairly well read in the mystery field. Despite the incendiaries found at the crime scenes, no evidence had been uncovered that would lead them to the killer. Cole believed these crimes were not being done as simple random acts of violence and there was not only a connection to the long-dead homicidal De-Witts, but that each crime was also leading to a particular conclusion. The Chicago Police chief of detectives was working hard to find out what that conclusion would be.

Cole exited the Siebert Towers. The crowd had dissipated and only a few diehard cop watchers remained. He was crossing Randolph Street to his police car when he heard the boom of a motorcycle exhaust. Turning in the direction from which the noise had come, he saw his son's red Honda exit the Grant Park underground garage and speed north on Michigan Avenue. Cole recognized Morgana De-Witt riding on the back with her arms wrapped around Butch.

17

The weather changed. In less than a week, the average daily temperature in Chicago dropped more than forty degrees. A cold front swept through the Midwest, and snow fell in upper Minnesota, Wisconsin, and Michigan. Thunderstorms and high winds battered Chicago, and the weather could only be classified as "nasty." But rain, cold, and wind notwithstanding, this November day was one of the most beautiful of Blackie Silvestri's life, because he returned to work.

Judy Daniels, hair swept back in a wavy red ponytail, a

smattering of freckles across her nose, and windowpane granny glasses pushed down on her nose, was at work in her cubicle at police headquarters. Since these mystery novel copycat murders had begun, she had been spending twelve to sixteen hours a day on the job. This had severely limited her ability to experiment with various disguises, so she was forced to rely on her old standbys like this red wig and freckles. That was no fun, and her mind had been alive with ideas she planned to try when she got more time.

Judy was downloading a report from the computer that had been e-mailed to her by Barbara Zorin when she heard someone cough outside the cubicle. The sound was so familiar that she initially ignored it. When she realized whose throat that gravelly sound came out of, she leaped to her feet and dashed out into the corridor. Blackie Silvestri and Manny Sherlock were waiting for her.

"Blackie!" she screamed, flinging herself into his arms and planting a kiss on his cheek. "You even shaved." She turned to the tall sergeant before hugging him as well. "Sergeant Manfred Wolfgang Sherlock, you long, tall drink of water. Boy, did I miss you guys." She stepped back and took them in from head to toe. "You've both lost weight. I heard about the workouts with Butch, and now you look like candidates for the Chicago Marathon."

"Never felt better in my life, Judy," Blackie said, patting his flat midsection. "The day might just come when we do run in the marathon. Now that we've got the greetings out of the way, I gotta go check in with the boss."

Leaving Manny behind, the lieutenant headed for Cole's office. Judy noticed the spring in his step. "Talk about making a complete recovery."

"Tell me about it," Manny said. "You want to bring me up to date on what we're currently working on?"

"Come on in," she said, stepping back inside her cubicle. "I've got a ton of stuff for you."

Blackie sat in Cole's office and watched rainwater run down the exterior windows. The chief was on the telephone when the lieutenant came in and had motioned Blackie to a chair. The lieutenant could tell that Cole was talking to either the superintendent or the first deputy. The topic was the homicide of C. J. Cantrell. The conversation was over in less than five minutes.

"Welcome back," Cole said, rising and extending a hand to his old friend. "You look ten years younger. Those workouts have done wonders for you."

"I've got you to thank for that, boss. Maria says I'm acting more like I'm twenty years younger, if you know what I mean."

They laughed before getting down to cases.

"We're receiving a lot of heat on the Cantrell Murder, as you probably heard," Cole said. "He wasn't very well liked by the LaSalle Street crowd he hung around with when he was alive, but in death, he's become something of a martyr in the financial world."

"The 'honored dead,' to quote Bogie."

Cole frowned in confusion.

"It was a Humphrey Bogart line in *Casablanca*," Blackie explained. "I've been watching a lot of late-night cable television lately."

"I want you and Manny to go over the reports already filed on Cantrell's death and take another look into his background in case there's anything the investigating detectives missed."

"I read in the papers where Cantrell tried to block Morgana De-Witt's inheriting the DeWitt fortune. There was potentially a nasty court fight brewing, but Franklin Butler outfoxed Cantrell, which left him out in the cold. Had our 'honored dead' financier been a real threat to DeWitt and Butler that would have been a motive for murder."

Cole didn't respond right away. "Take a ride down to DeWitt Plaza and talk to Butler and Morgana DeWitt. You never can tell what you'll come up with."

"Sure thing, boss. I'll take Manny with me."

Before Blackie left the office, Cole said, "It's good to have you back."

"It's good to be back."

After Blackie left, Cole leaned back in his chair and closed his eyes. He was indeed glad to have Blackie and Manny back on duty, because it would shift some of the workload of the chief of detectives' office from his and Judy's shoulders. Those who saw the chief of detectives' post as merely administrative had occasionally criticized Cole's hands-on management style. It had been argued that the same principles used to efficiently manufacture the proverbial widget could be applied with equal efficiency to criminal investigations. To Cole, such an approach was not only ridiculous, but it also smacked of negligence. As he saw it, he wasn't just a working cop, he was the main detective responsible for making sure that each and every investigation of an unsolved crime committed in Chicago was thoroughly investigated. For the past eight years that he had been the chief of detectives, he had done a job that both his supporters and detractors admitted was phenomenal to the point of brilliance.

But it wasn't his dedication to the job that was sapping Larry Cole's strength. He was concerned about his son.

Butch was Cole's only child. He hadn't intended it that way, because when he married Lisa, they had planned a bigger family with as many as four children. Then they went through the divorce, and Cole had never seriously considered remarrying. For most of his life, Butch had lived in Detroit with his mother. This had not diminished the extraordinarily close bond between father and son, and after Butch graduated from high school, Cole had talked Lisa into allowing Butch to move back to Chicago to be with his father. This she had done grudgingly, after obtaining a sworn promise from Cole that he would keep Butch out of danger. He hadn't been quite able to do that, but Lisa had been unaware of their son chasing bank robbers around Chicago on his motorcycle last year. Of course, she had been mildly upset when Butch told her he was going to become a police cadet, but she had come to the realization that their son was rapidly becoming an adult. He would have to be allowed at this stage of his life to make some decisions on his own. Such a gradual granting of independence was part of the maturing process—a process Larry Cole was struggling to come to grips with.

Butch Cole had always been an obedient, high-principled, respectful young man. He had never given his mother or father any trouble, and they were tremendously proud of him. In fact, at times they had separately questioned whether Butch was a bit too perfect. That was one of the contributing factors to the problem Cole was going through now.

Something was going on in Butch's life. Something that Cole's cop instincts were telling him was not good for the kid. Something that Cole wanted to find out about without prying into his son's life.

In the past week, Butch had begun staying out late and leaving the apartment early in the morning with no explanations given. Cole had the occasion to talk to Captain Gary Harmon at the Second District on a matter related to the mystery novel copycat slayings and had discovered quite innocently that Butch not only was doing a good job, but had been involved in the attempted escape of the armed prisoner. Cole had been unaware of that incident. Harmon also told Cole that the notoriously severe Commander Stephanie Robinson-Smith was very pleased over how well the young cadet was performing. Knowing the commander as Cole did, such a pronouncement meant that Butch was doing a truly phenomenal job.

Butch was taking nine semester hours at Roosevelt University, which was his father's alma mater. He was majoring in Psychology, and Cole had seen his son hitting the books on his off days. In fact, he thought that Butch was working too hard, with the long hours he spent at the Second District and in school. However, father and son still spent time together and had dinner at least once or twice a week.

So what was Larry Cole's problem? It came down to him seeing Butch with Morgana DeWitt the night of C. J. Cantrell's murder. Since then, Butch had begun keeping the odd hours, and Cole suspected he was spending that time with Morgana DeWitt. The dilemma facing Cole was what, if anything, he was going to do about it.

His intercom buzzed.

"Yes," Cole answered.

It was Judy. "I'm ready to go over the twenty-four-hour report with you, Chief."

"Come on in."

Cole sat up and willed himself to concentrate on the business at hand. However, he was still concerned about his son and Morgana DeWitt.

Blackie Silvestri and Manny Sherlock had been in DeWitt Plaza on official business many times before. Dating back to the serial-killing couple being in residence to a madwoman named Eurydice Vaughn kidnapping Larry Cole from this place, the two cops had investigated crimes in the luxury high-rise on the Magnificent Mile with such regularity that it could qualify for its own crime rate. One of the more amusing cop stories that Blackie told after he'd had a few beers was about the first time he accompanied Cole to interview the De-Witts. It was a fairly harmless mission requested by then First Deputy Superintendent Terry Kennedy. The eccentric but deadly

Margo had unwittingly disclosed to Kennedy and his wife that she knew the fate of a child who had disappeared in Lincoln Park on the previous day. After the little boy was found dead in the Lincoln Park lagoon, Cole and Blackie were dispatched to find out what she knew about the child's death. As required by law, they had advised the De-Witts of their Constitutional rights. Much to Cole and Blackie's surprise, Margo and Neil got to their feet and raised their right hands, as if they were taking an oath. At the time, it had been amusing. When they discovered that Margo had killed the child, the incident was far from funny.

Manny parked the police car on the north side of the plaza and they entered the lobby to find few shoppers in evidence at this time of the day. They crossed to the commercial elevators, which whisked them to the twenty-fifth floor. After showing their identification to the security guard on duty, they took another elevator to the forty-seventh floor. A few minutes later, they were seated in the waiting area of the combination offices of the DeWitt Corporation and Franklin Butler, attorney at law. "Someone" was supposed to be along to escort them to the acting chairman's office. The cops had been waiting for a short time when the staccato clicking of a woman's heels on the hard floor carried to them from an adjacent corridor.

Susanne York, clad in a tight-fitting black leather pantsuit, walked up to them. "Lieutenant Silvestri and Sergeant Sherlock," she said, giving them a careful once-over, "the chairman will see you now."

Blackie rose and was about to follow the statuesque woman when he noticed that Manny was still seated.

"You coming?" the lieutenant asked.

"Sure thing," the sergeant said, leaping to his feet.

Blackie didn't know what was wrong, but as they made their way through the spacious corridors of the executive wing, Manny never took his eyes off her.

They reached a set of double doors adorned with a gold engraved plaque that read, FRANKLIN BUTLER, ESQUIRE. She knocked once before entering. At the entrance, she stepped back and motioned them inside with a partial bow. It was only then that she met Manny's gaze with one of her own that was as cold as a gust of January wind off Lake Michigan.

"The chairman is a very busy man, so I trust you won't take up too much of his time." With that, she turned and walked away rapidly.

Butler's office appeared to have the dimensions of a football field. His desk was some distance away on the opposite side of the room. The attorney was on the telephone and didn't look up when they walked in. Manny reached out and grabbed Blackie's arm.

"I've seen that woman before."

"I could tell by the way you were staring at her. I ought to tell Lauren on you."

Manny rolled his eyes in exasperation and whispered, "Her photograph was on the wall of that secret compartment in Wrigleyville. If I'm not missing my guess, she's wearing a disguise."

"Gentlemen," Butler called to them, "please come in."

Before crossing the office, Blackie said, "We'll deal with this guy first, then we'll check our escort out."

Morgana DeWitt's life had changed dramatically in the past four months. Although she had been relatively well off all her life, she now found that she was among the one hundred richest people in the world. Her holdings in the multinational DeWitt Corporation were so vast that Franklin Butler told her it would take an independent accounting firm a minimum of eighteen months to produce a report listing not only her worth, but also what she actually owned. To Morgana all this talk about money and property was interesting up to a point, but she didn't plan to spend the rest of her life absorbed with her own wealth.

Despite the celebrity, which came with her money, she had managed to remain a fairly anonymous figure. That was primarily thanks to Franklin Butler, who had put security arrangements in place to protect her from the press, the inquisitive, and the nosy. In fact, if Butler had his way, Morgana would have been placed under virtual house arrest in the DeWitt Plaza penthouse.

Susanne York and that trio of military types who had taken her from the police attempted to follow her wherever she went. That angered Morgana, and when she voiced her objections to Butler, his response was, "You're now a very rich young woman, Morgana. There are people out there who would like to kidnap you and hold you for ransom. In my experience, such people kill more victims than they release unharmed."

"I can take care of myself, Mr. Butler," she argued.

"I'm sure you can," he responded with that smug attorney arrogance. "My people will just be there blending into the background to make sure that no undue complications develop."

She had seriously considered firing Butler, but she realized that she needed him. At least for the time being. She didn't want to spend her life chained to the business world. So Butler was necessary. However, Morgana didn't need Butler's henchmen and henchwoman following her around. That she would not tolerate, no matter what Butler said about kidnappers.

The first thing she did was move out of Dewitt Plaza and into her own town house in a trendy area of North Sheridan Road. She purchased the property for $1.3 million drawn on her bank in Switzerland. The DeWitt Corporation belonged to her, but she wasn't yet ready to begin tapping into its resources, no matter how much red tape Franklin Butler cut through for her. Then there was the issue she was forced to confront squarely in her own mind: Her parents had been serial killers.

Butler had voiced only mild objections to her moving out of De-Witt Plaza and into her own place. Morgana had assumed that this was because he planned to have his minions follow her wherever she went. She decided she would have to deal with this on her own.

She moved into the new penthouse in early October. She had yet to purchase any furniture, and on that first morning, after she had spent the night on a mattress on the hardwood floor of her living room, she had gone out for a walk to check out her new neighborhood. She hadn't gone a block before she spotted them. The black and white pair, who had impersonated police detectives, were sitting in a shiny Lincoln a half block from Morgana's town house. Although she had expected them, she became furious. She started to charge right up to the car and read them the riot act, but something stopped her. An odd chill enveloped her, which she had experienced only once before in her life. That was on the day she discovered Carlos Perfido was posing as stage actor Richard Banacek. The chill had remained with her when she made the calculated decision to kill him while he was performing on stage. Now, as she became aware of her watchers on North Sheridan Road in Chicago, the same chill returned. Of course, she didn't plan to kill them, just make a game of eluding them.

That first morning she wandered around the congested northside of the city, eating breakfast in a restaurant on Lincoln Avenue, taking a taxi to the zoo, and then returning to her town house in the early afternoon. She spent a couple of hours at home before taking in a movie at the Biograph Theater. Before returning to her place, she went to a pizza parlor and had the house specialty. By ten o'clock, she was in bed.

Her two bodyguards were with her all day. They didn't make any attempt to conceal their presence, and it was quite obvious they were bored silly. After she returned home, they once more parked down the block and settled in for the night.

Over the next few days, they were with her everywhere that she went. It wasn't always the phony detectives, as occasionally there was a tall, thin, stern-faced man present. To ease them into a false feeling of security, Morgana established a set pattern of behavior. In the morning she would leave the town house no later than 10 A.M. She would then go shopping until midafternoon. She would return home before six and on most evenings remain there. Each night they returned to their same post down the street.

As time passed, additional personnel were assigned to follow her. It was a simple matter for her to obtain the license plate numbers of the cars they drove and run those numbers through the DeWitt Corporation mainframe computer. They came back as registered to DeWitt Corporation security.

Finally, in early October, she decided to give them the slip. Her town house was almost completely furnished, and she was shopping for a few odds and ends at a State Street department store. The usual crew was on duty, looking bored as usual. It was a simple matter for Morgana to slip away in the crowded store. When she was certain she had eluded them, she spent the afternoon visiting the Shedd Aquarium on the lakefront.

Morgana was about to catch a taxi back to her town house when she noticed a tall woman exit the aquarium behind her. It took the young billionairess only a single glance to see that this woman was sixtyish and had wrinkled skin and silver hair. She was wearing a dated dress and orthopedic shoes. She also suffered from a bone disease that caused her to walk in a stooped fashion. That same brief glance told Morgana this woman was Susanne York wearing theatrical makeup. Now this game of cat and mouse became infinitely more interesting.

After being given the slip, her male watchers became more attentive to the point of aggression. They no longer remained politely in the background while Morgana went about her daily chores. One of them walked less than six feet behind her wherever she went. She still managed to give them the slip by entering ladies' rooms or the changing rooms of clothing stores. Once out of their sight, she would head for rear doors or emergency exits and make her escape. Butler began adding women to the security force, and she still disappeared on them. But Susanne York proved more difficult to get away from.

To Morgana DeWitt, the York woman was easy to spot due to the garish outfits she wore. From the "granny" outfit Morgana spied her in outside of the Shedd Aquarium to a black Western outfit that she looked grossly out of place in without a horse to a tacky glamour girl ensemble highlighted by a wide-brimmed hat and oversized sunglasses, the tall woman was easy enough to spot. However, Morgana found her more difficult to shake.

Back in her town house, Morgana analyzed the problem that Susanne York presented. Actually, she saw the York woman's continued presence as a challenge. A challenge Morgana planned to overcome.

For the next few days, she ran her watchers ragged on a marathon of all-day shopping sessions and sightseeing tours around the Windy City. She walked, took cabs, caught buses, and even rode a subway. At will, she was able to lose her forced escorts, but not Susanne York. Then Morgana noticed two things about the woman wearing the flamboyant outfits. One was that she liked to call attention to herself; the other was that she would occasionally break off the tail abruptly and then take it up later. It was at this point that Morgana decided to turn the tables on her challenging adversary. She decided to follow Susanne York.

Morgana would sometimes lose sight of Susanne York, but each time that she did, she learned something more about her quarry.

Once, when York ventured by cab into one of the seamier neighborhoods of the Windy City near Humboldt Park, Morgana in her own taxi watched her enter a predominantly Hispanic bar. Susanne emerged a half hour later with a wiry, dark-haired male who was a head shorter than the statuesque woman. They got into a rusting old Cadillac and drove away, leaving Morgana to record the license plate number before breaking off her surveillance.

The next day Morgana was out walking and became aware of Susanne York following her again. They continued like that in tandem for a while, and Morgana was about to give her the slip once more when they came across the cordoned-off area of Lincoln Park, where Chief Larry Cole was in charge of the investigation of the man who had been burned alive. Morgana recognized the booby-trapped car parked in the bus stop as the same one she had seen Susanne York get into the night before. That was an interesting bit of intelligence, which she filed away for future reference.

The game of cat and mouse between the DeWitt Corporation heir and her watchers continued. At times, Morgana made no attempt to elude them, then just as quickly would mysteriously vanish from sight. The one thing that was a constant with her was tailing Susanne York. That's how Morgana happened to be outside the Siebert Building the night C. J. Cantrell's body was found hanging from the upper floors. And since that night, and her meeting with Butch Cole, Morgana's life had changed dramatically.

Morgana DeWitt's Sheridan Road town house faced Lake Michigan. From the windows of her living room, she could see gray waves crashing against the rocks north of Belmont Harbor. It was a cold scene. A chilling, uninviting scene; however, it didn't bother her, because for the first time in her life she was happy. She had no idea how long she'd been standing there, but it was just starting to snow when Butch Cole came into the room.

He was dressed in his police uniform, which included a navy blue waist-length Eisenhower jacket. He was also carrying his leather Windbreaker as protection against the frigid weather.

"I'm on my way to work, Morgana," he said. "I'll give you a call this evening."

Clad in a black turtleneck sweater and jeans, with her hair pulled back into a ponytail, she turned to face him. Since the night they ran into each other downtown, they had been spending a great deal of time together. The young heiress had converted a room on the top floor of her town house into an ultramodern gymnasium, and the place had come with a sauna, steam room, and whirlpool. Butch had started working out at her place at least twice a week.

"Did you eat the salad I fixed for you?" she asked.

He nodded and gave her that shy smile, which she thought was the most wonderful thing about him. He responded, "It was great, just like everything else you cook."

"And it was healthy," she said, crossing the living room and taking his arm. "You Americans eat too much fat," she said with authority. "Although you don't show it now, when you get older, it will begin to collect around your midsection."

"It hasn't on my dad," he argued. "I think he's in better shape than I am. There's also one thing that you forgot."

"What's that?"

"You're an American, too, Morgana."

Now it was her turn to smile, which was something she had rarely done in her life before she met the young Mr. Cole. "I guess that I am."

As he began putting on his coat, she said, "It's a pretty raw day outside. Not the kind of weather you should be out riding a motorcycle in."

"I'll be warm enough with my helmet on."

She hesitated a moment before saying, "Could you do me a big favor?"

"Sure."

"This is the start of the flu season, and you told me last week that you haven't gotten your inoculation yet."

"I'll get around to it on my next day off. My dad and I take a couple of thousand units of vitamin C every day, so that should keep the bug off me for a while. Now, what about this favor?"

"I want you to leave your motorcycle here and take my car. That way you'll be out of the elements and I won't worry about you catching cold." Before he could argue, she said, "Please don't say no, Butch. It's a long way out to that police station on the south side. You're coming back this evening for dinner after you get off, and you can pick up your bike then. I won't let anything happen to it. Now please say yes."

"When did you get a car?"

"It was delivered while you were in the shower after your workout. I ordered comprehensive insurance coverage, and you'll be able to test-drive the car for me."

He thought about it for a moment before shrugging. "Okay. But I'm bringing it back tonight."

"Great," she said. Then she led him back to the garage, which was attached to the town house.

When Butch Cole saw the car, he was stunned. It was a brand-new 2007 BMW roadster. It was of the exact same shade of fire engine red as his motorcycle and had a black convertible top. In the overhead lights of her heated garage, it sparkled with the same brilliance as it had on the showroom floor.

"Morgana . . . ," he protested.

"You promised, Butch. Look." She dashed around to the passenger side of the two-seater, opened the door, and pulled a card from behind the sun visor. She handed it to him. "The Midwestern States Insurance Company of Illinois issued a policy that covers both of us, so you don't have anything to worry about."

"Okay," he said, "but I'm not going to need insurance, because I'll be driving this buggy very carefully."

"Buggy?" she said with a frown. "Oh, you mean the car. 'Buggy' is a slang word."

"You got it," he said, giving her a wink. Then Morgana DeWitt and Butch Cole parted by formally shaking hands.

She watched him back carefully out of the garage into the narrow alley. Then he put the car in drive, and the powerful engine vibrated with power. Through the windshield, she could see his face split into a broad grin. Then he was gone with a burst of controlled speed.

For a time, Morgana stood in the cold outside the open overhead door. It had been fairly easy for her to sell him on driving the BMW. She had foreseen his possible objections and skillfully dealt with them. She hoped not, but she couldn't simply come out and tell him that the car was his. It was a gift from her, but he would be too proud to accept it. Then there was his father, the great Chicago Police Chief of Detectives Larry Cole. The man who had killed Morgana's mother.

Right now that really didn't matter to her, she thought as she stepped back inside the garage. Butch Cole was the only real friend she had ever had. In fact, she felt closer to him than she ever had with Isaac Weiss, whom Carlos Perfido had killed all those years ago. Her only contact with the handsome young man at this point was a formal handshake. Someday she planned for that to change.

She was about to close her garage door when she became aware of two men standing out in the alley staring in at her. She was not unduly alarmed as she turned and came face-to-face with Blackie Silvestri and Manny Sherlock.

"Good afternoon, Ms. DeWitt," Blackie said, flashing his badge. "We tried your front door bell, but there was no answer. We'd like to ask you some questions, if you don't mind."

"Not at all," she said, maintaining a cool front. "Come in."

With that, the two cops entered the garage and Morgana shut the overhead door behind them. As they crossed the cement floor, she was aware that they both stared with recognition at Butch Cole's motorcycle.

Blackie Silvestri and Manny Shealock sat across from Franklin. Blackie knew Franklin was tall, but, Christ, he tooked like Goliath sitting at his desk.

Blackie thought sitting at a desk made you shorter.

"You got lucky at that Morgana DeWitt trial, Franklin."

"It wasn't luck. I am a good attorney."

"Could you tell us where you were the night he was killed?" Silvestri asked.

"I was here in the office working."

"Alone."

"I always work alone."

"How did Ms. DeWitt feel about Mr. Cantrell?"

"You'll have to ask her that yourself."

After he gave them Morgana's new address, the cops left. Then Susanne York came in.

Franklin Butler had hired Susanne York after he became the chief counsel for the DeWitt Corporation shortly before Margo's death. Susanne, who had earned a law degree at the University of Chicago, worked initially in the corporation's legal affairs department before becoming Franklin's executive assistant.

When Butler was growing up in the South, there had been poisonous snakes infesting the woods around his home. They were not necessarily deadly so long as a bite victim received prompt medical treatment. As a child, he had learned to coexist with snakes. Doing that consisted of being very careful when you were around them. If an adder or cottonmouth was encountered in the wild, you were to stand very still and hope the snake didn't feel sufficiently threatened to inflict a venomous bite. He sometimes felt that his snake-charmed childhood had trained him to cope with Susanne York.

"What's the matter with you, Susanne? We've almost achieved our goal, and you're starting to get squirrelly on me. We've got to protect our mutual interests on this thing. If we don't, the whole plan could fall apart."

"I need to protect my own interests and do something about Sergeant Sherlock."

"I forbid it," Butler said with finality before returning to his paperwork and adding, "If you want to protect your own interests, you'll curtail your violent nocturnal activities. They will really succeed in getting Sergeant Sherlock and the rest of Larry Cole's crew directing their attention toward you."

She started to reply but thought better of it. Finally, she got to her feet and silently left the office.

Once more alone, Butler realized that Susanne York was an effective tool. In fact, in their early years together with the corporation, she had displayed an extraordinary allegiance and belief in him. He had put that to good use in facilitating his rise to his current position. Now she was becoming a liability he couldn't afford. Perhaps what she said about Sergeant Sherlock recognizing her could be worked to his ultimate advantage. That and the woman's fanatical devotion to the dead Margo Dewitt. And if that didn't work, Franklin Butler had other ways of dealing with her.

Larry Cole pulled into the driveway next to the John G. Shedd Aquarium in Museum Park on Lake Shore Drive. There were three police vehicles already there: a marked cruiser, an unmarked detective car, and a police wagon. The wind blowing off the lake kept the number of pedestrians in the area to a minimum. His head bent against the elements, Cole climbed the steps to the building entrance. Manny Sherlock was waiting for Cole in the rotunda.

"Blackie sent me to escort you to the lower level, Chief," Manny said. "We were on our way back from interviewing Franklin Butler and Morgana DeWitt when we monitored the call. We've got another weird murder on our hands."

Cole didn't say a word, because he didn't have to. This place, the shark tanks, and the fact that a homicide had been reported in the aquarium said it all. Another mystery novel copycat murder had occurred.

The Shedd Aquarium maintained a wide range of aquatic exhibits on the lower level. Manny led Cole to the exhibit labeled SHARK GROTTO. A pair of uniformed officers, Blackie Silvestri, and an aging, myopic gentleman wearing a stained white lab coat waited.

Before Blackie could say anything, the man in the white coat rushed up to Cole and demanded, "Are you the person in charge?"

With a scowl, Blackie quickly intervened. "Dr. Fabian, would you please take it easy? This is the chief of detectives, but he can't help you until he knows what's going on here."

"Dr. Maurice Fabian and I have met before, Blackie," Cole said. "I attended the Chicago Museum Curators' Dinner at the Hilton and Towers last spring with Dr. Silvernail Smith of the Field Museum."

That information stunned Dr. Fabian into silent confusion. "Yes," he stammered. "Dr. Silvernail. He won the City Council's Curator's Award. You say that you were there, sir?"

Cole smiled. "My date at I sat at the same table with you and your wife. I was the cop."

"Yes, the cop and Dr. Silvernail," Dr. Fabian mumbled, as if trying to convince himself of what had occurred months ago.

While the aquarium director remained preoccupied, Blackie briefed Cole. "The maintenance crew was cleaning the shark tanks, boss, and found the remains of a human body. It's difficult to say how long ago the victim became fish food until we get what's left of it to the morgue."

"The body has been in the tank less than a month, Blackie," Cole said. "It was put there to make sure that it would be discovered when the next regularly scheduled cleaning cycle was to take place. The fish on display were recently born tiger sharks."

This revelation startled the cops and focused Maurice Fabian's attention back on Cole. "The *Chondrichthyes* are extremely adaptable aquatic creatures," the doctor said with authority. "The ovoviviporous types give birth to three-foot-long offspring capable of consuming the same prey as their full-grown parents. The larger ones will generally not consume their young, but sharks are extremely aggressive carnivores, which have been known to attack members of their species. That's why we kept the pups separated from the elders."

"I know, Doctor," Cole said. "The baby sharks were of the species *Galeocerdo cuvier.*"

The doctor's mouth dropped open as he said an amazed, "That's right! They are tiger sharks! I didn't know you were a student of the *Chondrichthyes,* Chief Cole?"

"I'm not," Cole replied. "I read about them in a mystery novel."

The red BMW drove like a dream. To Butch Cole, the ride was so smooth, it was almost as if he were flying as he drove south on the Dan Ryan Expressway from Twenty-second Street. Midday traffic was light, and he was moving along at an exceptionally good pace when he happened to glance at the speedometer. He was doing seventy-five miles an hour in a fifty-five-mile-per-hour zone. He quickly slowed his speed and checked the rearview mirror in case a state trooper was coming up behind him. Finding that he had eluded official scrutiny, he emitted a sigh of relief and slowed down to the posted speed. At Fifty-first Street, he exited.

As he entered the Area One parking lot, he found himself faced with a dilemma. Where was he going to park this beautiful sports car?

The lot behind the police station was the size of a city block. Over a thousand cars were crammed into its confines on a daily basis and had a high accident ratio due to the heavy traffic volume. Butch didn't want the BMW dented by some careless cop running late for roll call. He was considering parking out on the street when a high-pitched whistle split the cold air. Turning, he saw Sergeant Q. Davies motion to him from the sidewalk adjacent to the parking lot entrance. Butch drove the roadster over and rolled the window down.

"Now this is what I call a sleek machine, lad," the sergeant said.

Butch smiled and explained, "It belongs to a friend of mine."

Davies laughed. "I should start hanging with you, Cadet. I could use a 'friend' like yours." He paused for a moment. "I wouldn't park it in the lot. If you do, some idiot rushing off to a hot date will back into it." Davies looked around. On the west side of the station, there was a reserved parking section for the brass. Davies said, "Park the BMW in the tactical lieutenant's spot. She's in Hawaii on vacation."

Butch was uncertain. "Are you sure it's okay?"

"Yes, Cadet. Now park the car and let's go to work."

Butch left Morgana DeWitt's BMW red roadster in the Second District tactical lieutenant's reserved parking space.

Larry Cole had his crew pull the security videotapes from the Shedd Aquarium. Blackie went to the photo unit in the crime lab at Chicago Police Headquarters and collected the enhanced copy the technicians had made. Returning to his office, Blackie popped the tape into his department-issued VCR and settled in to watch.

Dr. Maurice Fabian at the aquarium had given them a feeding schedule for the sharks and the times that the tanks were cleaned. The medical examiner's office was unable to establish an exact time of death, but the pathologist had been able to provide a broad estimate based on the conditions of the bones found at the bottom of the shark tank. That would indicate the body went into the shark tank in the past two weeks to thirty days. Blackie activated the PLAY button on the remote.

Two hours later, he emerged from his office with the tape in his hand and headed for Cole's office. It was obvious to those the lieutenant encountered that his first day back on the job was not turning out very well. At the door to the chief's office, Blackie knocked once before entering.

The tape revealed that the dark-haired young woman had been standing at the fish tank staring in at the sharks for seven minutes and thirty-two seconds on the afternoon of October 8. Then a man entered the shot and stepped up to the railing beside her. After watching the sharks for a moment, he turned and flashed a seductive smile. She continued to stare into the tank without looking at him or acknowledging his presence. The tape wasn't equipped with sound, but it didn't have to be, as there was no mistaking his seductive "playboy on the make" manner.

"The guy's name is Ross Stevens, boss," Blackie said. "He's been pinched a couple of times inside Museum Park, Burnham Harbor, and Meigs Field for criminal trespass and once for assault. According to his sheet, he's basically harmless, but he has been known to aggressively annoy lone females in and around Museum Park to the point that they call security."

"We have anything else on him?" Cole asked.

"He's a LaSalle Street commodities broker. Makes a quarter of a million bucks a year. Has a condo in Lincolnwood and drives a year-old Porsche."

"You would think that he could find better ways to spend his time."

"Well, we don't know how he's been spending his time for the past month, because he vanished right about the time he tried to put the moves on our favorite billionairess there. Stevens's mother reported him missing on October tenth."

On the TV screen, Morgana DeWitt turned away from the masher and walked out of camera range. With a shrug, Ross Stevens followed. That left only a tall woman with gray hair in the shark grotto security camera shot. Cole and Blackie paid her little notice.

"The security cameras picked Morgana up at the beluga whale ex-hibit twenty-two minutes later," Blackie said. "Where she was in the aquarium in the interim is a mystery. The cameras down there don't cover everything. Ross Stevens was wearing a navy blue corduroy blazer and what looks to have been a gold signet ring with the initial S on his right hand. The crime lab recovered a gold signet ring with that same initial from the bottom of the shark tank."

Cole picked up the remote and freeze-framed the shot. On the screen, Morgana DeWitt was looking down at the beluga whales with the same intensity she had employed to study the sharks.

18

I t had been an unusually slow night for Captain Gary Harmon, the third-watch commander in the Second District. This had given him the opportunity to catch up on some long-overdue paperwork. He also had a chance to study a series of composite sketches Sergeant Manny Sherlock had left for him. Those sketches had been prepared by a Crime Lab artist, and they depicted six women. One of them Harmon was extremely familiar with. He had provided the description on which the composite was based. It was the woman who had kidnapped him on the day Morgana De-Witt escaped from custody. The picture was fairly accurate, but with that Farrah Fawcett hairdo and oversized sunglasses, it was difficult to see her face. For all that he could tell about her features, she could have been wearing a mask. Harmon flipped through the other pictures.

Each could have been a composite drawing of his kidnapper. Then they could also have been renderings of completely different women. Sherlock wanted Harmon to compare the sketches and see if he could come up with a possible match. For the identification to have any evidentiary value, three of the drawings would have to be of subjects selected at random. But as the captain examined them, he was forced to admit that they were all very close. Very close indeed. However, there was one that he kept going back to. It depicted a woman with her hair drawn back into a bun. She wasn't wearing glasses, but she reminded him more of his kidnapper than any of the others.

Harmon made a note to call Manny Sherlock. If the captain could take a look at this woman in the flesh, he might be able to identify her. Just as he had that thought, his desk phone rang.

"Second District, Captain Harmon."

"Gary, it's Larry Cole."

"Hey, boss, how's it going?"

"Good. Anyone ever find out who kidnapped you or who those fate cups were?"

"We got nothing—I'm still looking at mug shots."

Harmon remarked to himself that Cole didn't sound so good.

"What can I do for you?"

"Is my son working tonight?" Cole asked.

Harmon could tell that the chief was not in much of a mood for small talk. "Yeah, Chief. He's working the report station on the desk."

"Do me a favor," Cole said. "Could you have him come into your office so that he can take this call in private? I wouldn't want his coworkers to know that his dad is checking up on him." Although the last was said lightly, Cole still didn't sound as if this was a casual call to "check up on his son."

"Hold on, boss." With that, the captain put Cole on hold and used the intercom to summon the cadet to his office.

Larry Cole hung up the telephone after talking to his son. He was in their apartment overlooking Grant Park and the Chicago lakefront. For a moment he glanced out his living room windows at the scene below with the rows of streetlamps on Lake Shore Drive and the flood-lit splendor of Museum Park in the distance. But the Windy City's nocturnal beauty was lost on Cole. All he could think about was Butch and his relationship with Morgana DeWitt.

Cole crossed the living room to the bar. He picked up a bottle of cognac, poured two fingers into a brandy snifter, and then set the glass down on top of the bar. He decided that he actually hadn't wanted a drink to begin with. Leaving the glass, Cole sat down on the couch. The lights in the living room were off, but he was too distracted to turn them on. He had faced problems many times before in his life. In fact, he had faced numerous crime problems of a horrendous nature, such as those posed by Margo and Neil DeWitt. But this was the first time he'd ever faced a problem originating from his son.

Butch Cole was an only child. He had never caused his mother or his father the slightest bit of trouble. After Margo DeWitt had kidnapped Butch, Cole's ex-wife had become so distraught that their son might face danger from his father's enemies that she had divorced Cole and moved to Detroit. Those had been frustrating, lonely years for Larry Cole Sr., because he'd been forced to stand by in silence while his family broke up. Then Butch had reached young adulthood and decided he wanted to live with his father. Everything had proceeded without a hitch from that point until now.

Cole had been staring out the window for some time. He realized that as a parent he was securely impaled on the horns of a dilemma. How was he going to handle this conflict between what he wanted and what Butch apparently wanted? Having spent most of his life as a cop, Cole realized that he had a tendency to be autocratic; however, his son was not a criminal, and he was not going to be treated like one. Over the years, Cole had watched Blackie raise two children: Maureen and Bobbie, who had both come out very well. And Cole couldn't recall a single instance in which Blackie had raised his voice to his children. So Larry Cole Sr. and Larry Cole Jr. would have to work this out between them like two adult males. The senior Cole had asked his son to come home straight from work so that they could talk. Butch had replied that he had to run a brief errand first and then he would be there. Cole had noticed a wariness in Butch's voice that had never been present before. At least not when he was talking to his father. Cole vowed that he would not let Morgana DeWitt or anyone else drive a wedge between him and his son. Somehow he and Butch were going to work this out.

Morgana laid out cheese, fruit, and a bottle of fruit-flavored mineral water on the dining room table of her brownstone. This was going to be Butch's after-work snack. She didn't particularly care for his nickname. The sound it made when spoken out loud reminded her of someone calling a dog. Morgana was not an animal person. As far as the name went, she didn't like Larry Cole Jr. either. She preferred the more formal Lawrence. Actually, she would rather use the French pronunciation of Laurence. She planned to wait awhile before making her thoughts on the matter known to him. When he got used to driving the BMW, she would begin occasionally referring to him as Laurence. Of course, she would never admit that she didn't like his name. To do so might make him think of her as a conniving, manipulative female.

Satisfied that her preparations for his meal were in readiness, she checked her watch. On cue, the chime sounded, indicating that the garage door had just been opened. With a smile, Morgana went to greet Laurence.

She bounded down the rear steps and entered the stone-floored room to find him getting out of the red roadster, which was dripping with moisture from the still-falling rain. She walked toward him shivering as a cold gust of air blew in from outside—he had not activated the remote door-closing mechanism. She caught a glimpse of his face in the overhead lights and could instantly detect there was something bothering him. She had just stepped around the front of the BMW when three masked figures ran into the garage from the alley. From the orange-and-black jackets they wore, signifying them as gang members, to the black knit ski masks obscuring their features, she could tell they were trouble.

The intruders moved quickly, with the two largest of the trio rushing Butch and the smaller one heading toward Morgana. This last one brandished a nine-millimeter handgun, and she could tell by the build and gait that it was a female.

"Freeze right there, bitch!" the gun-wielding intruder screamed.

Butch Cole became aware of the intruders' presence just as the two males reached him. The pair shoved him roughly against the garage wall, and one of them swung a fist at his head. He saw the intended blow coming and ducked the punch, but the other one followed up with another swing that landed hard against his left temple. He was stunned, and before he could recover, the masked pair began methodically raining blow after blow on his head and torso. Fighting to remain conscious under the vicious onslaught, Butch tried to defend himself, but he was now having trouble making his arms and legs work. Then, just an instant before he lost consciousness and fell to the floor, he heard a gunshot, which seemed to come from a great distance. Then he passed out.

Judy Daniels, her hair in a boyish brush cut and her eyebrows and eyelashes lined with heavy mascara, was the first member of the chief of detectives' staff to arrive at the North Sheridan Road garage crime scene. Wearing a black hooded raincoat with her badge clipped to a chain around her neck, she was cleared by the officers manning the wooden barricades at the alley entrance. She then ran down the alley to Morgana DeWitt's garage.

The area was clogged with marked and unmarked police cars and a Chicago Fire Department ambulance. Judy found the overhead garage door still open with the interior cordoned off with yellow barrier tape. A smattering of detectives and crime lab technicians was huddled beneath the narrow garage overhang, attempting to take advantage of the sparse protection from the elements, as freezing rain was falling steadily. In the dim available light, the waterlogged cops appeared particularly grim. Then Judy's blood ran cold when she looked inside the garage and spied the two bodies covered with rubber sheets lying on the bloodstained cement floor. The blood perfectly matched the red of the snazzy BMW parked there.

"Are you Sergeant Daniels?"

She turned to find Captain Michael Zefeldt from the crime lab standing in the alley, his thinning hair plastered to his head by the rain.

"Yes, I am," she responded.

"Chief Cole's son is in the ambulance with Miss DeWitt," he explained. "The kid's got a few bumps and bruises, but for the most part, he's fine. Miss Dewitt has a superficial cut on her hand that didn't require any stitches."

Judy glanced back at the bodies on the garage floor. The captain explained, "There were three offenders. Two males and a female who have all been identified as members of the Insane Popes gang from the north side. They were wearing ski masks and apparently tried to mug the chief's son and Miss DeWitt. The female gangbanger was carrying a nine-millimeter automatic pistol."

Judy frowned. "But how did—?"

Captain Zefeldt sneezed before managing to say with a shrug, "Morgana DeWitt took the gun away from the female offender while the two men were fighting with Cadet Cole. She shot all three of them. The two males were dead when the first police unit got here. The woman was still alive, but just barely. They took her to Northwestern Memorial, but her chances are not good."

Due to a combination of the elements and what she had just heard, Judy shivered. She then thanked the captain for what he had just told her and went to the fire department ambulance to check on Butch.

Having spent three combat tours in Vietnam, Franklin Butler seldom exhibited signs of external stress. Being a very demanding individual by nature and a professional soldier by training, he was capable of generating a pronounced degree of controlled fury when expressing his displeasure. But when he learned that Morgana DeWitt had been attacked on her own property by a trio of armed thugs, Butler's cool, controlled demeanor deserted him.

"Where in the hell were Gaskew and Goolsby?" he shouted into the telephone in his office. He listened briefly before interrupting the DeWitt Corporation security chief. "They are professionals. They weren't supposed to allow her to give them the slip."

A few minutes later, his Lincoln limousine was speeding through the wind- and rain-swept streets of Chicago en route to Northwestern Hospital. He was attempting in vain to contact Susanne York on his cell phone. Finally, when they were less than five minutes away from the hospital, Butler snapped the instrument shut and leaned back against the soft leather cushions. He took a deep breath and willed himself to relax. This was either a major snafu on the part of his people or it was something else altogether.

By the time his chauffeur pulled into the hospital driveway, Butler had a theory as to what had occurred and why. And he didn't like what he had come up with.

Franklin Butler entered the hospital and officiously bullied his way into the area of the emergency room where Morgana DeWitt was being treated for what had been described to him as a "minor laceration to her right hand." The lawyer was aggressively searching for his client in the individual treatment rooms when he came face-to-face with Lieutenant Blackie Silvestri.

"Good evening, Counselor," Blackie said. "Looking for your client?"

Butler stood toe-to-toe with the cop. "Although that is none of your business, yes, I am."

"I wouldn't be so sure about it being none of my business," Blackie said coldly. "She did manage to kill three people tonight."

"My understanding is that she did so not only in defense of herself, but also your boss's son," Butler countered.

"So I hear. But before she goes anywhere tonight, State's Attorney Kim Wong is going to want to talk to her."

"Then I arrived just in the nick of time, didn't I, Silvestri?"

They borrowed a conference room on the main floor of the hospital adjacent to the emergency treatment area. Chief Larry Cole made the decision to keep everything within the self-contained confines of the hospital as opposed to transferring the investigation to Area Three Detective Division headquarters. He did so for two reasons: One was to ease the media impact that would develop when Morgana DeWitt's name was mentioned in connection with a triple homicide; the other was because Cole wanted to protect his son as much as he could. However, as the official types, led by him and Cook County State's Attorney Kim Wong, who had been the prosecutor at Morgana's murder trial, filed into the carpeted conference room, Cole realized there was no way he could minimize Butch's involvement in such a high-profile case.

The room was set up with a raised speaker's platform at one end on which was arranged a table and four chairs. The beige walls were lined with vinyl chairs equipped with aluminum legs. Besides the chief of detectives and the state's attorney's presence, there was also Blackie Silvestri, Judy Daniels—still dripping water from her visit to the Sheridan Road garage crime scene—and two detectives from Area Three Violent Crimes. The group pulled up chairs and arranged them in a haphazard semicircle in front of the platform. They had been waiting less than a minute when the corridor door opened and Morgana DeWitt, the webbing of her right hand covered with gauze and a couple of thin strips of white surgical tape, came in. Franklin Butler accompanied her. As they proceeded to the raised platform and took seats, Cole rose and left the conference room. A moment later, he returned with his son, who was still wearing his police cadet uniform.

Other than a bruised left cheek that was beginning to turn a deep shade of purple, and a swollen lower lip, Butch didn't look too bad. But it was obvious to those who knew him that he was tense and emotionally overwrought. When he took a seat in the chair that his father motioned him to, the cadet put his head down and stared at the floor.

When Butch entered, Morgana started to rise and go over to him, but Franklin Butler placed a hand on her arm and gently restrained her. This and whatever he whispered in her ear made her return to her seat without protest.

Once everyone was settled, Kim Wong stood up and addressed Morgana DeWitt. "I have already met you and your client, Mr. Butler," she said.

Butler merely nodded, while Morgana did not acknowledge the state's attorney's presence at all.

Kim Wong continued. "This inquiry is required by law to ascertain the circumstances surrounding the shooting that occurred earlier tonight. Because of the anticipated publicity, the state's attorney's office, in conjunction with the Chicago Police Department—" She paused to nod in the direction of the police officers present. "—have decided to conduct that inquiry here at the hospital as opposed to having it take place in a police facility. At least at the present time. I hope that is acceptable."

Butler cleared his throat before saying. "As there is no court reporter present, I assume that what we discuss here will be off the record."

"Actually, it will be part of the official investigation conducted by the Area Three Detective Division," Cole said. "These detectives will take notes on this phase of the investigation for inclusion in their report."

The pair of Area Three detectives present pulled notebooks from their pockets and stood by attentively, waiting to take notes.

"Then my client's responses will be summarized?" Butler said.

"As accurately as we possibly can make them," Cole responded.

Butler snorted by way of reply.

The pleasantries over, Kim Wong began her interview. "If I may, I'd like to begin with you, Ms. DeWitt."

Morgana stared straight ahead without acknowledging the state's attorney or anyone else in the room with the exception of an occasional glance in Butch Cole's direction.

"Could you tell us what occurred this evening?" Kim Wong asked.

Before Morgana could respond, Butler said, "I would like to stipulate for our 'summarized' record that my client is aware of her rights and that she is being currently advised by counsel."

"Whatever you say," Kim Wong said.

After a brief hesitation, Morgana began to speak.

"I had prepared an after-work snack for Lawrence when I heard him drive into the garage. I went down to greet him and was just entering the garage when three people wearing masks rushed in. Two of them, who I am certain were males, attacked Lawrence, while the woman accosted me with a semiautomatic handgun. It was quite obvious that the men were planning to seriously injure Lawrence by the way they were beating him and with the woman pointing the gun at me, I felt that I had to do something."

At that moment, the young billionairess paused. Something about her suddenly changed. She had become visibly harder, colder, and in the blink of an eye, infinitely more dangerous. Then she concluded her statement with, "So I took the gun away from the woman and killed all three of the intruders." Then add softly, shyly: "In Paris, I was privately tutored in small arms and tae kwon do. I have a black belt."

Cole studied Morgana a long hard minute with narrowing eyes. *What the hell is my son getting into?* he wondered bleakly.

19

B ecause there was a chance that Butch Cole had sustained a concussion, he was admitted to Northwestern Hospital for overnight observation. He was given a private room, a gown, coarse terry cloth robe, and a bag of toiletries. The bruising was discovered to be a great deal more extensive than was thought during the original emergency room examination, and when he removed his uniform shirt, there were ugly blotches covering his torso from the waist up. Throughout the admittance procedure and settling him in his room, his father was at his side. However, there was an odd silence hanging over the two men.

Cole carried the toiletry bag and robe from the nurse's station to the room. Setting it down on the night table, he began unpacking the items inside.

"I'll do that, Dad," Butch said.

"Sure thing." Cole stepped back. For a moment, he stood there not knowing quite what to do next.

"I'm going to change out of my uniform and brush my teeth," Butch said, picking up the bag and retreating into the bathroom.

Cole stood alone in the room for a time before crossing to the window and looking down at the streets below. He couldn't shake the feeling that he had somehow failed his son. Of course, he would have to tell Lisa what had happened. She wouldn't like it and would probably become a bit hysterical. But Butch was no longer a child, and he had made his choice of occupation on his own. Cole also realized that Butch had made more than just the decision as to his choice of job.

Butch came out of the washroom all scrubbed and ready for bed, which made his facial bruises stand out in sharper contrast. Cole forced himself not to stare at the injuries.

Seeming to sense what was on his father's mind, Butch said, "They're a lot worse looking than they feel." Despite himself, he winced at the pain.

"You'll heal quickly enough."

Butch sat down on the edge of the bed.

"Don't you want to get under the covers?" Cole asked.

Butch merely shook his head by way of reply.

Cole hesitated a moment before saying, "You want to talk about what happened tonight?"

Butch shrugged.

"Do you know why those three people attacked you and Morgana?"

Before answering, Butch emitted a deep sigh. "She's rich, Dad. Maybe they figured that she was an easy mark and I just got in the way."

"We were able to identify them. The woman with the gun was Connie Ramirez, aged twenty-six. Her two male companions were Joey Pressman, twenty-five, and Kyle Shannon, twenty-two. They're members of the Insane Popes street gang, and each of them has a criminal record for minor street crime. The Popes are not much of a criminal organization to speak of, but they do have connections to a few right-wing white power groups around the Midwest. The gang engages in a little low-level street dope peddling and lightweight extortion on the near northside. Primarily, the Insane Popes and the three deceased muggers are no more than a bunch of street punks going nowhere fast."

Throughout Cole's narration, Butch kept his head down.

Cole forged on. "The two who attacked you were bad actors, but they're definitely small time. What I'm saying is that I don't believe they were smart enough to attempt a robbery up on north Sheridan Road."

A tear rolled down Butch Cole's face and dropped onto the floor.

"Butch?" Cole stepped forward and placed a hand on his son's shoulder.

The young man turned his battered face up to look at his father. "I'm sorry, Dad."

Confused, Cole said, "Sorry for what?"

"Letting you down tonight. I should have been more of a man. Not let those two punks beat me up. If it hadn't been for Morgana—" Then his words were choked off by emotion.

Cole put his arms around his son and held him tightly. Now there were also tears in the chief of detectives' eyes. Father and son remained in that position for a very long time.

Pending a formal inquest, Morgana DeWitt was released without charges. The billionairess was given a ride back to her brownstone in Franklin Butler's limo.

"Don't you think it would be better if you spent the night at De-Witt Plaza?" the attorney asked.

The young woman was sitting back against the rear seat, staring at the passing street scenes of the Windy City. She appeared relaxed to the point of serenity. She responded, "Why? So that you can provide me with better protection?"

"That's really not fair, Morgana," Butler said stiffly. "I assigned twenty-four-hour security, and you did all that you could to make their jobs impossible."

"That wasn't difficult, because they are so incompetent. However, Susanne York is quite formidable. It is quite a task for me to elude her. By the way, where was she tonight?"

"I'm certainly going to find out," Butler said.

"And while you're at it, I want to know everything that you can about the thugs that attacked Lawrence and me. We were not, as Ms. Wong from the state's attorney's office implicated back at the hospital, mere targets of random street violence."

The Lincoln pulled up in front of Morgana's town house. Before the chauffeur could get around to open the back door, Morgana had bounded out and was standing on the sidewalk. She looked back inside the limousine and said, "I want that information as soon as you can get it for me, Mr. Butler. Especially the whereabouts of Ms. York."

Before he could respond, she turned her back and ran up the steps to the front entrance and vanished inside.

Butler stared at the expensive brownstone for a long time. He planned to indeed carry out his employer's orders and find out what had occurred here tonight—and why. He also planned to make sure all possible obstacles to his original plan were minimized from this point on.

. . .

The late supper Morgana had prepared for Lawrence had to be thrown out. She carted everything from the dining room into the stainless steel kitchen and dumped the food into the garbage disposal before placing the dishes in the dishwasher. Then she went down to the garage.

The red BMW was still parked in the same spot where Lawrence had parked it before the attack. The garage door leading to the alley was closed. The bodies had been carted away, but there were still a few telltale bloodstains visible on the cement floor. The police had left the place untidy. Not necessarily messy, but not in the pristine condition she preferred. For a moment, Morgana stood in front of the BMW in the exact same spot she was when the three intruders charged into the garage. She briefly relived the event with all its violence and fury. And in that instance, she realized something: She had enjoyed a tremendous sensual rush during those seconds it had taken to kill the three attackers. She also realized that there had not been even the slightest vestige of fear or hesitation in her being. She had viewed the masked thugs as merely things with no more humanity than pop-up targets on a carnival shooting range or the images of electronic video airplanes on an arcade video game screen. When it was all over, she had experienced a definite letdown, because the moment of exhilaration had been all too brief. Perhaps Morgana had indeed inherited some traits from her infamous parents, Margo and Neil DeWitt.

She quickly pushed the memory of her parents from her mind as she did each time she thought of them. She went to bed at 1 A.M. That night she had the first of a series of dreams that verged on nightmares. In each of them, Morgana and Lawrence were attending a circus. A strange and terrifying circus.

PART 3

"Psycho Circus!
"Welcome to the biggest, most exciting, most electrifying
extravaganza-extraordinaire in the world—the
greatest sado-erotic show on earth! Welcome to . . .
"Psycho Circus!!!"
—*Susanne York*

20

November 6, 2006
6:56 P.M.

I t was overcast but dry as the Lincoln Town Car—carrying DeWitt Plaza security specialists Goolsby and Gaskew—sped out of Chicago into the Wisconsin countryside. Dressed in dark pin-striped suits, white Brooks Brothers button-down shirts, and conservative ties, the two men looked like Wall Street bankers. Granted, they had unnaturally broad shoulders for bankers, and their thick blocklike arms stretched the fabric of their coat sleeves. Goolsby—a large-frame, perpetually scowling black man—appeared to have had his nose broken four or five times, and his bullet head was clean shaven. Gaskew's high wide cheekbones and lantern jaw—if one looked closely—evinced major reconstructive surgery, and a long jagged scar traversed the side of his head beneath his neatly trimmed blond hair. Both men looked weathered and hard-used, and the armpits of their suits—despite some compensatory tailoring—bulged ominously. Nor did they appear particularly happy in their current assignment. The two ex–Special Forces—despite the high wages paid them by Franklin Butler—were bored with what they considered the meaningless mission Butler had sent them on.

They were to locate and kill Susanne York.

"This will turn out to be another waste of time," Goolsby grumbled.

"The target may be hiding out there."

"What do you want to do afterwards?"

"I don't know," Gaskew said. "By the time we finish, it'll be what? Nine thirty, ten P.M.?"

"Then what will we do?"

"How many years did you spend in the military?" Gaskew asked. "Instead of rushing into things, let's take the rest of the night and the next day off. We'll tell Butler we're following a slim lead in Milwaukee. We'll kick back and enjoy ourselves."

Goolsby didn't respond right away. For a moment it appeared as if he was going to berate Gaskew over this goldbricking. But he smiled and said, "You got a point. The Chicago cops don't know about this circus farm. The only connection it has with the York woman is that the tiger used in the play was rented from this wild animal circus farm. Slim chance she'd be hanging around up in Cheese Land, though. I still say it's a waste of time."

"So we'll take the next day off."

The wild animal farm was not easy to find. As it was well off the main highway from Chicago, twice the two security specialists had to stop and ask directions at local service stations. Only after an interminable trip down a gravel road did they finally come to a gate set in a tall rusting barbwire fence. They had to break the gate's lock with a tire iron, and the only suggestion of a road was the ruts left by the animal trailers. Fields of cornstalks surrounded them on all sides.

"Something tells me the owners don't want this place found," Goolsby said.

"No shit."

"You trust that road?" Goolsby asked.

"We'll take it slow."

Despite their caution, they scraped the underside five times. Once they got stuck. Goolsby had to push, while Gaskew rocked the big car back and forth to free it. At the end of the ghost road, around a sharp turn stood a stand of trees. Beyond the trees and cornfields loomed a faded brown circus tent, in front of which, in red and white script, an equally faded sign read:

BEWARE OF WILD ANIMALS! INTRUDERS WILL BE EATEN!

"According to Franklin's information," Gaskew said, "the owner, Doc Matson, fell on hard times, sold off most of his assets, and died. The absentee owners board wild animals from traveling circuses and zoos. Most of the time, Butler said, the only caretakers are illegal aliens—Mexicans, primarily. Hardly a lucrative business."

"Who are the absentee owners?"

"Who else? DeWitt, Inc."

"What?"

"Franklin told me that while he was in New York fighting a takeover battle with Cantrell, Susanne York bought the whole show. When Franklin returned, he discovered the company owned a circus farm. Said it was the only thing she'd ever done without his permission, so he let it slide. For a while."

"But no more."

"No more."

"You didn't say why she bought it."

"She's not very tightly wrapped."

"Which is why we're here."

"Franklin's got a thing about loose lips and loose ends."

In front of the big round circus tent stood three Latino workers in dirty Levi's and ripped T-shirts. They had long straggly hair, short scruffy beards, and disastrous dental work.

"These people are illegal aliens," Gaskew said. "We should get over on them no problemo. Let me handle it. I speak some Spanish."

"Go head-on, boss."

"Who's in charge here?" Gaskew bellowed. He repeated the question in Spanish.

The workers tensed, but none of them looked at the two men.

Becoming more aggressive, Gaskew approached the oldest of the workers. "*Qué pasa, amigo?* Who's *el jefe* around here?" The boss.

The man's fists tightened. Worn and seamed, his face was brown as old saddle leather, but his eyes were fearful. He finally nodded toward the tent.

"*Gracias.*"

As they approached the tent's entrance, Gaskew noticed that the tent was far larger than it had appeared. Ignoring the sign, he pulled open the tent flap and entered.

A blast of warm air, reeking of excrement, hit him full force, and Gaskew felt sick. He looked over his shoulder and considered going back outside. He noticed the workers had stopped working and stared at them.

Again, Gaskew considered leaving the tent—and not coming back. He suddenly had very bad vibes about this job, and he hated to ignore his instincts. Nonetheless, he led Goolsby into the big tent. The interior was so poorly lit, he couldn't make out much detail. At last, they reached the main ring.

"Get your piece out, Goolsby. I don't like this."

"I'll affirm that."

They were starting to pull their TEK9 machine pistols out of their shoulder rigs when Gaskew heard a stirring behind them and what sounded like heavy . . . *purring*. A woman was walking toward them. Gaskew could barely make her out in the murky gloom. Still, he had an eye for beautiful women and knew even in the dark she was stunning. Decked out in black circus tights and a black revealing halter top, she was less than a dozen paces away.

Unfortunately, the lion pair flanking her was frighteningly visible . . . even in the Stygian gloom.

The great cats were more frightening when they charged.

Gaskew's last thought was that he had never seen animals that big move that quickly. . . .

Chief of Detectives Larry Cole was approaching State and Rush Streets when the police dispatcher directed a CSI unit to Susanne York's apartment near the Towers. After issuing her address, the dispatcher reported over the radio:

The perpetrator incinerated the victim and half of her apartment with an incendiary device—apparently a thermite bomb. We've asked the firemen not to destroy our crime scene. Try to get there on the double.

Recognizing the name of the victim—Susanne York, Franklin's executive assistant—Chief Cole pulled a U-turn on Rush Street and turned on his siren and flasher. Since Susanne worked for Franklin at DeWitt, Inc., she was, in effect, an associate of Morgana's, and people had a bad habit of dying around Morgana.

Cole pulled into a parking space across from Morgana's apartment building just as the bomb squad pulled out, leaving the scene with their own lights blazing and sirens blaring. *Where are they racing off to?* Cole wondered.

When Cole reached Susanne's apartment, he immediately recognized several of the CSI officers by name, rank, and face. Still he ID'ed himself, badging his black pin-stripe suit before entering Susanne's apartment.

Having gone in with the firemen, the bomb guys had already cleared the apartment for booby traps and left.

"Where did the bomb squad run off to?" Cole asked a rookie, a red-haired freckle-faced kid who didn't look old enough to vote or drink.

"They got called to a multiple homicide on the South Side. Some militiamen blew up most of a house."

"They cleared the crime scene here too quickly," Cole said to the kid.

"They were ordered away and didn't have much choice. That house bombing was pretty bad. We're keeping it off the radio until the bomb guys clear it. They have every bomb squad in the city working it."

Cole shrugged and looked away, scrutinizing the smoke-filled apartment.

Even so, he tried to read all murder scenes the same. He tried to look and listen to what the body and its surrounding scene said to him. He tried to see and hear and smell it the way those who preceded him in the case saw and heard it—the people who discovered the body, the uniformed cops whom they summoned first, the friends and relatives who knew the deceased before he or she was killed, the forensic tech who got to the scene before Cole and saw it while it was new and fresh. Cole tried to see beyond the myriad details, put them all together, find the unifying thread, and glimpse the greater whole.

He tried never to start with a preconceived perpetrator, then cherry-pick details to support his belief . . . to indict and convict according to his prejudiced opinion. He wanted the Crime Scene to tell him the truth—the way it was.

In this case, thirty-plus years of crime scene experience told him Morgana was the killer, but would the crime scene say she was. . . .

The rest of the Crime Scene Investigation was just getting under way, and the work wasn't pretty. Everything in the apartment—walls, ceilings, furniture, carpeting, drapes, wall pictures—was befouled by smoke. White-clad investigators with white-masked faces and white latex gloves examined the carpeting for hair, blood, skin, saliva, fingernails—anything with DNA in it. Others searched for shell casings and powder signatures. Despite the smoke and soot, other investigators looked for fingerprints. Sketch artists sketched, while photographers armed with still cameras and camcorders surveyed the interior, having just finished up with the murder scene.

The thing that got to Cole, however—that always got to Cole at such scenes—was the stench of the burnt victim.

His physical reaction to the smell of burnt flesh went back to Vietnam—to the first time he had searched an NVA underground bunker after Phantom jets had razed it with napalm. By the end of his tour, he had rooted through enough burned-out VC and North Vietnamese bunkers and tunnels and smelled enough charred flesh to last him a hundred lifetimes. For the first five years he was back in the States, he could not look at barbecued food.

He'd hated the stench then; he hated it now. . . .

Pulling a black bandanna out of his hip pocket, he covered his nose and mouth and waited till his stomach settled. Wiping the smoke-sting out of his eyes, he headed toward the murder scene— Susanne's bathroom.

Christ, it *was* Vietnam all over again—as if all the burn fatalities of that whole bloody war were in front of him, rolled into one, concentrated in Susanne's thermite-blasted bathtub—there in her sad fire-scorched remains, burned and blackened beyond recognition.

Again, Cole pulled out the black bandanna, fearing he would lose his lunch in the soot-covered toilet.

Howard Barry—a tall rawboned captain with a master's in forensic science—joined Cole in the bathroom. He was wearing a white crime scene mask and gloves and handed a mask to Cole. It didn't help the smell.

"Someone gave her a thermite bath," Barry said. "They put her in the tub and torched her to hell and gone. She probably got to watch, knowing what was coming, the poor kid."

"How do you know they didn't sneak in and burn her?"

"No water in the tub or steam vapor on the ceiling and walls. Also a tub full of water would have retarded the conflagration, and she was completely incinerated."

"Maybe she hadn't turned the water on yet."

"How many people you know climb into dry tubs, then turn on the water?"

Cole nodded. "Point taken." Leaning over the charcoaled remains, he tried to discern facial features. Nothing.

"The sides of the tub and the close confines of the bathroom held in the heat. The thermite not only charred the flesh but the teeth and bones beneath. It pretty near disintegrated her. The lab guys could spend months trying to officially ID this one. They might never do it—not forensically."

"Don't forget to dig down into the bathtub drain," Cole said.

"We'll check it. The blast might have blown some intact tissue samples down there."

"I'd get another bomb squad in here and have them check that body and drain for booby traps. Her killer could have more thermite tamped down in that drain and rigged to blow. We're dealing with a psycho."

"The bomb guys checked and cleared it already. Hell, they went in with the firemen. They always go in first. They radioed back their all-clear while we were still in the car."

"They still ought to be here. I'd call them back and make someone from their department clear it in person. I don't like this clear-and-run stuff. That kind of corner-cutting gets people killed."

"You don't trust anyone, do you, Cole?" Barry said with a hint of a grin.

"The killer is obsessed with booby traps and loves setting them off. Make the bomb boys turn that body over and probe the drain."

"They checked it out. I'll show you right now, you don't believe me."

"Not while I'm around."

Cole waved to the CSI people on the way out. He was in his car and heading toward Rush Street when the second thermite bomb detonated in the already flame-blackened bathroom.

That night Chief Larry Cole sat in the backseat of a black-and-white police car with his son, Butch. Two uniforms were in the front. A Hispanic officer Cole knew only as Sanchez drove. His partner, Henry Monroe, was also black—also a fellow Vietnam vet and a thirty-year veteran on the force. All four cops, including Butch, wore bulletproof vests. They were entering the door of a murder suspect—a woman suspected of killing people with booby-trapped firebombs. That the door was at a fancy address didn't mean much to Chief Cole. He'd learned long ago that a wealthy socialite could kill you just as dead as an impoverished sociopath.

The DeWitts had taught him that. They'd once even kidnapped Butch, and he was now dealing with their legacy.

Cole's son knew Morgana better than any of them, so he was accompanying them to her palatial penthouse apartment on Lake Shore Drive. Despite the lavish digs—in Cole's mind—she was still a murder suspect.

Not much rattled the chief after thirty-plus years in the Chicago PD. His son's choice in women, however, had gotten under his skin.

"Give us a moment of privacy, boys."

Henry Monroe rolled up the bulletproof glass separating himself and Butch from the front seat.

"I should have dragged that asshole captain out of the bathroom by the scruff of the neck," Cole said to his son.

"It was his crime scene, Dad. If you'd ordered him around without proper authority and you were wrong, he could have filed a grievance against you."

"It wouldn't have been the first."

"Or the last. How did the bomb squad miss the thermite under the body?"

"The bomb wasn't under the body—which was what I tried to warn the chief about. It was stuffed under . . . the bathtub plug. I saw that happen once in Nam. The VC used C 4 instead of thermite, and when some guys lifted the drain plug, they got blown to pieces. Our killer did the same thing here. When the bomb squad looked under the body and didn't find it, they considered the crime scene safe. Meanwhile, the thermite bomb was still there."

"Under the drain stopper."

"Right. The bomb was spring-loaded, the bomb's pin chained to the stopper's bottom. Some CSI guy pulled the plug after they removed Susanne's remains. When he pulled the pin, the bomb blew."

"Just like a grenade?"

"A thermite-grenade that took out two CSI men."

"What's that got to do with Morgana?"

"We got an anonymous phone tip that Morgana fire-bombed Susanne's apartment then rigged the drain bomb. We got the call before the drain bomb was made public."

At first, Butch was speechless with shock. *This can't be happen-*

ing, he said to himself. *Not Morgana. This has to be a bad dream.* "Dad, the killer could be framing her."

"Or someone fears her. Look, son, whoever did this has presumably been on a crime spree—and killed a lot of people."

"It's not her style."

"She and Susanne didn't get along."

"So she also killed the two CSI people?"

"Maybe she wanted to make it look like a deranged psycho—not a well-mannered young woman."

"It's not her, Dad."

"She *is* capable of murder, Butch. She proved that at the play when she tried to kill Perfido. She would have succeeded if she'd been quicker on the trigger and a better shot."

"She had all the reason in the world to kill him."

"And she tried."

Butch stared out the window in silence.

"Butch, I respect the fact that you like Morgana. Maybe you even think you love her. But you respect the fact that you're a pro, and pros don't shoot from the hip in their judgments or take anything for granted. The graveyards teem with people who trusted the wrong man and loved the wrong woman."

Butch remained silent. He understood his father wanted the best for him, and he wanted to remain objective but doubted very much that he could.

But then the chief didn't *know* Morgana.

Franklin sat at his massive mahogany desk, staring down at Rhonda Oliveri seated across from him—the woman the temp firm had sent to replace Susanne, his deceased executive assistant. She looked like she'd been sent from central casting—central casting for the porn industry. Once more, Franklin admired her long platinum-blond hair, her black heavily mascaraed eyelashes—thick and stiff as rake prongs—her pouty collagened lips glisteningly red, enough air in her voluminous breasts to float the *Andrea Dorea* . . . and he sighed.

Rhonda was a dead ringer for . . . Marilyn Monroe.

She was also an insatiable vixen, and now Franklin could not keep his eyes off her. Again, he pondered her black six-inch stiletto spikes with matching net stockings, her red leather miniskirt with its scoop-neck top of scarlet spandex, which left over five inches of midriff exposed . . . a midriff hard and tight enough to strike kitchen matches off of.

Damn, you ought to keep her on permanently, Franklin said to himself.

Rhonda couldn't type, take shorthand, operate a computer, or even make coffee. Still, she had not disappointed him. Especially when he recalled how he'd spent the afternoon sampling her ample wares on his leather couch.

"I don't know much about office work."

She'd then unceremoniously shaken three ounces of cocaine out of a sterling silver talcum-powder flask—with the letters RO lavishly engraved on it in ornate Gothic script—across his mahogany desk. Removing a two-inch sterling silver straw from her shoulder bag, she helped herself to two long-winded snorts of pure Bolivian marching powder, one in each nostril.

"Would you care to imbibe?" she'd asked in that same eager Marilyn Monroe squeal. Giving him a sultry come-hither Marilyn pout, she handed him the silver straw.

Damn, he'd never snorted so much coke so fast in his life.

He was in all kinds of arousal for the next three hours. He'd spent those hours with Rhonda on the leather couch—with the door bolted and the phone turned off—locked in the throes of hell-fired fornication . . . as well as a few other kinds of hell-fired ecstasy.

Remembering some of their more perverse activities ignited a sudden flash of fear in Franklin. His wife had put divorce detectives on him in the past. Rhonda couldn't be in her employ, could she? No way, he decided—not with all the coke she snorted. She carried enough blow in her bag to get her ten years in the joint—minimum. No reputable detective operated like that, and his wife would definitely hire reputable detectives.

And no detective could fuck like that, for sure.

In truth, he did not care. Rhonda was the hottest, wildest, strongest, and most of all, kinkiest fuck he'd ever had. He wasn't letting that one go, and he wasn't letting his wife and her threats to expose his chicanery and steal their kids ruin it.

Four times! Four times Rhonda had made him come—and gotten him high!

God, Rhonda was hot!

What *had* her previous employment been . . . ?

In fact, he now had difficulty looking Rhonda in the eye. He'd never met a woman like her. She stared at him with a look of utter omniscience, as if she knew *everything* about him . . . things about him he would never know . . . as if she'd peered into his soul. Her cockiness turned him on—and at the same time . . . frightened him. Which was bizarre. Franklin specialized in menace—it was an art he cultivated—and he was brilliant at intimidating clients and employees. But not her. With her, he could barely maintain eye contact.

Probably the coke—a few of those unmentionable things we did.

Most clients who sat before him were terribly intimidated—often afraid. Of course, they did not understand that he had mounted his desk and chair on a carefully concealed platform that allowed him to look down on his visitors. The added height and the downward cast of his menacing stare enhanced his sense of personal power. Nor was the effect illusory. Franklin was what he often appeared to be—a dangerous feral animal. Today his features were more ferocious than usual.

"Someone calling himself Chief Cole says that he needs you to ID Susanne's body," Rhonda said.

"You said when you called CSI to confirm Susanne's death, they claimed she was burned beyond recognition."

"That's what they told me."

"Then how can I ID her?"

Rhonda shrugged. "Chief Cole said he wants you there."

"I think I need a lawyer. It doesn't make sense."

"You are a lawyer."

Franklin stared up at the ceiling. Jesus, four times in three hours he'd made it with her, and every time he stared into those sinfully seductive eyes, he felt desire well up in him like a volcano in hell. Luckily, he had her cell phone number. Maybe he'd call her later, take her out for dinner, then bring her back for some . . . *dick*-to-phone. The woman was a witch—no doubt about it. Too bad he had to deal with that asshole Cole first. Better get that meeting out of the way, he decided. No percentage in pissing off the cops.

He struggled to clear his head. Susanne was dead, and God knew who did it to her or why. He had to have his wits about him.

Again, he looked at Rhonda's legs and cleavage. His brain lost another fifty IQ points.

Stop thinking about your dick, he muttered to himself.

"Killing Susanne makes no sense," Franklin said, leaning back, trying not to stare at her prurient appendages. "That cold-hearted bitch was a natural-born killer, not a murder victim. If I'd thought I could get away with it, I'd have killed her myself."

"Chief Cole still wants you to come down. He was quite insistent."

"I better find out what he wants."

Franklin took his private elevator to the underground garage's third floor, where he parked his silver Ferrari convertible in his reserved space, three down from the elevator. That he paid more for that space than many people paid for each month for their apartments was an irony that always pleased and amused Franklin. As he climbed in behind the wheel and shut the door, he saw what he assumed to be the garage attendant approaching him from his blind spot. Turning his head, he started to say, "About the ding on the left rear bumper last week—"

He never got to the rest of the sentence. A woman in a black plastic raincoat—wearing a matching ski mask and gloves—pointed a pistol at his nape. The gun looked more like a *Star Wars* toy—something that fired laser beams, not bullets—than a real gun, Franklin noted with mounting apprehension.

Then a dart was thrumming in his nape.

Well, he thought, *at least it's not a lead slug or a lethal laser.*

His last thought was that the shooter looked amazingly like Rhonda. In fact, dressed in black and without the platinum wig, Rhonda looked more than a little like Susanne.

But then he'd never looked closely at any woman's face—only at their bodies.

No more of that now. Lights were exploding in that Stygian darkness surrounding him in dazzling polychromic starbursts. Popping, sizzling, sputtering, the fiery fragments faded, went out, and were gone.

Then he knew no more.

The bomb squad met Chief Larry Cole and his team at Morgana's door while several other units surrounded the outside exits.

"The manager wouldn't let you in?" Cole asked John Lee Simpson, the bomb team's leader.

A stocky Irish ex-heavyweight who was slowly going to fat, Simpson looked at Cole and shrugged. "The manager claimed maintenance lost the key."

"Seems unlikely," Cole said.

Simpson sighed. "The son of a bitch manager stays bought—you have to give him that."

"Morgana must have bribed him pretty well," Cole agreed.

"Who says it was Morgana bribed him?" Butch asked.

"You're saying whoever planted that bomb paid him," Cole said his son.

"Stands to reason."

"It does, and I'm sure he's expecting a future payment."

Morgana had not been home, and the bomb squad had entered via a lock-punch. They'd also left Morgana's living room in chaos—couch cushions slit and emptied; TVs, stereos, and air conditioners eviscerated; flowerpots turned upside down. Glancing in the bedrooms, bathroom, and kitchen, Larry Cole could see everything was turned inside out—closets, cupboards, drawers. He could also see the bomb squad had come up with nothing.

The balcony, however, told a different tale. On the floor next to an overturned, emptied-out rubber tree pot sprawled a disassembled thermite bomb. The squad had defused its detonator and ripped out its wires, which now spewed across the balcony floor like straggly squid tentacles affixed to an electronic mini-alarm and a stick of thermite.

Standing on the balcony, staring out over Lake Michigan, Butch glanced at his father.

"Something's cockeyed," Butch said. "Morgana wouldn't stash the evidence where we were sure to find it. It's the same as signing a confession."

"Why are you so positive?"

"You've had dealings with her, too. She may be many things, but she's not stupid."

"The compulsion to commit crimes is intrinsically self-destructive. Since the penalty for getting caught is prison or worse, criminals are by definition self-destructive."

"You keep assuming Morgana's a criminal."

"Which is my job and your job."

"What about her presumption of innocence?"

"Son, courts presume innocence. As cops, we presume guilt."

From the roof of the building across the street, Morgana studied the activity in her apartment. Through binoculars she'd already watched the bomb squad empty out her balcony rubber tree. She'd also watched the bomb squad carefully dig the thermite device out of the rubber tree's pot. She'd even watched the bomb boys lock it gingerly in a steel case, clear the building, then defuse and disassemble the bomb.

So the bomb squad confirmed her worst fears. She had suspected for some time that someone was setting her up. Her suspicions were based on little things—the manager's sudden inability to look her in the eye when before he couldn't stop coming on to her, flowerpots slightly out of place, too many phone calls followed by abrupt hang-ups, the unshakable feeling that people were shadowing her and staking out her building. She had tried to talk herself out of her conspiracy theories. She had tried to dismiss her suspicions as paranoid delusions. She knew now she was not paranoid and that someone was not only framing her for Susanne's murder, but they were implicating her in the killer's other bombings.

She knew who forged the best passports and driver's licenses in all of Chicago.

She also knew Chicago's finest practitioners of identity theft.

They were the same people who helped her trace, track, and confirm Banacek's true identity.

Anticipating that she might need a new identity and a quick getaway, Morgana had ditched her security detail several days before on the Marshal Fields department store escalators and elevators, then met with her forger and identity thief.

Three days later, with her fraudulent IDs in hand, she'd again lost her bodyguards—this time with a series of bewildering U-turns during the Rush Street rush hour—and headed straight to the BMW dealership. She had bought a gray BMW—under one of her new assumed names—on the spot, paying cash.

The new BMW was a different model from her old one and would be her getaway car.

She liked the BMW for its speed, handling, and for its nondescript design. In her mind, BMWs blended in with the countless cars around them, making them them hard to spot. Chicago also boasted a lot of BMWs. For upwardly mobile drivers, BMW was the car of choice.

Immediately after purchasing her new BMW—straight out of the showroom—she had driven it straight to the long-term airport parking lot, then cabbed it back to the dealership to retrieve her old BMW, which was parked on the street.

The new one would still be at O'Hare. . . .

Since Cole would soon have an all-points bulletin out on her old BMW, Morgana abandoned it in her apartment building's parking lot. Decked out in a red wig, a matching Cubs cap with the bill pulled down over her eyes, and Wayfarer sunglasses, she cabbed it to the O'Hare long-term lot, paid the driver, and got out of the taxi.

As she strolled toward her new car, Morgana thought about the woman she had hired with the help of her lavishly remunerated identity forger and thief. She had kept her on call twenty-four hours a day, and she would be catching the first available flight to Zurich, Switzerland, under Morgana's name and with her passport. From there, she would commence an all-expenses-paid whirlwind tour of the continent. The police would need time to activate their search for Morgana, and tracking the fake Morgana through all those cities and countries would eat up weeks, if not months.

Morgana slipped behind the wheel of her new BMW. Once again, she made sure that her new fake driver's license—which she had used to purchase the car—matched the registration. It did. The fake documents duplicated those of a real driver who owned the identical BMW with an identical license plate, so if Morgana was pulled over, she could survive a computer check.

To confirm the license's and registration's credibility, the forger had even hacked the police computer in front of her and run them through. They were good as gold.

She drove to her new residence—a well-appointed suite at a residential midtown hotel, which she had leased three weeks earlier, wearing her red wig, pulled-down Cubs cap, and Wayfarers, again using fake IDs, matching passports, and hard currency. She'd assiduously stocked the suite's kitchen with food, medicine, clothes, a computer, a fax machine, and a BlackBerry—none of which could be traced to Morgana. Several hundred thousand dollars in cash, ATM money cards, and credit cards—all under a variety of aliases, superbly documented by her flawlessly forged IDs—also awaited her in the suite's safe. The money and the banks accounts were all real, and the names on the new IDs matched those on the accounts. She'd also taken out safe deposit boxes under those aliases. In the boxes, she'd stashed two million dollars in twenties, fifties, and hundreds.

Again, the FBI would waste a lot of time if they tried to trace the account holders' real identities.

If necessary, Morgana could disappear for years.

Sitting down at her computer, Morgana went to work.

Morgana had never been satisfied that the assassin Carlos Perfido's appearance in Chicago in a play financed by Cantrell had come about by coincidence. In fact, she'd long suspected that Carlos had targeted her for assassination eight years long years ago, when he had killed her adopted uncle. The fact that Cantrell—who was also trying to seize the DeWitt fortune—would be behind the hit fit nicely. Cantrell probably found out that Franklin had a DeWitt heir he was going to spring on him—by which Franklin could consolidate complete control of the corporation—and so moved to eliminate the problem.

How did Cantrell find out about her? The obvious candidate to leak the information was Susanne. She was playing against everyone— and playing them against each other.

Susanne's ultimate aim would be to destroy her. Killing Carlos at the theater—with security tapes showing Morgana entering the theater—would have framed Morgana for murder and blocked Franklin from achieving complete mastery of the corporation.

Butch had spoiled their frame-up by discovering Morgana had the wrong caliber "binoculars." In fact, Butch had spoiled it by noticing Morgana in the first place.

How did Susanne know I'd end up in Chicago? Morgana wondered. That wasn't a hard question to answer. The detective who traced Carlos to Chicago had discovered someone else was doing the same thing. Also Franklin had learned who Morgana was—the DeWitt heir. Anyway the detective had reported that he'd gotten an anonymous tip—from a woman.

After Susanne found out Morgana was coming to Chicago, Susanne had laid out bread crumbs for her to follow. She might not have known Morgana planned to shoot Carlos that night, but given the time and money Morgana had put into locating Carlos, her presence in the theater—recorded on security tapes—would have been enough to make her a prime murder suspect.

Killing Cantrell and others, leaving a trail of insane homicides and police deaths, was Susanne's next game plan. . . .

So Morgana had a good idea who was setting her up now: Franklin and Susanne. Morgana wasn't sure what Susanne's ultimate motive was—or who she was, what drove her—but Franklin was clearly after her for the DeWitt corporate fortune. DeWitt, Inc., was a $50 billion corporation—which was the only reason Franklin had joined it—and Susanne had to know he was ripping it off. Even so, Morgana couldn't imagine Franklin cutting anyone in on his ill-gotten gains, not for long. He would eventually kill them. Susanne could, of course, be in on the scam with him for a time—but not for long.

Franklin had not been content with his multimillion-dollar salary, gargantuan bonuses, and lavish perks—not when billions more stared him in the eye. Morgana knew him. She'd seen him in action. He would extract, extort, borrow, leverage, scam, beg, inveigle, cajole, and steal every nickel he could get his hands on. He would liquidate De-Witt, Inc., like a cracked egg. When he finished with it, the firm wouldn't have enough left in its balance sheet for the birds to carry away. Franklin would burn it down to bedrock and sow its fields with salt, like Carthage. He would make the looting of Enron look like Sunday-go-to-meeting.

When she'd first begun investigating his DeWitt money trail, she had visited Franklin's office and installed a small video bug, which had recorded his DeWitt computer "passkey." This cyber "Open Sesame" allowed him to enter every file, document, and financial account in every department within the corporation—as well as granted him unlimited power-of-attorney to transact money transfers from those accounts.

Which he had done with abandon.

Not content with her own sleuthing, Morgana had hired a Swiss firm of financial detectives, who—armed with Franklin's personal passkey—had probed both Franklin's and Susanne's money trails. They'd hit pay dirt with Franklin. He had bled over a billion dollars from the corporation, concealing it in paper companies and black-hole accounts in a string of offshore tax havens, spanning the globe from Liechtenstein to Singapore to Johannesburg to Buenos Aires to the Cayman Islands.

And he'd stashed so much money overseas that Morgana guessed he was planning one day to leave the States for good.

The money-running and -laundering was so secretive, devious, and complex that at times Morgana caught herself admiring Franklin—at least for his energy, ingenuity, brazenness, and chutzpah. Franklin was pathologically fearless.

She had hoped that after she e-mailed the FBI her evidence on Franklin, they would teach him the meaning of fear.

Well, no time for that now.

Morgana had to worry about her own welfare.

Curiously enough, she and her detectives had found next to nothing on Susanne. Except for a small checking account and a corporate credit card, this personal assistant to one of the world's most powerful CEOs was a cipher. She was almost nonexistent—the invisible woman. After the thermite bomb had burned Susanne beyond recognition, it was as if she'd never been.

Again, Morgana probed her files. After poring over every personal transaction Susanne had made at DeWitt, Morgana noted only one oddity—a series of collect calls from a phone near or in Kenosha, Wisconsin. All the other calls were from major cities with easily recognizable area codes such as 212 or 213. Even more bizarre, Susanne had refused to accept the Kenosha calls. She had instead dialed the number up on her cell phone—immediately after each refused call.

Why? She wasn't trying to save pennies for the $50 billion firm—not with her boss robbing it blind. Perhaps Susanne worried someone at DeWitt would notice the calls. Or maybe when the FBI eventually closed in on Franklin, they would spot and trace those calls. That was it. She didn't want anyone *knowing* about the calls.

Morgana dialed up the number. After a half dozen rings, a gas station attendant in Kenosha picked up and identified himself and the phone. She'd called the gas station's roadside pay phone.

After explaining to the man that she was checking her daughter's incessant calls to that number, she asked him if he knew anyone who received frequent calls. He said no—unless her daughter was communicating with "the Mexicans out at the circus farm."

"What circus farm?" Morgana asked.

"It's actually been closed up for the last several years, except the owners do board wild animals for traveling circus acts."

With the Kenosha connection, Morgana began an Internet search of the city's public records.

Within three hours, she solved the mystery. The real Susanne York had died in a hit-and-run accident three months before Franklin's Susanne went to work for DeWitt. Franklin's Susanne had simply assumed the deceased woman's identity.

Pulling up the dead woman's picture from a Kenosha newspaper archive, she noted that Susanne bore enough of a resemblance to the deceased to actually pass for her—so much so that she wondered whether Susanne had helped the deceased into her untimely grave.

Questions buzzed through her head like angry hornets. What was Susanne hiding? Whom was she hiding from? Was it the police? What alarm bells would her real name set off?

She no longer believed Susanne was dead. The burnt body was too convenient, too coincidental. No, Susanne had disappeared again—no doubt under another assumed name. Susanne was awfully good with her makeup. Perhaps she was even sporting a new made-over face.

None of which explained why Susanne hated Morgana so much. Jealousy, love, money? None of those emotions were relevant. Morgana had never harmed Susanne.

So why did Susanne want to destroy her?

Morgana was correct: Susanne was still alive and still consumed with hatred. Her wrath, however, reached beyond Morgana. She had planned to capture Franklin as well as Morgana, then finish them both off at her leisure . . . ruthlessly . . . violently . . . sadistically.

She had always recognized that Morgana would be the more elusive of the two. Franklin, in fact, had been embarrassingly easy to snare. A little animal tranquilizer and he was putty in her hands. Morgana, on the other hand, had evaded both herself and the Chicago PD. She had gone to ground so completely, Susanne was clueless as to her whereabouts.

Vanishing without a trace was an art Susanne herself had mastered. She recognized almost immediately that traditional police methods would not locate Morgana. If she wanted to finish her off, she would have to flush her out.

She would need an irresistible lure.

Butch.

While she was still running DeWitt, Inc., with that imbecile, Franklin, she had convinced one of their computer geeks to clone Morgana's BlackBerry—insisting it was a company project. She now used that clone to send him a text message, asking him to meet her— Morgana—by the Lincoln Park Zoo parking lot at 9 P.M. Telling him to come alone, she said she had proof of her innocence.

With Butch in hand, she would have the means to settle with them all in one fell swoop.

Butch stared at Morgana's text message. He did not want to circumvent his father or the department, but he couldn't let Morgana down. Despite his father's skepticism, he still believed in her innocence. Furthermore, he knew of no department regulations that said he needed backup to meet with an unarmed suspect, and he knew in his soul that Morgana would never harm him. If anyone pressed him later, he could argue he was still a cadet. He didn't know any better.

Since his father was out of his office, Butch called the chief's voice mail and left a message for him, saying he was attempting to reach Morgana.

He then sent Morgana's cell phone a text message of his own. Halfway through the message, however, his phone went dead.

Susanne put the phone down with a small wry smile. Convincing Butch's phone service provider that his cell phone was stolen and in need of a block was shamelessly simple, and her timing had been perfect.

Butch would never know what hit him.

As Susanne had anticipated, deceiving Morgana was no day at the beach. Receiving the partial text message, Morgana knew immediately that she had not contacted Butch and that he was walking into a trap.

When she failed to reach him on his cell phone, she called his provider and learned his phone had been stolen and that his line was now blocked. Jumping into her car, she drove ten blocks up the street and called Chief Larry Cole from a public pay phone.

Reciting the phony text message and Butch's partial reply, she told Larry Cole his son's phone was now blocked and that he was in trouble.

"You aren't out of the woods either, Morgana. Come to my office and turn yourself in. I'll do everything I can to help."

"Do everything you can to help your son."

"Morgana, I want to help you, too."

"Forget me, Chief. Find your son."

She hung up and returned to her BMW.

Larry Cole may have had doubts about Morgana, but he did not question for one second that Butch was in trouble. Nor did he doubt that someone had deliberately disabled Butch's cell phone and that if he did not get it back online—and warn his son—his son's problems might prove terminal. Too many people died around Morgana.

He punched up the phone company's director of operations—Ray White. After explaining to White's brain-dead assistant that he had a police emergency and needed to speak to White immediately, White's assistant sounded off:

"Once when my husband was beating the living hell out of me, I called 911, and when I asked for help, your police department put me on hold."

"I'm sorry, ma'am, but this is also an emergency—just as yours was—a life-and-death emergency."

"Yeah, sure. I'll see what I can do."

With a derisive laugh, she put Chief Cole on hold.

. . .

Butch rode into the Lincoln Park Zoo's parking lot at nine on the big graphite-gray Honda ST1300 motorcycle Morgana had bought him for his birthday. Most of the cars had departed, and the lot was nearly empty. He spotted Morgana standing beside a new BMW. She was staring at the zoo's gate, her back to him, but he recognized her hair.

He pulled up behind her, turned off his Honda, and swung off. He walked up to her, shouting:

"Morgana, what's going—?

When the woman turned around, Butch saw immediately that even though her hair matched the cut and color of Morgana's, her facial features were different—sharper, more angular . . . and more sinister. The woman's upper lip was pulled back over her teeth, and one side of her mouth was hooked in a feral sneer. Her eyes glinted cruelly, filled with sin and wickedness.

"You've been a bad boy, Butchie," the woman said softly. "Mama's going to have to spank. Mama's going to have to spank . . . *very hard.*"

"I don't know what you're talking—," Butch started to say.

She leveled a strange-looking gun at his chest and shot him with a sleek, streamlined, aerodynamically shaped dart. Glancing down at his chest, Butch watched with dismay as it vibrated just below his left clavicle like a diminutive arrow. Looking more closely, he noted that its four-inch tail section was contoured like a syringe and, in fact, contained a rapidly shrinking supply of liquid—no doubt some sort of drug.

Butch tried to yank the dart out, but he could not lift his arms. Yes, it was some sort of drug. Falling like a lightning-blasted tree, his head hammered the concrete parking lot so hard, it bounced, the combined force of the double shocks only heightening the knockout power of the tranquilizer.

. . .

Back in her hotel room, Morgana remembered that all the text messages sent to Butch's cell phone were automatically forwarded to his e-mail. Since they'd spent so much time together, he had sometimes used her computer to access his e-mail, and she knew his Internet e-mail account number.

Sitting at her hotel desk, she accessed his e-mail on her computer and instantly learned where Susanne had directed him.

Immediately following that e-mail, however, was a final directive addressed to *herself*.

The message said that Susanne had apprehended Butch, then listed map coordinates for Morgana to punch into her BMW's navigation system. The message warned Morgana to "come alone."

Goddamn, Susanne had been a step ahead of her all the way.

Butch's rendezvous point wasn't far and getting there didn't take long—not when Morgana was flooring a BMW. Pulling into the near-empty parking lot, the first thing she spotted was Butch's Honda. A note taped to its seat advised her to check her computer for map coordinates. The note reminded her to come alone. She knew Susanne all too well not to comply.

If she showed up with the police, Butch would die.

Chief Larry Cole roared down the off-ramp near the park in time to see a gray BMW rocket up the opposite on-ramp like a Phantom jet detonating off the deck of a carrier. Within seconds, it was gone.

All he got off the license plate were two digits—a 5 and a 3.

Not enough for an all-points bulletin.

Reaching the rendezvous point, the chief found Butch's Honda. Except for two pieces of Scotch tape on the seat, he found nothing unusual—just an abandoned bike.

Morgana must have been in the BMW, he suddenly realized. As

the darkness settled in, he knew it was too late to call for helicopter support—and Morgana was going too fast for him to catch her, and night was falling.

Putting out an "all points" on the BMW anyway, he offered up a terse prayer.

Butch came to, his vision red, blurred, and pulsing in time to the throbbing in his head. Each throb in his temples hit like a drop-forge.

Slowly, memories returned: the woman by the BMW whom he'd mistaken for Morgana, the strange-looking gun, the dart thrumming in his chest . . . and then the blackness.

What the hell had happened to him?

. . . *Other memories tortured Butch as well . . . Trussed up in a chair, his wrists were shackled to the arms, his ankles to the legs, his waist to the back . . . A dazzlingly beautiful, sinfully sensuous woman— with long red-gold hair, luridly crimson lipstick, black spike heels, matching net stockings, and a bloodred gossamer-thin scoop-neck top— was climbing onto his lap and making love to him . . . She whispered:*

"You know you love me, baby. You know I'm good for you. Let me do it to you! Let me be the lover Morgana never could be . . . I'll fly you places you've never been, take you to worlds you've never dreamed of . . ."

Retrieving a vial of coke out of her stocking garter, she helped herself to a healthy snort straight out of the bottle. When she placed the vial under Butch's nose and he shook his head in disgust, she laughed shrilly:

"More for me, sweetie."

Suddenly, her mouth—wet, torrid, and irresistibly seductive—was everywhere . . . on every throbbing orifice of his body . . . He tried to be faithful to Morgana . . . He tried to fight off the voluptuous vixen's voracious mouth with every ounce of his willpower . . . But his desire was overwhelming, and she was too desirable . . . He was falling . . . falling . . . falling . . . into a scorching abyss of lewd lust and libidinous betrayal, the power of his passion all-consuming . . .

When she was done with him . . . when she had used him like a whore . . . had her fill and wrung him dry . . . she brandished in his face her drug-filled syringe . . . and shoved it in his shoulder just below the neck . . .

Treating him to one last peal of high-pitched vibrating laughter . . . filled with mean merriment and illimitable derision . . . like the echoing tinkle of an infinitely insolent bell . . . she pressed the plunger home . . . Butch threw his head back, groaned, and then was tumbling down the abyss . . .

His last memory was of an overhead klieg light, an accompanying boom mike, a high-angle camcorder, and a whore from hell plying her infernal trade.

Smile, Butch, *he thought,* you're on *Candid Camera*. . . .

Chief Cole huddled with his men. No one had spotted Morgana since she eluded the chief at the Lincoln Park Zoo, but Morgana had given the chief one quick voice mail message from a phone booth, saying:

"I'm going to try to rescue your son alone. I can't bring cops, because if I do, Susanne will kill him. The rendezvous point, however, is south-west of Milwaukee. That's all I can tell you. I know it's not in Illinois and out of your jurisdiction, but if you can arrange with Wisconsin to have some cops deploy in that area, and if at some point it's safe to send in the cavalry, I'll call and let you know."

Entering Cole's office, Judy Daniels listened to Cole replay the message and listened to his men moan about the missing BMW.

"I was staring so hard at that disappearing license plate," the chief said, "I didn't even stop to check out what model BMW it was."

"Didn't Butch say it was a hundred-grand car?" she asked her chief.

"So?" Cole asked back.

"You ever heard of a hundred-grand car that didn't have a LoJack? You know, the car alarm system that transmits a signal when activated to the LoJack control center? There can't be that many gray BMWs heading out of Chicago and into southern Wisconsin with the license numbers five and three."

"What am I doing for brains?" Cole said to his deputy. "Call Lo-Jack. Get that car system activated and get me into a chopper. Call the Wisconsin State Police, tell them we're in hot pursuit, and arrange for backup where Morgana said."

With an effort tantamount to erecting the Mayan temples and excavating the Suez Canal, Butch opened his eyes. The light was painfully bright, his vision blood-tinged.

Christ, how long had he been out?

What had the hell-bitch shot him with?

A deafening roar shook him like the crack of doom. He recognized it instantly. He had heard it in a hundred jungle movies and in the Lincoln Park Zoo: a lion's ear-cracking ululation.

Where am I?

With an even more agonizing effort, Butch rolled over onto his side. His vision slowly focused. Surrounded by vertical bars, he was imprisoned in a cage. Elevated at least six feet off the ground, the cage stank of . . . manure.

With superhuman effort, Butch crawled to the bars, propped himself up on one elbow, and scrutinized his surroundings, inside and out. His mini-prison was mounted on a red sideshow wagon, which was parked inside a big round circus tent—at least 150 feet in diameter and seventy-five feet high. A steel cyclone fence encircled the main ring. Thirty feet high, topped by coiled razor wire, the fence was hooked up to a diesel-powered electrical generator.

No way Butch was escaping that circus.

A couple of tough-looking hombres strode up to his wagon, opened his cage door, and motioned him out. Except for a difference in height, their appearances were markedly similar. They both sported long black unkempt hair, short straggly beards, and jailhouse tattoos. Their frayed Levi's, ripped T-shirts, and filthy bodies were in sore need of laundering.

"Out of the cage, amigo," the taller of the two said.

"Por favor," mocked his partner.

Again, the lion's roar reverberated through the tent, and Butch considered staying where he was. But his warders were insistent.

The taller of the two banged on the cage door. This time Butch noticed he hit it with the buttstock of a 12-gauge Winchester pump—the barrel and stock crudely cut down, the stock beveled to a pistol grip. He smiled at Butch nonstop, but his twisted grin was hardly reassuring. Four front teeth were missing, and his right eye stared sightlessly—Butch believed mindlessly—into space, rheumy, cretinous, and confused. His nose looked like a badly busted knuckle.

His partner—who was at least eight inches shorter than his perpetually smiling friend—sported the same long dirty disheveled hair, the same sparse ratty beard but boasted thirteen Mexican Mafia tattoos around his neck. Unlike Smiley, Shorty never smiled. His eyes—black as pitch, empty as the abyss—were singularly mirthless, seething with moronic malice. He also motioned Butch toward the door—sparking it this time with his thick crackling cattle prod.

Lion roar or not, Butch was exiting the cage.

Half-led, half-dragged to the main ring, the still groggy Butch found Franklin waiting for him. In the ring's center a scantily clad woman—in a black leather micromini, matching spandex, and thigh-high riding boots heeled with sterling silver five-inch rowels honed razor-sharp—sneered at him. Her outfit was gaudily adorned with glittering spangles. Staring at him with conceited condescension, she presented Butch with a stately bow. Doffing her black top hat, a luscious mane of freshly dyed red-gold hair cascaded down her back. Keeping her nickel-plated Ruger magnum—.44 SuperHawk—leveled at both of them with one hand, she focused her digital camcorder on them with the other.

"Welcome to the Circus Maximus—our grandiose update of the Roman arena," she said to Butch, giving him a seductive wink. Straightening, she carefully placed the top hat on her head.

"What do you want, Susanne?" Butch asked, recognizing her in spite of her flamboyant makeup and garishly dyed hair.

"I want you two to fight my lovelies," she said, pointing to the far edge of the circus ring with her magnum pistol. "You will find your weapons over *there.*"

Again, the deafening yowls of jungle cats ripped through the big top.

Christ, there was a pile of weapons along the edge of the circus ring. Swords, round military shields, what appeared to be a black rope net and a trident. Gladiator garb was stacked beside them, and behind the clothes and weapons someone had mounted a thirty-foot-by-thirty-foot . . . *theater screen.*

In fact, Butch now saw that three thirty-foot-by-thirty-foot theater screens were mounted at intervals around the perimeter of the main ring.

"I'm sure you'll look quite striking in your gladiator gear. Get changed now, and be quick about it. Don't force my assistants to hurry you up. Roberto's cattle prod is a real ball-burner."

Her blood-chilling laugh rang through the tent, and somewhere a lion echoed her hellish howls. The two men trudged off toward their weapons pile and gladiator attire.

"I think I'm going to be sick," Franklin said.

"Buck up," Butch muttered, trying to project a bravery he did not feel. "To survive, we're going to have to work together."

Morgana's navigational system directed her out of Chicago. Every fifty miles or so, it brought her to a spot—usually a diner or an old gas station—where she met one of Susanne's thugs: hideously tattooed psychopaths acquired from the psycho wards of Mexico's most brutal prisons. These brain-damaged gallows birds would give Morgana the next set of coordinates after confirming she had not been followed.

Loading those coordinates into her navigational computer, she followed them to the next stop.

Not that Morgana had any illusions about overwhelming Susanne with superior firepower. Bent on revenge, Susanne had planned meticulously. She would have guns, a small army of killers, and a plethora of ingenious surprises.

Morgana had a few surprises up her own sleeve, but the closer she got to Susanne's lair, the flimsier her own plans started to look.

More and more, she believed she would have to improvise.

A huge, hulking ex-NFL star, Franklin would have looked awesome in his gladiator gear. However, the armored tunic, short leather breeches, and breastplates were too big for him. The steel helmet was a full size too small for his behemoth eight-$1/2$ size head and hurt his forehead and temples. In his gargantuan hands, the short legionnaire's sword and his round eighteen-inch shield were like a pocket-knife and a dinner plate.

Butch had no illusions about his own appearance or prowess either.

Butch was just about to ask Franklin where Susanne had disappeared to when he spotted her. Dressed in her black spandex, micromini and black top hat, she was climbing the ladder to the trapeze platform sixty feet overhead. She had handed the Magnum to one of her killers, but over her left shoulder was a coiled blacksnake whip; over the other shoulder, two coiled ropes. Every so often, she stopped to zoom her camcorder in on the tiger and his martially garbed prey or to help herself to a forceful snort of cocaine from the small vial she'd stashed in her miniskirt's waistband.

While she clambered up the ladder, two of Susanne's psychopathic killers wheeled Butch's nemesis into the ring—a full-grown, six-hundred-pound Bengal tiger, half-mad with hunger, pacing his cage and yowling dementedly. After wheeling his cage in—directly under Susanne's trapeze platform—Susanne waved down at her two psychopaths and shouted: "Here it comes!" She dropped them one end of her coiled rope. After removing the padlock from its cage door, they lashed the rope to the top of the tiger's cage door and turned on the electrical generator. To test the fence's electrical charge, Smiley spat on it, his spittle sparking and crackling.

"We have to forget everything and focus on the tiger," Butch said to Franklin.

"If we don't kill him," Franklin agreed, "he'll eat us alive."

Butch nodded his agreement.

"Look, I'm bigger than you are," Butch said. "You do the heavy lifting. Let's see if when he moves on us, you can tangle him up in that net."

Franklin returned his short sword and shield to the weapons pile and picked up the thick rope net and three-pronged triton-lance. Leaning toward Franklin, Butch whispered in confidence:

"I'll draw him off—threaten him with my sword and shield. And when he lunges at me, you hit him from the side with this rope net, dropping it over his head and shoulders. Try to pull it under his feet. While he's tangled in the net, I'll attack him with my broadsword, you with your trident. It can work.

Franklin stared at Butch, incredulous.

"I say it could work," Butch repeated.

Franklin began ticking off his Power Points one at a time, point-ing at himself first: "*(a) I'm* a lawyer." Pointing his finger at Butch, he said: "*(b) You're* a kid." Pointing at the cage across the ring at the big cat, Franklin shouted: "And *(c)* he's . . . *a goddamn no-shit tiger, and I'm supposed to stop him with a fucking fish net and a spear?*"

"I tell you it could work. You have a better plan?" Butch asked.

"No."

"Then we go with mine."

"Why are you so sure it might work?" Franklin said Butch, his face a contorted mask of skepticism.

"I saw the movie *Gladiator* seven times."

"So?" Franklin shouted. "I saw it, too—the DVD. The director's cut. That still doesn't qualify me to kill tigers."

"Yeah, but I saw it seven times . . . *in the theater!*" Butch roared.

Morgana kept the BMW's pedal to the metal and reached the aban-doned farm in record time. Once during the trip when a cop had sneaked up behind her, she had turned off her lights, cut down an un-lighted country road, and outrun the cop, racing invisible as night. The cop had grudgingly given up his blind pursuit.

Except for that slight detour, she had raced toward the old aban-doned farm as fast as she knew how.

Susanne was up on the trapeze artist's platform, sixty feet above the ground, a digital camcorder in one hand, a portable microphone in the other. As she zoomed in on the people and animals below, she roared into the heavily amplified mike, her voice thundering through the big top:

"Ladies and gentlemen! Children of all ages! Welcome to the biggest show under the big top! And I don't mean a few dumb-ass tightrope walkers or stupid-looking clowns or even a troupe of high-flying trapeze artists. I'm talking about a life-and-death drama to make Barnum and Bailey look like Dumb and Dumber, turn Siegfried and Roy into Abbott and Costello and reduce the bloody spectacles of the Roman Coliseum to Hare Krishna street-chanters. I now present Butch and Franklin versus Manfred the Man-Eating Tiger! And by capturing this extravaganza on broadcast-quality digital, we will preserve it forever for a worshipful posterity. This will be the greatest movie ever made. We'll make *Gladiator* look like *Snow White and the Seven Dwarfs* and *Deep Throat* a ludicrous remake of *The Sound of Music!* We'll be bigger than Halley's comet!

"So come one, come all. Room for one more inside the big tent. Welcome to the biggest, most exciting, most electrifying extravaganza-extraordinaire in the world—the greatest sado-erotic show on earth! Welcome to . . .

"Psycho Circus!!!"

Glancing around the ring, Butch saw three commercial-quality digital camcorders mounted atop the theater screens, supplemented by overhead boom mikes and klieg lights.

Shit, Susanne *was* making a movie!

"Why are you doing this?" Butch shouted up at her.

The tiger seconded his question with an earth-shattering, nerve-fraying yowl.

"I guess, Butch, I do owe you an explanation," Susanne squawked into the mike in her little girl's voice. "As a child, I was captured by the DeWitts, just like yourself. Unlike you, however, I was tortured hideously, mentally abused and sexually violated. I did escape, but when the police found me, I had lapsed into a coma. Since I never died, and never revealed the names of my tormenters, I was never on the DeWitt's list of victims."

"Why didn't you tell the police what they did to you?" Butch shouted up at her.

"Don't you understand? I didn't want justice for the DeWitts. I wanted revenge *pour moi*. Even as a child, I wanted to brutally torture, sexually mortify, and viciously kill the DeWitts. I wanted to do to them everything they had done and tried to do to me—only replicate it on an infinitely grander scale . . . with more perverse ingenuity and sadistic savoir faire. It was all I lived for, all I ever dreamed of. The only thing that kept me alive during those subsequent years was my study of revenge—what I would do to them when I grew up and caught them—and let me tell you that list of atrocities was fiendish."

"What does your revenge against the DeWitts have to do with Franklin?" Butch asked.

"As a young woman barely sixteen, I had left high school to become a secretary. Lying about my age, I went to work for Franklin. I'd been there about three months when he lured he me into his office, locked the door and exploited me *sexually* . . . using and abusing me in every perverse way! When I threatened to turn him in, he laughed in my face, saying he was too powerful, that he ran the firm, that he was above the law. To prove it, he pulled down my pants and spanked my bare bottom with a black leather paddle. Then he fired me. I knew then there was nothing I could do to him legally. He was too powerful, and it was my word against his. When he fired me— believe it or not—he wrote this on my letter of dismissal: 'Dismissed for not putting out enough.' Working for him was like suffering the perversions of the DeWitts all over again, and he not only got away with degrading me, he went on to become ridiculously rich and prodigiously powerful. All I got was boffed, my butt beaten red, and the door. I didn't even get severance! I didn't even get *unemployment!*"

"Why didn't you turn *him* into the police anyway and take your chances?"

"I was obsessed with destroying the DeWitts, and I was afraid that to save his skin, he might give them up to the cops—you know, 'trade up.' Then I would be cheated out of my justly earned *personal* revenge. And in any event, when Franklin took over DeWitt, Inc., I saw a better opportunity to wreak my revenge. Disguising my identity, hair color, and facial features, I went to work for Franklin as his executive assistant, knowing he could get me close to the DeWitts. I now planned on a double treat. I intended to sink my tingling talons into the DeWitts *and* Franklin. When I'm done with you and Franklin, your lovely Morgana will be next."

Taking out a second vial of coke, she treated herself to a stupendous snort.

"What did Morgana ever do to you?"

"The DeWitts were rich. DeWitt, Inc., made Franklin rich. When Morgana got her inheritance, DeWitt money made her rich. They made everyone rich except me. All I got from the DeWitts was used and abused. Then adding salt to my wounds, Susanne took you from me."

"You never *had* me. We were never lovers."

"But *I* loved you. Ever since I saw you in the theater . . . the night I killed Carlos."

"You were the woman with the cats? You were disguised?"

"You got it, bubba. One look at you, and I was smitten. But did you do anything about it? N-o-o-o-o-o. You just stood there staring at me like a stupid dork. You never wrote. You never called. You never sent flowers, candy, greeting cards. You never courted me. I even bumped into you on the street once, and you looked right through me. It was as if I were chopped liver, dirt under your fingernails—dog shit on your shoes. I was *nothing* to you. And then Morgana—after making off with the DeWitt fortune—stole you from me, and I knew I'd lost you forever . . . *to her!*"

"I didn't *know* you."

"No, that wasn't it. Your companion distracted you from me. You were with the luscious Morgana DeWitt—another DeWitt fucking up my life!—and you only had eyes for her. Once again, the DeWitts had ripped me off. Once again, I lost and the DeWitts won."

"You had no claim to me," Butch blurted out in frustration.

"But I *wanted* you, and if I couldn't have you, no one else could either. Them's the rules, bucko. Get the picture?"

"That's why you want to hurt me."

"In part. By abusing and killing you, however, I will also get back at your father. You see, your father hurt me—quite unforgivably, when you get right down to it—so now I will hurt your father . . . *by hurting you*. Now, when I send him and Morgana the DVDs—of you being eaten by both a tigress *and* a tiger both, if I might say so—your father will suffer the unbearable horror of my revenge, and Our Poor Little Rich Girl will fathom the ecstatic extent of her lover's betrayal in the arms of her most-hated enemy. I'm doing the same for old Franklin there as well. When he and I had our little tryst, I smuggled a small digicam into his office in my shoulder bag. Through an aperture in the bag's side, it captured every sadomasochistic indignity I visited on the poor boy on his office couch in living color and quadra-sound. When I inundate his wife and children with droves of DVDs depicting Franklin and me engaged in the most degrading sado-pornographic sex acts imaginable, they, too, will curse his memory."

Franklin shuddered uncontrollably.

"I still don't understand how my father hurt you?" Butch asked, staring up at her, incredulous.

"He hurt me most abominably. . . . He killed the DeWitts. He robbed me of my revenge. *He took away my fun!*" Her raucous guffaws exploded though the big top like rolling thunder.

"So you'll hurt them by debauching, then murdering me?"

"Don't worry, sweetie. It won't end there. In case you haven't guessed, after I have mortified them mentally, emotionally, spiritually— have broken and tortured them in every way known to God, Lucifer, and mortal man—I plan on killing them as well . . . in the most unspeakable ways I can think of. And as you know, *Mama always keeps her word!*"

"Suppose we win?" Franklin asked. "Suppose we defeat your tiger? Do you let us go?"

"Victory over Manfred only makes the game more . . . challenging. It only promotes you to level two."

"What's level two?" Butch asked.

"Wheel up level two!" Susanne shouted.

Her tattooed gaggle of raggedy psychopaths pulled forward another red circus wagon and parked it inside the center ring's gate. They next removed the padlock from the up-down sliding cage door. It contained two large yowling lions.

"Meet . . . *Leo and Lois!*" Susanne boomed.

Susanne threw down a second line, which they affixed to the top of the lions' cage door.

A second cat cage? Butch glanced around the ring's perimeter, suddenly suspicious. He had the sneaking feeling that Susanne might have other animal surprises up her sleeve.

While the ring was brilliantly lit, the surrounding area was shrouded in ill-lit gloom. Staring into that Stygian darkness, however, Butch could now see—in between the movie screens—three other cat cages, propped up on red sideshow wagons. In a big double cage paced two more lions. To their right, a large leopard snarled against the bars, its jaws gaped, its feral fangs bared. On the left side of the lions, camouflaged in dim shadows, the amber eyes of a black panther blazed like balefire behind its own cell-like bars.

Christ, he now saw a fourth cage as well. In it coiled . . . coiled . . . coiled . . . *an anaconda*!

"I hate snakes," Butch muttered under his breath to Franklin, pointing to the python cage. "I almost died from a snake bite once. I really don't want to fight . . . *a fucking python!*"

"You're worried about the python?" Franklin shot back at Butch, his mouth twisted in an evil sneer. "We're never going to get to him. The tiger's going to . . . *eat us first.*"

At which point, Susanne's mad echoing laughter tore through the big top like a banshee-shriek from hell.

No sooner had Morgana jumped out of her BMW than two white pit bulls, a black rottweiller, and brown mastiff—the size of a small Shetland pony—leaped out of the rear of a panel truck at her. Two more of Susanne's grungy-looking psychopaths bounded after them in hot pursuit.

The dogs charged her—snarling, slavering, jaws black and gaping as the abyss, the very hounds of hell.

Chief Larry Cole was up in his chopper, roaring over the Wisconsin cornfields, making a beeline toward Morgana's LoJack-equipped BMW. He'd been able to commandeer only one small chopper at the PD's helioport. Everything else was in maintenance or in midpursuit.

Nor had the Wisconsin State Police seemed eager to cooperate on the phone.

The chopper held only four people—Chief Cole, the pilot, Judy Daniels, and Blackie Sylvestri. Not that Blackie much helped. Still recovering from his hospital stay, he complained incessantly of air sickness and acrophobia.

"Can't you set me down, Chief? I never should have come up here. I'm going to barf all over this chopper."

Through his police binoculars, Cole spotted their destination. Christ, Morgana was in a parking lot surrounded by a pack of mad dogs, two goons with guns—and not one goddamn Wisconsin Smoky in sight.

"Can't this damn thing fly any faster?" Cole shouted at the pilot.

"And now," Susanne thundered into the mike, "ready, action, camera!" Bending over the trapeze platform, she focused the digital camcorder on the actors and animals below. "I've starved my lovelies for over a week, and they are now hideously hungry. Since they're dying to put on the old feed bag, let the games begin."

Hauling up the rope a length at a time—all the while keeping the camcorder focused on her victims below—she lifted the tiger's cage door.

At the sight and sounds of the police chopper, the two men fled not only the scene but the circus, charging through the Wisconsin cornfields. As for the attack-trained dogs, when Chief Cole reached Morgana, he found her on one knee, scratching the bellies of the four dogs, who now rolled on their backs and yelped with contented pleasure. Looking up at the chief with a demure shrug, Morgana said:

"I've always had a way with dogs."

"Then bring them with you. We have to find Butch, and we may need them."

Suddenly a lion's roar, a tiger's yowl, the hilarious howls of an unimaginably demented woman, all accompanied by the symphonic strains of a full orchestra—playing . . . *the theme from* Gladiator!— detonated out of the big top.

Gun drawn, Chief Cole led the charge toward the music, the cat yowls, and the harpy's hellish horselaughs . . . all erupting from the big tent.

The theme music from the film *Gladiator* thundered out of five outsize loudspeakers while intercut excerpts from *Gladiator*'s most grotesquely violent gladiatorial battles blazed across the thirty-foot-by-thirty-foot theater screen mounted next to the electrified fence surrounding the center ring.

Complementing the *Gladiator* excerpts, a pornographic film of Susanne on the lap of a naked man shackled to an armchair also ran on one of the theater screens. Looking more closely, Butch suddenly realized the man was . . . *himself*!

Shit!

His gaze quickly turned to the other screen. Christ, Marilyn Monroe had grabbed Franklin's three-inch ponytail in her one hand, his left ear in the other, and was coercing Franklin into violent cunnilingus, all the while mugging moronically for the camera, pouting her lips in lewd lurid circles and singing in her famous cutesy-pie voice: "Happy Birthday, Mr. Pres-i-dent."

Physically ill, Butch averted his eyes.

Just in time.

The tiger's cage door was opening.

Manfred the Man-Eating Tiger lumbered out of his cage and into the main ring with a nerve-shattering roar. If Manfred had looked big before—inside his cage, pacing and yowling—he now looked preternaturally huge. Nor did he seem at all deterred by Butch's three-foot-long sword and two-foot-diameter shield or by Franklin's trident and rope net. He studied them with supreme conceit, with infinite condescension. With eyes heavy-lidded and half-asleep, he stared at them as if they meant nothing to him . . . as if he had all the time in the world . . . as if he had nothing left to lose and nothing left to love . . . as if they were his merely his . . . next meal.

He stared at them like a gambler holding straight aces . . . a lockup hand.

With another nerve-fraying, hair-frying yowl, Manfred strolled toward them.

He looked more than relaxed.

He almost looked . . . *tired.*

Five of Susanne's greasy-haired, straggly-bearded, foul-smelling psychopaths assaulted Cole's team with guns and knives as they entered the tent. Chief Cole had his police-issue Beretta out and reflexively emptied it into the gunmen. When he, Judy, and the limping Blackie turned to take on the three knife-fighters, he saw—to eternal amazement—that they were too late. Morgana was already dispatching them. A rapid cadence of pelvis-crushing crotch-kicks followed by three larynx-cracking throat jabs, culminating in a series of heart-stopping sternum-snapping sidekicks, and the three men were rolling in the entranceway, sobbing, moaning, groping their crotches, clutching their windpipes, and massaging their broken breastbones.

"I hope Butch knows what he's getting into with that girl," the chief muttered to Judy.

Butch feinted an attack from the left, and—as he'd hoped—the big tiger diverted his attention away from Franklin and went for the fake. Weak from protracted starvation, the cat was moving with surprising slowness, which gave Franklin an opening. Knowing it was now or never, do or die, Franklin flung the rope net over Manfred's growling mouth and yanked it under his legs, tightly entrapping his paws and jaws just before he reached Butch.

Staring up at Butch with feral fury, Manfred gaped his monstrous mandibles and treated Butch to another earsplitting roar and a terrifying glimpse into his black malodorous mouth.

Which was a major mistake on Manfred's part.

Hurling himself at the great cat—as if all the furies in hell were clawing at his back—Butch let out a truly spectacular yowl himself and plunged his three-foot sword-blade straight into Manfred's malevolent maw. Manfred's yowl came to an abrupt halt . . . and the great cat died.

"Damn you, Cole!" Susanne screamed from her lofty trapeze platform. "Damn you to hell and back!" Yanking on the second rope, the second cage door levitated, and the roaring, yowling lions stumbled out—also half-dead from hunger.

"Stay back to back with me!" Butch yelled at Franklin. "It's our only chance."

Chief Cole needed more sleep and a better doctor. That police sawbones was treating him for high blood pressure, but the chief increasingly believed he needed a hernia operation. Or maybe it was just sleep deprivation. Cole could still pump a lot of iron for a man his age—four hundred pounds with reps—but he was averaging three hours' sleep a night. Since Butch tied up with Morgana, all the chief did was worry. That kid was going to be the death of him.

Christ, his side hurt. Maybe he'd ruptured an intercostal muscle.

By the time he reached the fenced-off circus ring, his vision was blurring from pain and fatigue, and his breath was coming in spurts. He did see the two lions bound out of the cage. He'd unfortunately emptied most of his clip into the two armed psychopaths. Firing at the cats, the hammer hit the magazine's last round, the slide slammed back, and the gun was empty. Even worse, he rushed the shot, and it ricocheted with a spark-filled whine off the fence and the tiger cage.

By the time he slapped another magazine into the butt and racked the slide, he saw that more shots were unnecessary.

The two starving lions—having witnessed the efficiency with which the gladiators had dispatched Manfred—deemed discretion the better part of valor. Furthermore, they were so unimaginably hungry they could barely walk, let alone charge. Instead of risking bloody death for their next meal, they fell on Manfred, quickly ripping out choice morsels. Leo went straight for the tiger's liver, while Lois tore off his . . . cojones.

Averting his gaze in disgust, the chief next found himself staring at a theater screen. To the stirring refrains of *Gladiator*'s theme music, Russell Crowe was battling a tiger.

Cole averted his eyes again, in time to see a redheaded vixen ferociously fellating his son on the big screen. Flinging back his head, Butch groaned like a stuck pig.

Cole quickly turned to the third screen. Marilyn Monroe was forcing the naked Franklin over her knee. The big hulking ex-NFL star fought Marilyn valiantly, but she threw her right thigh over his kicking legs. Scissoring her ankles together in a tight-as-a-vise death grip, she yanked back his head back by his three-inch ponytail and proceeded to beat his bottom halfway to death with a black leather paddle.

Damn, she could hit. Cole wondered whether Marilyn had whaled on Joe "the Clipper" DiMaggio like that. She walloped Franklin's backside like she was possessed—like she was hammering the final spike on the Trans-Siberian Railroad . . . all the while, laughing like a loon.

Through it all, the ex-football star roared like a gored water buffalo and bawled like a baby.

Cole's horror was interrupted by a banshee-shriek from hell. Looking up from the theater screens, he saw Susanne on her trapeze platform cut loose with a second bloodcurdling scream—hair-raising enough to wake the damned. Grabbing the platform's trapeze, she swung almost balletically across the length and breadth of the big top. Gracefully arcing her glide path, she angled neatly over the thirty-foot fence and dropped almost angelically into the center ring.

She stared at the feasting lion pair with supreme disgust. "I've never been so humiliated in my life!" she howled at her two felines. Pointing at Butch and Franklin, she yelled: "Kill!"

Leo ignored the command. Lois, however, did look up. Turning her head, she gave Susanne a hateful glare of hungry defiance and a soft, insolent growl.

Susanne turned into hell itself. Cursing them with every disparaging epithet in her obscenely depraved soul, she denounced them—among other things—as "fit for nothing more than mangy rugs, dog food canneries, and basement walls." After defaming the mating habits of their mothers and the unnatural propensities of their sodomizing fathers, she reared back and cracked the whip with a feral fury and almost preternatural power at Lois's rebellious head, the whip's concussive cracking not so much a crack but a shotgun blast.

Her aim, however, was off.

The whip's popper took out Lois's angrily upturned eye as dexterously as a pair of forceps plucking a raisin from a scone.

A heartbeat later, Lois was disemboweling Susanne, and Leo was ripping out Franklin's throat.

Morgana screamed at Butch at the top of her lungs: *"Get in the tiger cage!"*

It was only three feet away.

Seconds later, when the lion pair turned on Butch, they found him hunkering in the center of Manfred's pen, the cage door slammed shut and padlocked.

Shrugging irritably, growling gruffly, the two returned to their sumptuous, long-awaited repast.

Epilogue

Butch, Chief Cole, and Morgana sat in the chief's office. All three had finished giving their statements to both the Chicago Police and the Wisconsin State Police. To the chief's consternation, however, neither his son nor Morgana seemed particularly relieved or even grateful to be alive.

In fact, Butch was peeved.

"Dad," Butch said, clearly hurt, "did the Wisconsin State Police have to show Morgana the *entire* DVD of Susanne raping me?"

"I told you they were out of their office on a coffee break

and left it lying on a desk. They had a TV with a DVD player hooked up. She sneaked in and ran it without their permission."

"It didn't look like rape to *me*," Morgana said.

"Susanne drugged me, tortured me, took me against my will. That's not rape?"

"Yes, it would be—except while you were *allegedly* being taken against your will, your tongue lolled out of your mouth," Morgana muttered, "and your eyes rolled back. Your hips pumped up and down like locomotive pistons."

The chief poured them each a cup of coffee. "Butch has a point. He *was* drugged and coerced."

Butch mustered the most pitiful stare he could manage. "It didn't mean *anything* to me."

"You mean it didn't mean anything to you . . . *five times*!" Morgana's stare was hard enough to hurt.

"Stop it, you two lovebirds," the chief said. "I'm starting to think you deserve each other. Morgana, your boyfriend was almost devoured by a tiger and two lions, and all you can do is complain about . . . nonconsensual sex. Butch, Morgana risked her life and liberty to save you, and you're mad at her because she sneaked a look at a DVD. You two are getting what you deserve—*each other*."

"Is it true the ASPCA is bringing charges against me?" Butch asked. "For cruelty to animals?"

"You did kill an endangered tiger," the chief pointed out.

"It was him or me."

"And you can prove it," the Chief concurred. "You have everything on DVD."

"Including Butch's starring role in Susanne's remake of *Deep Throat*," Morgana snarled.

"Can't we look on the bright side?" the chief said. "We're all alive. Except for a few comedic columnists, the papers are treating all of us like we're heroes. Frankly, Morgana, this petty jealousy is . . . petty. Let me say again Butch could have been eaten by a yowling cat."

"Okay, okay," Morgana said with a sheepish smile. "Agreed?"

"Agreed," Butch said. "Truce?"

"Truce." Morgana walked over to his chair, took his hand, and kissed his cheek. "I love you," she whispered in his ear.

The chief rolled back his eyes. "I need a drink." Getting a bottle of Jack Daniels out of a filing cabinet, he dumped out their coffee in his waste basket and filled their mugs.

"To the lions," Morgana said. "For ridding us of Susanne and Franklin."

"As law enforcement officers," the chief said, "we're not supposed to drink to violent death, but what the hell." He raised his mug. "I'll drink to Morgana. I could learn to like you, girl."

"I'll second that," Butch said, raising his mug.

"To the Coles," Morgana said, raising hers.

"Now anyone for a trip to the Lincoln Park Zoo?" Chief Cole said.

"What on earth for?" Butch asked.

"Lincoln Park?" Morgana moaned.

"Yeah, why not? I have a burning urge to visit the cat cages."

DATE DUE

APR 2 0 2009		
APR 2 6 2010		